A GOOD FAMILY

Seo Hajin

A Good Family

STORIES

TRANSLATED BY ALLY H. HWANG
AND AMY C. SMITH

 DALKEY ARCHIVE PRESS

Originally published in Korean as *Chakhan Gajok*
by Munhakgwa Jiseongsa (Moonji Publishing Co., Ltd.), 2008.

Copyright ©2008, Seo Hajin
Translation copyright ©2015, Ally H. Hwang and Amy C. Smith

Library of Congress Cataloging-in-Publication Data

So, Ha-jin.
  [Short stories. Selections. English]
  A good family : stories / by Seo Hajin ; translated by Ally
H. Hwang and Amy C. Smith. -- First edition.
    pages cm
  ISBN 978-1-62897-118-7 (pbk. : acid-free paper)
  1. Families--Fiction. I. Hwang, Ally H., translator. II. Smith, Amy C.,
1978- translator. III. Title.
  PL992.74.H26A2 2015
  895.73'5--dc23

                                    2015030557

LIBRARY OF KOREAN LITERATURE

Partially funded by the Illinois Arts Council, a state agency
Published in collaboration with the Literature Translation Institute of Korea
Dalkey Archive Press publications are, in part, made possible through the
support of the University of Houston-Victoria and its program in creative
writing, publishing, and translation. www.uhv.edu/asa/

Dalkey Archive Press
Victoria, TX / Dublin / London
www.dalkeyarchive.com

Cover: design and composition by Mikhail Iliatov
Printed on permanent/durable acid-free paper

Contents

What Grows out of Sadness

1. A Sign

Two days after they moved to the new place, a couple of pigeons nested in the corner of the veranda. The pigeons, constantly flying up to the eighth floor with bits of straw in their mouths, built a cozy, smelly house. Seeing that one of them had stopped flying around the nest and settled into it, her husband guessed that it was a female sitting on eggs. Unlike the woman, who detested the bustling sound they made every morning and the stench of the whitish, mushy excrement that hardened in piles, her husband enjoyed watching the birds, regarding them as extraordinary and amusing. One morning he called her, "Look at this. These eggs seem to have gone bad." It was only then that she realized the female pigeon hadn't been seen for several days. "Do you think it could have fallen? Could it be dead?" Her husband seemed full of pity as she stood before him, holding a broom. He looked at her with vacant eyes. She neatly cleaned out the now useless nest, spraying water from a long hose.

The woman, Hee-sook, was an ordinary person. Until the age of fifty-four, she always thought she could find nothing about herself that was not ordinary. She was born the first child of a father who ran a private transportation business in a small city, lived an untroubled childhood, and graduated from a women's college in Seoul, which was admittedly somewhat rare at the time. Just as she began working as a bank teller in her hometown, as her four siblings were busy in middle school, high school, and college, her father declared that he was closing his failing business. She felt a little nervous, wondering, 'Will I be expected to support the entire family now?' But her father was industrious and highly confident. He bought a small commercial building, easily took care of his four children with the rent it brought in, and even had enough left over to buy small gifts for his wife, who was suffering from a mid-life crisis.

"Family, beyond all else, means responsibility," her father often said. She understood her mother's shy enjoyment in showing off a new necklace or scarf, but she couldn't help feeling that it was somehow ridiculous.

So it was. Being happy about a husband's small gift and smiling, or being sad about little day-to-day things . . . If such a thing was *ordinary*, Hee-sook was nowhere near ordinary. But she was a person who learned how to fit in, showing the appropriate feelings at the appropriate moments, to the extent that she herself didn't realize this fact for a long time. While she spent her time and energy on marriage, housekeeping, childbirth, and raising children, her twenties, thirties, and forties flew past like water. 'Getting used to the current, feeling it smooth or wild and, sometimes, flowing backward, isn't that what we call living?' she thought. So she didn't complain about taking care of her husband's three sisters' and younger brother's weddings and the ancestor memorial rituals every season, and she didn't have any particular complaints about her father-in-law's frugality, and how he wouldn't even get her a washing machine and checked the contents of the refrigerator all the time, or the fact that her husband seemed to show no interest in her at all.

Sometime last spring, or perhaps last winter or fall, it must have planted itself in Hee-sook's body. It was in her ovary that the cell first began to grow, like a monster savagely multiplying and exposing its violent gluttony, and the cells the size of red beans spread here and there in the peritoneum. She, of course, was unaware of all this for quite some time. Until the day her abdomen swelled up.

When she went to see an internal medicine doctor in town, he said, "Well, you might just be getting a big belly."

When she told him that she had recently lost ten pounds, he said with empty laughter, "Your waistline is always the last place it shows."

After a week had passed and her abdomen was still growing, making her short of breath, she called a friend from school who worked in the department of internal medicine at a university hospital. The call went through, and a woman with a pretty voice said, "I will connect you in just a moment." Even though she had never expected to see her again and didn't want to see her in this condition, now she waited to talk to her friend. Could it be that she somehow sensed that something horrible and serious was going on in her body? That was something no one could know.

"Well, well. It's been a long time. What leads you to call me today?" Her voice, beautiful as ever, had a slight edge to it, but Hee-sook took a deep breath and spoke calmly.

"A strange thing. My abdomen keeps getting bigger."

After a short pause, her friend took up the role of doctor again, "When did it start? How does it feel? Are there any other symptoms?" she asked Hee-sook systematically.

"Well, I feel weak . . . I lost some weight, about ten pounds."

Her friend responded airily, "It might be nothing. Come see me in the afternoon."

Although her friend was booked for the afternoon, she managed to get Hee-sook in first. The faces of the people sitting in the chairs that lined the waiting room like solid blocks looked exhausted and shattered. Hee-sook felt a little guilty.

"Come in. Have a seat," her friend said, closely observing her face with suspicious eyes. And then she asked, "Can you describe it? How does the swelling feel? How are you feeling?"

"Well, it feels like my abdomen is filled with something. It keeps sloshing around and feels weird."

Laying Hee-sook down on one side in her office, she pressed on her abdomen and chest here and there, as if she were poking her, and asked when her last regular check-up had been.

"Maybe it was last fall? My annual exam."

A dark look passed across her friend's face, but then she calmly said, "I can't say anything definite right now. It could really just be a fat belly. But let's get you examined. Come back tomorrow. We'll set up an appointment for that. I want you to fast, starting tonight."

Hee-sook wanted to ask if she could really do it tomorrow but she only ended up saying, "Thank you," and left the office. The people in the waiting room looked at her with empty eyes. She thought she could sense a hint of animosity and she quickly withdrew from the hallway. She was out of breath after walking fast for just a few hundred feet. Had there been a sign? There could have been but she never saw it. Neither did her husband and son. In the afternoon, when she said, "I went to see a doctor," her husband asked, "Why? Are you sick or something?"

"Well, it's . . ."

Before she could answer, his mouth burst open in an excited cry, "Wow, it's going, going. It's gone! That's it! I knew it!"

Watching the white ball flying over in a perfect parabola on the screen, she closed her mouth. Her husband had always been into baseball. Since before they were married, back before she knew him, he had been a huge fan, never missing a single high school or professional game since junior high. Even though she couldn't understand how he could spend so much time watching the players throw, catch, hit, and run, doing so much just to score a run, she didn't say a word. For her, baseball was something she knew nothing about, not even how many players were on a team, and it was something she would rather not know about.

She recalled how she had passed out very suddenly about two weeks ago. It was while she was standing in front of the elevator after finishing her prayers in the hospice ward. In that moment, she felt as though a sudden cold wind brushed past her head and she fell down unconscious. Since she was in a hospital, a nurse who knew her moved her to the emergency room, but she woke up before they even reached the entrance. A young doctor made her lie down even though she said, "Oh, I'm fine," took her blood pressure and pulse, thrust a glowing device with a small round light before her eyes, and ordered her, "Bend your knees. And stand up."

"Have you strained yourself recently?" asked the doctor.

"Well, I might have," she answered mildly. She had spent the last several weeks moving her family out of the place where they had been living for the past ten years, due to the city's reconstruction projects, trying her best in the lottery for a new apartment, keeping up her volunteer work, going back and forth to *Byeokje*[1]

1 A town in which a central crematorium is located.

as if it were her home, because many patients happened to be dying at that time, and in the meantime cooking *v* with the ingredients her mother had given her and sending some of it to her in-laws, and . . . She didn't think that had been exceptionally tiring, but she wanted to get out of the emergency room as fast as possible. Being in the hospital when she wasn't volunteering felt strange to her. During the eight years she had been working with the terminal cancer patients, praying and singing for them, pushing their wheelchairs and walking slowly with them, she had been so healthy that she never even took cold medicine.

The next day she was put into a machine for a PET scan, something she had heard about many times but which was still unfamiliar to her. *Kwing*, the sound of something going round and round reverberated in her head, and when a needle pierced her arm, a burning sensation spread throughout her whole body.

"They explained it to you, right? It's contrast. We inject it to have a clear picture; the feeling will go away soon. Hold your breath, breathe out, breathe in, hold it, and breathe out again." While she was holding her breath and breathing out, following the voice from the speaker, she was filled with anxiety.

"It was uncomfortable, right? It's all done now," a pretty nurse informed her kindly.

Three days later Hee-sook went to see a doctor with her son, who happened to be on break from the army. The doctor, who was supposed to be an expert in that field, and was recommended by her friend, was a middle-aged man with a mustache and a dark face. It was hard to read his expressions because of his mustache. Sitting in a small chair in his office, Hee-sook took a deep, nervous breath.

When she asked her friend about the test results later on, she said, "Well, I'm not sure. Your new primary care doctor will tell you." Her voice didn't sound clear or cheery. "Get the information and come to my office if you have time," but it sounded like she was the one who didn't have time.

Hee-sook thought about how she was used to living with prayers as constant companions in her life. For her children and

---

2 A special soup made of loach fish and vegetables, which requires a complex technique.

husband, for her fellow volunteers who didn't mind washing old bodies withered like cucumbers and helping them move their bowels, happily tolerating the stink, for her father-in-law, other in-laws and family members, and for her own father who had been at the hospital for only three days, never revealing his illness . . . Had she ever prayed for herself? She couldn't remember a time. Or maybe all of those prayers had been for herself.

The fluorescent lights came on behind the pictures, and the doctor pointed at one of them, "It's your ovary . . ." The doctor hesitated. The air in that not-so-spacious room felt like it was swaying with the pulsing fluorescent lights. The doctor looked at her with an equivocal face. Something surged in her heart. She knew at that moment. That something was happening in her body, that she probably could not turn it around, and that she might never go mountain climbing again.

"The thing is . . . This is a rare case. It started in your ovary and spread to the peritoneum. Onset began, well, I can't confirm when at this point. Only that it spread very fast. Once we do the operation, I think we'll be able to tell your exact condition, but even if we can remove the cancer cells, it will be difficult to get it all because, as you know, the peritoneum is something we cannot remove." Her doctor was a man of circumspection. He pronounced each word slowly and carefully and seemed to be reading their faces the whole time.

"But, I mean, my mother . . . was really healthy." Her son looked dumbfounded. For some reason, he detested doctors. His GPA had been good enough to get into medical school, and when he decided to study chemistry in college, casually breaking free from all the expectations of his teachers and father, her husband had been disappointed and angry. But Hee-sook wasn't. She thought it was unfair to be too involved in her son's life just because she had given birth to him and raised him.

She felt like her mind was vacant and blank, turning white. 'That is absurd . . . but . . .' She couldn't describe her own emotions. The woman had never realized that even feelings—sadness, surprise, or pity—required practice.

"Then, am I going to die?" Her voice cracked as she spoke. He slanted his head and smiled at her.

"Cancer is different in every case, depending on the person. Some people seem like they won't live more than a year but survive for ten years or more, so if one takes care of oneself, there are cases where people end up dying of old age."

"Isn't there something like a general prognosis? What is the prognosis for ovarian cancer?" It felt weird to be so calm, as if she were asking for someone else and it felt like her voice wasn't coming out of her own throat.

With a slightly troubled face, the doctor talked slowly. "Well . . . these generally don't have such a good prognosis. You could say the prognosis is very different than for, say, skin cancer."

"I think I'm dying," Hee-sook turned her head towards her son. After she said it, she realized too late that it wasn't an appropriate thing to say as a mother.

"What are you saying? Why are you . . ." Pausing, he burst into tears. He sobbed like a small child. She held his shoulder and thought regretfully, 'I shouldn't have brought the kid.' She resented that her husband's schedule had sent him off on a business trip just in the nick of time.

"Let's schedule the surgery; we can find out more information by opening you up." Ending with that and asking, "Do you have any more questions?" the doctor left the office. Behind Hee-sook, who said, "Thank you," and followed him out, her son murmured, "Thank you, my ass. Who the hell does he think he is?" Her son was convulsing with anger. 'That doesn't help me at all,' Hee-sook thought. 'Should I talk to my friend? She would probably be honest with me.' Hee-sook had always found her straightforward and practical.

2. Compassion

"What was it you said? Oh, you went to the hospital, right? Did you say you were sick?" Three days later, in the evening, Hee-sook's husband, who had just returned from a business trip, was looking tired. It was only natural that he didn't have the slightest idea what was going on because she had never said anything about it: that her belly had swollen up or that she had been given a PET scan. It was, of course, Hee-sook who dissuaded her son from calling his father, telling his brother who was studying abroad, or postponing his return to the base. As always, he quietly obeyed his mother.

"Couldn't it just be menopause? My friends tell me their wives are all out of sorts these days. Why don't you take some pills? The vitamins that, who was it, Min-woo brought last time, they're supposed to be premium quality. Try those."

It was Sun-woo, not Min-woo, but now wasn't the time to bring that up, nor the time to criticize him for not being able to remember the names of his thirteen nieces and nephews.

"I . . . you see. I was told I have cancer, peritoneal cancer." Her voice had no highs and lows. Her husband, who was undressing, dropped his tie from his hand. His eyes instantly turned red. He stiffened like a statue. Hee-sook slowly approached her husband and picked up his tie, reaching around his foot.

The next day the couple went to see her friend. Her friend gave a truthful and detailed explanation and the point was this: cancer cells had been discovered. There would be an operation. The results could not be known at this time . . . Hee-sook's husband wanted to know why, how in the world this kind of thing happened. But her friend said, "That kind of question doesn't help. What's important at this point, you see, is to stay calm. You have to trust your primary care doctor and follow his instructions. Once we have the biopsy results, I'll give you my opinion."

Her attitude was so detached that it came off as coldness. Hee-sook's husband became angry. He looked blankly at his wife's friend, like a fool, because he was angry but could not be angry; there was no one to be angry at.

On the way home he felt a little ashamed. He realized too late that he hadn't consoled his wife. She was only fifty-four. Wasn't that too young to die? He was mortified and felt it was all unfair. His wife was healthy and diligent and the most sincere person he knew. It had never once occurred to him even in his wildest dreams that she might die before him, and he was choked with anger and incomparably ashamed of himself for looking like such an idiot in front of her. Naturally, he began to feel guilty that maybe he had caused her illness. He didn't think he was a particularly difficult husband, but he couldn't be sure. His wife was not the sort of person to nitpick and complain.

In the passenger's seat his wife closed her eyes and leaned back. "*Yeobo*,"[3] he said.

Suddenly her eyes opened wide. "What is it?" she asked. The moment he saw her eyes, he burst into tears. He turned the steering wheel and pulled onto the shoulder.

"Let's try another hospital. Isn't there a chance the diagnosis could be wrong?"

She looked at him with clear eyes. Those eyes that captivated him, those beautiful, limpid eyes had dark circles under them. "The doctor . . ." and she tightly shut her parched lips. Forcing himself not to reach for her hand, he gripped the steering wheel tightly. She never changed her mind or thought twice once she had decided something, and she didn't regret things, either. She frightened him when she was like that, and she was like that right now. He didn't know what else to say. The beams of summer sunlight pricked his eyes.

At night he couldn't sleep and he watched his wife sleeping, breathing evenly. He was thinking about the changes that her body—her corporeal form that fell so gently into sleep—would go through now. The moonlight sneaking through the window sat on her shoulders. He was about to touch her shoulders, brightly shining in the moonlight, but drew his hands back. He was afraid to touch her. 'She is sick. She might die . . .' Something he had never even imagined until a few days ago had suddenly happened to him. 'This is wrong,' he thought.

'There's got to be some way, some kind of treatment, a good treatment.' He was by nature an optimistic person. 'When the morning comes, I'll call someone and ask. I'll find a way out of

---

3 The familiar term that spouses usually call each other; it is not a term of endearment.

this.' Warily, he lay down beside her. The serenity of her breathing passed over him. 'How can she sleep so peacefully?' he wondered, gratified, but puzzled.

The next morning he woke up early as usual, but his wife wasn't awake yet. He went to the kitchen and opened the rice cooker. It was empty. He removed the covers from the two pots on the stove, and saw that they contained seaweed soup and marinated beltfish. 'Where would the rice be?' He searched the pantry and the refrigerator but didn't see anything that looked like rice. Finally, he found a rice jar under the sink. He went into the bedroom, looked at his sleeping wife, and came back into the kitchen. "So, would this be enough water?" Talking to himself, he put washed rice in the rice cooker and pushed the button. Beep, it made a weird tone. "White rice cooking initiated." The rice cooker spoke with a pretty woman's voice. "Well, then," he said, looking curiously at the red rice cooker.

As he opened the refrigerator, taking out the containers of *kimchi*[4] and other side dishes, he heard her waking up. He went to the room at once, "Why don't you sleep a little longer? I'll do the cooking from now on." A faint smile crossed her face. She didn't ask, "Do you know how to make rice?" or "Did you find the rice?" or anything. She silently covered herself up with the sheet and lay back down. He began to feel awkward, so he left the room. It was strange for him to start the day before his wife, but he would have to get used to it sooner or later. He would probably have to get used to a lot of other things, too, but he thought, 'Let's just do what I can for now.'

3. Underway

The operation took a very, very long time. After seven and a half hours, the door of the operating room opened, and a group of doctors came out. "Doctor, how . . ." Hee-sook's husband blocked

---

4 A traditional Korean staple; pickled vegetable, most commonly made with Napa cabbage, red pepper flake, garlic, and fish preserve.

the way of the primary care doctor.

"It went well. There's no need to be too concerned." Looking extremely fatigued, the doctor pushed past him and moved to the end of the hall.

"We'll set up an appointment for tomorrow and give you all the details then. Today's operation was really difficult." Hee-sook's husband attached himself to the other doctor, who was kindly explaining the situation to him.

"First, before that, just roughly . . . the situation . . ."

"Dad, over there," his son grabbed his arm.

Pushing the operating door open, a bed escaped. Hee-sook was lying on the bed from which several bags of fluids were hanging. As soon as he saw her colorless face and cracked lips, tears streamed down his face. "*Yeobo, Yeobo, Yeobo . . .*" He stood by the bed and touched his wife's forehead. She was cold.

"We're moving her to the ICU now, so you can wait for her there. And you might want to stay near her room tonight. Her pulse stopped, though just for a little while. We had a serious situation," an intern pulled him away. He followed the bed alongside his son.

The middle of the night. When Hee-sook awoke, the wall clock read four o'clock in the morning. The room was dark, and for a moment she was totally bewildered. 'Where is this? Where am I? Am I dead? . . .' She could hear the rhythmic beeping of machines above her head. She looked up and saw an IV attached to a needle in her arm. She thought of the cold air in the operating room and the moment when her consciousness faded away as she was counting one, two, following someone. With a heavy arm, she felt the tube clinging to her nose and chest. A young man in the bed next to hers moaned. His entire body was wrapped in white dressing.

"You're awake. How are you feeling?" A nurse approached Hee-sook.

"I'm feeling . . ." It wasn't easy for her to tell how she was feeling. She felt as though something had left her body and she was a little cold, but she also felt like she was suspended in mid-air, the way it felt when she ran a fever. But all she said was, "I feel fine."

"You're in the ICU and the operation seems to have gone well. Your husband was outside until a little while ago. Do you want me to find him for you? Visiting hours start at seven a.m." She was a kind nurse. *There's no need to do that. That's OK.* A strange voice came out of Hee-sook's throat. She closed her eyes. She had learned more about the prognosis for peritoneal cancer from the Internet. The postings people wrote about their grandmother or mother consistently said one or one and a half years was the limit. One year . . . the time it took to pass from fifty-four to fifty-five. What was going to happen to her during that time? If that was all she had left, what should she do? Oddly enough, she wasn't sad or afraid. Hee-sook gradually began to think about her year as if it were someone else's story.

"We excised the cervix first and, of course, removed the ovaries. We removed a fair amount of ascitic fluid. You should breathe more comfortably now. Fortunately, the cancer doesn't seem to have metastasized to other organs. The liver and stomach are clean. We took out all the cancer cells we could remove. The problem is the cells in the peritoneum. We're going to put you on chemotherapy . . . If you have any questions, feel free to ask." Her primary care doctor seemed kind, but he was very perfunctory. Hee-sook's husband cautiously asked how much of the cancer would be removed by chemotherapy. The doctor looked at him blankly.

"What I'm asking is, if you give her chemotherapy and the cancer cells are removed . . . whether that means she can recover."

His speech became more measured. "In the case of this patient, it is hard to say. As you know, we're talking about living cells. Each person and each case is different. It varies a lot, depending on the willingness of the patient to fight and the care provided by the family. Anyway, prepare yourself and . . . this is just the beginning."

"I could have guessed what Doctor Shim would say without you telling me. He's highly capable in his field but a little self-protective. He takes principles and statistics very seriously. He doesn't say anything unpleasant. Sometimes he goes too far and doesn't say what's helpful."

Although her tone was decisive, she maintained a gentle expression on her face. Hee-sook looked at her friend with longing in her eyes. "I would like you to tell me exactly how it is. You know." This was the only reason she had come to see her. What she needed was not consolation. She wanted to know the exact facts.

"You . . . are still the same." Her friend's lips, which seemed blown-up and looked like the only living part of her face, moved slowly. "I'll be straight with you. I think you have about a year and a half. In the case of ovarian cancer, the fact that it went this far means you probably won't have longer than that." The words were chopped up in pieces and dropped in front of Hee-sook. "If I were you . . . if I were in your shoes, I wouldn't get surgery. I wouldn't do chemotherapy, either. My mom, you know about her, right? When she was diagnosed with liver cancer, that's what she did. She went to *Jochiwon*, ate whatever she wanted to eat, did whatever she wanted to do and she passed away peacefully. Two years. I don't think the amount of time really makes that much difference."

A few feet away from the office, Hee-sook's husband clicked his tongue. "Is that really your friend? What kind of doctor is she?" He barely swallowed the words that threatened to escape his lips, "You two are so similar."

"I asked her to tell me the truth. It's not her fault." There was no feeling in her voice. He walked away, hanging his head like a shamed child.

The chemotherapy ran in three-week cycles. Admitted to the hospital the day before the treatment, treated for two days, left to vomit for two days and then sent home, Hee-sook lost a fair amount of hair. When she woke up, a pile of hair stuck to her pillowcase. When she was about to be released after her third round of chemo, she asked her husband to shave her head.

"Me?" He looked as if he might cry.

"I wouldn't be comfortable going to a hair salon. Wouldn't

it work if we cut it with scissors and then used your razor?" She covered her shoulders with a sheet, brought in a small chair and sat on it. Her face reflected in the mirror was small like a child's. She looked through the mirror at her husband's hand, which was trembling as he held the scissors. *Shrick*, the scissors sounded, and a handful of hair fell to the floor. The hair had lost its sheen and it looked like animal fur.

"You look cute with your head shaved. You look like a child monk. Why don't we take a picture to commemorate it? It'll be fun to look at it later, don't you think? Where's the camera?"

Hee-sook looked blankly at her husband's back as he was opened the wardrobe. 'A person who is simple-minded, honest, and innocent as a child . . .' The fact that her husband hadn't changed a bit from the man she knew made her feel both fortunate and desolate.

4. Practice

Her condition appalled everyone who knew her. "What in the world? A person like her, what's happening to the world, what kind of nonsense is this?" Her sisters-in-law burst into tears and her brother-in-law said, "Oh. Well," and couldn't say anymore.

Hee-sook always used to wake up at six o'clock every morning and walk to the *Yaksootuh*[5] behind the house, breathing in the fresh air from the night. When she came back, she had breakfast with her husband and sons, who had gotten up in the meantime. It was always seaweed soup or dried fish soup or beef soup with cooked greens, fish, vegetables, and fruit, always food that was in season and purchased through the organic food cooperatives. For her son, whose skin was hypersensitive and prone to allergic reactions, and her husband, who had hay fever, she was very attentive, especially with food, and she filled their pillows with organic buck-

---

5 A natural spring that is known for having good, healthy water, usually located on a mountain.

wheat hulls and starched their cotton sheets.

"Nobody uses this kind of stuff anymore. Why don't you give it a rest?" Although her sisters-in-law nagged her once in a while, she insisted on it. They had been middle and high school students when she got married, and now they visited her almost every day. Their children, who were lined up in front of them, cried, calling out "Auntie," were scolded for their tears, and quietly left the room. After several visits to the hospital, the kids learned to walk quietly and speak in low tones.

"By the way, we got it back. That photo we took. You look really pretty, like a celebrity. Do you want to see it?" Hee-sook's husband asked her, sitting at the dining room table at the end of the evening. It was their thirtieth anniversary next month. It was her son who had suggested that they all take a picture before he got married, before the family expanded, and before his younger brother left to study abroad. Her husband bought her a sky-blue two-piece dress, and she went to the hair salon for the first time in years. Her husband gave her exaggerated compliments. It was before they knew she was sick. Her pale face floating in the dark background looked like a stranger's. The woman, whose long eyelashes looked artificial, smiled a big smile, her eyes slightly squinted, probably because of the lighting. Hee-sook softly stroked the faces of her two sons standing side by side in the rear in the picture. The grainy touch was delivered to her fingertips, and the lament rose within her heart like a wave. 'Maybe we'll use this as a portrait for my funeral. It might be unsuitable because of the big smile on my face.'

5. Wound

Time passed slowly. During the days of chemotherapy, as she wrestled with nausea, she felt like time stopped. Her once clear skin was turning yellow, and she developed spots under her nails that looked like the teeth of a comb. One afternoon, Hee-sook was visited by her doctor friend. She had just been released from the hospital after a chemotherapy treatment.

"How are you holding up?" Her friend's face looked blank, as if nothing had happened. A long time ago, when she and her friend were at school together, they used to send each other notes. While they were exchanging notes about trivial things—like 'Last night, my dad, well . . .' or 'My brother, you know . . .'— she and her friend took turns being at the top of their class. Later their friendship went astray and they began to hate one another, finally forgetting about each other, because of a tutor they shared, a college student.

The man, Jeong-soo, who was now her friend's husband, used to show up to lessons looking worn out, asking them in a dull voice if they'd done their homework, and tutoring them with a languid expression. The room smelled like sweat, cigarettes, and poverty when he was in it, and he would doze off during their breaks, leaning up against the wall.

"Whew, male stench." After he left the room, her friend would open the windows, shaking her head. She couldn't say it was a good smell, but Hee-sook somehow felt sad, feeling the trace of him disappear into the cold night air. Everything about him, the small dark patchy mustache, his blistered hands from *Kendo*,[6] and even the worn-out heels of his socks, stuck in her heart. It was probably not that he was actually special, but rather that she felt he was special. Because she had grown up with four sisters and always gone to girls' schools, he was the first man she had spent a lot of time with. Her friend, who went to church, had several male friends. Sometimes, out of nowhere, she would promise to introduce Hee-sook to them, but Hee-sook had no interest in boys her own age who wrote ridiculous, childish letters. Although at the time it was trendy to fall in love with older people like teachers, Hee-sook was sure that wasn't the case with her.

On the day they got the results of their college entrance exams, he took Hee-sook and her friend out to a western-style res-

6 A Japanese style of fencing.

taurant. Sitting across from him, holding knives and forks in their hands, they cut the meat and drank the beer. Wearing a suit, he still smelled like poverty, but nevertheless he paid for the meal, which was not cheap, and gave them each some pocket money. It was a long time before Hee-sook learned that the money had come from a large envelope that her friend's mother had given him.

Her friend's mother was highly self-interested and trend-conscious. At that time, most mothers could be found in the kitchen, wearing an apron, but her friend's mother dressed in a fine suit and was out all day. They soon moved from a small town to a small city, and then to Seoul.

During his four years of medical school, Hee-sook continued seeing him, though not often. They went on dates to the *kimbap*[7] shop, the movie theater, the café, and the night market. Sometimes they strolled around *Kyeongbok-gung*[8] when it was quiet or hurriedly walked the cold streets. At times like that he held her cold hand and put it in his coat pocket. She felt embarrassed thinking of how she wanted to hang on to his arm, and walked hesitantly, leaving her hand to him. He asked her in that awkward position if she wanted her hand back, "What, don't you like it?" She could only nod because it was hard to look at his face. She would stand in the streets of *Dongsung-dong*, hoping to run across him, and when she saw his face approaching from a distance, she felt happy.

The reason she couldn't simply be happy, the thing she couldn't and didn't tell anyone, happened not long after. He became incomprehensibly violent. Once, during a conversation, he suddenly stood up like a bolt and threw his fist at Hee-sook's cheek, who was sitting beside him. They were at a gathering with a friend of his. The *soju*[9] glass crashed to the floor, and everyone in the bar looked at her.

"Man, are you out of your mind?" His friend hurriedly pulled him outside. Hee-sook stood looking blankly at their receding backs. Her cheek was burning, but she didn't feel pain. 'What did I say? Was he that drunk?' Hee-sook grabbed her bag and slowly

---

7 Korean-style sushi, made of a seaweed wrap filled with rice, cooked vegetables, marinated meat, etc.
8 One of the palaces of the Yi-Dynasty; it is open to the public.
9 A traditional and popular Korean alcoholic beverage.

left the place. He called her the next day and told her he remembered nothing.

"But I'm really sorry. I've been so stressed out these days," he said. Just when it was almost forgotten, he hit her again. Once on the street, and once more at night in a nearby playground, when she was sitting on a swing with him, he punched her in the face without any reason or warning. They were talking gently—"I see. Is that so? . . ."—when out of nowhere, he suddenly became aggressive, and it happened. Though he was drunk both times, Hee-sook had no warning, because his speech and gait were normal. She ran away from him both times. She was terrified. The next day, he called and asked, "Did I do something? Did something happen?"

Instead of saying, "You hit me. It hurt," to a man who couldn't remember doing anything, she only said, "You were probably under a lot of stress." She felt it was useless to poke and pry and blame someone for something he didn't even remember doing, and she was afraid he would stop seeing her. So she waited for his impulsive, incomprehensible violence to settle down. Until the smell of poverty left him little by little, and he asked her unexpectedly one day, "Why are you with me?"

They were on their way out of a movie at the French Cultural Center. Hee-sook had just been thinking of suggesting they go to his favorite place, *Keunjeong-jeon*.[10] 'Why am I with you?' She wanted to give him a casual answer like, "Because I like you," but he looked serious and she wasn't sure what kind of answer he wanted.

"I mean, why do you date me?" he abruptly yelled at her. 'Is he angry because of what happened during the movie?' She thought of his hand covertly reaching over her shoulder, just as Marlon Brando's morose face loomed large on the screen. When his hand traveled from her back to her waist and then to her breasts, she had twisted away, startled. He had withdrawn his hand as though he'd touched fire . . . While she stood there thinking, he left her, crossing the street in long strides and disappearing into a taxi. She realized it was over when she got the wedding invitation inscribed with his name and her friend's.

10 Part of Kyeongbok-gung palace.

"Your son called me from the base yesterday, you know. He said he had heard from his father, and he put me on the spot, saying 'what were you thinking, telling her everything straight?' He went on, asking if I had some kind of grudge against you." Holding the cup of coffee she had made, her friend looked around the house. With its uncovered windows and empty walls, the house was barren. Like Hee-sook herself, the house stood as it was, without any decorations. Hee-sook said she was sorry, but her friend nodded. "No, he was kind of cute, actually. And I do hold a grudge against you."

Hee-sook's eyes opened wide.

"When you open your eyes like that you look exactly like you did before. You don't even look like a patient who just had surgery." Her friend smiled brightly. And then she asked Hee-sook suddenly, "You knew, huh? My husband's 'hitting problem.' You knew and you ran away, right?"

'What does that mean?' Unable to ask, Hee-sook stared at her friend.

"My husband, he told me about you after a fight. He said it was weird, that he was never like that before. It was because of you, he said. Well, it's not even funny. He said it became a habit because of you, because you accepted everything and didn't seem to mind, no matter what he did." Hee-sook's face became pale.

"When I thought about it after you got sick, I realized he wasn't entirely wrong. You never do or say anything that might hurt or offend anyone. I think it all turned back in on you. I'd say that in sickness one is truly alone . . ."

Hee-sook's murmur didn't even come out as words.

6. Regret

"What are you talking about?" Hee-sook's father-in-law didn't understand at first when his younger son told him about Hee-sook's illness. He was hard of hearing. Even with a high quality hearing aid, he couldn't hear clearly.

"*Hyeongsoo*[11] has cancer, father. Her doctor says it's terminal." The son spoke carefully, looking at his father and moving his lips accurately. Sitting in a massage chair his son had bought him, he froze.

"What . . . in the world . . . what . . . ?" The vein in his hand, holding the arm of the chair, bulged.

"Actually, it wasn't true that she went on a trip to Southeast Asia. She had an operation." It had been thirty years. Since she had married into his family at the age of twenty-four, until now at the age of fifty-four, Hee-sook had always been there when he called her. When he, who went to bed early, woke up in the early morning and called to her, "Hey," he would hear her long "Yes," and she would appear holding whatever he wanted: a cup of coffee or a half-bowl of ramen or hot red-bean porridge. Her eyes were still sleepy, but she was always neatly dressed. Sometimes she had to make noodles from scratch instead of the rice she had already cooked, because his tastes were capricious. Or she had to make rice-cake soup or soup with sweet rice dough flakes, but she never seemed to mind.

"So . . . if it's terminal, does that mean she won't survive?" He looked straight at his son. He wanted the truth. His wife had fallen and died on the way home from the bathhouse on a cold day. It had been more than ten years ago. After she was dead he found out she had already had two seizures. Nobody, not his wife, his sons, or his daughters, had told him the truth. The fact that he sometimes got annoyed and yelled at his wife, who suffered from heart disease, had filled him with regret for a long time. In his daughter-in-law's case, he wanted to know the truth.

"Her primary care doctor only said that the results of the operation weren't bad, but . . ." His son measured his response stealthily and continued, "My friend's older brother specializes in gynecology and happens to be friends with Hee-sook's primary care doctor, so I asked him, and he said we can reasonably expect a year and a half . . . He said that in her case the chemotherapy

11 The familiar term usually used by a man for his older brother's wife.

wouldn't make much of a difference. It would only be more painful for her, so we should let her do what she wants and eat what she wants and be comfortable . . ."

Cutting his son short, he abruptly exploded, "What the hell are you talking about? Don't you know what century we live in? There must be so many good medicines . . . we have to do whatever we can. We have no time to wait. Let's go! Which hospital is she at?" Jumping to his feet, he moaned, "Ow!"

"Father!" The startled son grabbed his shoulders.

"I'm fine. Let's get going." Even though his back throbbed with pain, he made a great effort to walk.

"She's not in good shape, father. She had chemotherapy today. She's been throwing up and feeling irritable . . . Even if she's unpleasant, please try to cheer her up."

Shoving aside his babbling son, he opened the door of her room. Her shaved head met his eyes first. Something in his heart surged. He staggered forward.

"Father . . ." Hee-sook raised herself up.

"No, stay where you are . . ." He couldn't finish. Her shiny skin and plump cheeks were sunken, causing him unspeakable pain. Tears rose up in his eyes.

"Father, please don't . . ." Hee-sook smiled faintly. He was sitting in a small metal chair, holding her hand. Her hand felt hot and feverish.

He said, "My hands are cold," and she said, "It's better to be cold, father." He didn't know how to speak or what to say. The feverishness entered him, warming his hand. He stood up and went to the bathroom, running cold water and washing his hands for a long time.

"Well, can I hold your hands again?" With his hands cold again, he soothed her hands as long as he could.

"This is . . ." The envelope that he thrust at her contained his checkbook and his seal.

"What is this? Father, we have money. And we have health insurance." She reacted with dismay. She knew very well how extraordinarily frugal he was.

"It's not for your treatment. Buy whatever you want, spend it in whatever way you want, get well soon and go on a trip if you want . . ." Finally, he burst into tears.

7. Downhill

Hee-sook woke up at the crack of dawn. Something, a sharp pain, woke her. Even after opening her eyes she couldn't tell where the pain was coming from. "What was that?" she mumbled, and when she tried to turn over, a moan escaped her lips. She couldn't move her body, it was stiff like wood. Trying to raise her arms and then her back, Hee-sook muffled a scream. Her right leg was swollen like a balloon. She stretched her arm and woke up her husband. Jumping up from his seat, he turned pale.

"What is it, *Yeobo*? What's happening to your leg?" In confusion, he hurled questions at her all at once, "Are you in pain? Do you feel anything? What should I do? Should I call an ambulance?"

"Who's going to be at the hospital now? Can you give me a massage first?" Hee-sook began to regain her composure. By coincidence, her primary care doctor had just left for a conference in Europe.

"What could happen in a week?" She was reminded of his empty smile before he left. She had to grind her teeth and remain patient. She endured the pain until morning. Every once in a while a groan made its way past her lips. At around ten o'clock two men and a woman entered her room. A man in a purple modernized *hanbok*[12] started massaging Hee-sook's leg. He pushed down on her feet and between her toes, patting her lower leg.

"Ouch, ouch," she cried.

"It will hurt. The pain means it's getting better. The poison has

12 Traditional Korean attire.

spread into your leg. It's going to be more difficult than your last treatment," the man said solemnly. He was the same person Hee-sook's husband had hired after her first operation. She was told he had come through terminal pancreatic cancer by practicing advanced "*Ki* training."[13] He had saved the life of a distant relative of a colleague of one of her husband's upperclassmen. The woman who had come with him opened the bag and handed him a syringe. He injected small amounts of the clear liquid here and there on her swollen leg. "This is ginseng extract. It neutralizes the poison." While they were patting her down, turning her over, and poking her, she closed her eyes as if she were dead. His breath reeked of stale tobacco smoke.

"Look, the swelling has gone down a lot, right?" the man asked, finished with the treatment.

"It looks like it. Thank you for your work. Let's step outside." Hee-sook's husband couldn't really see a difference, but he was grateful, at least, that she was able to sleep again.

"Would you mind making me a large, strong cup of coffee?" the man asked politely. Hee-sook's husband turned on the cordless kettle.

"May I ask as well?" the other two requested, so he poured two packets of instant coffee in each of the three mugs and filled them with the hot water that had just come to a boil. The three made slurping sounds as they drank their coffee.

"She's a lot worse than last time. You should've continued the treatment as I suggested . . ." The man in the *hanbok* said. It was because of Hee-sook that they stopped the so-called treatment. She said she hated the man's rubbing and massaging and stroking.

"What will the fee be for today?" Hee-sook's husband asked.

"Well, our teacher . . ." The man in the *hanbok* looked at the man in the black shirt. The man called "teacher" looked at Hee-sook's husband, almost staring as if he was angry. His eyes were bright and keen, which somehow made one feel small. They had already told the story of how the man had been practicing "*Ki* training" for the past thirty or so years at the base of *Jirisan*,[14] and that he was the best in his field.

---

13 A mind-body training similar to Chinese Chi training.

14 One of the biggest mountains in South Korea. San means mountain.

"Besides the payment . . ." After pausing for a while, he re-sumed speaking. "If you leave her like that, she's going to die."

"She's been getting chemotherapy . . . Now she's being inject-ed with zinc compound . . ." Hee-sook's husband told him.

"As you know, the chemotherapy is a poisonous substance. It ruins the body. It's not enough to just protect her body from the cancer, and it's foolish to expect her to recover when you're dam-aging her body." His voice had a unique sonority. "There is still hope in her. When I saw her just now her spirit was alive. Her willingness and her body's response . . . altogether she is an ex-traordinary person."

"So, what are we supposed to do? If we move her to *Jirisan* as you suggest, she . . ."

"If she doesn't want to, she can get treatment at home. It's complicated for me to come, but what can we do? Her life de-pends on it. I'll come twice a week. There's something you need to prepare. You saw it a little while ago. You have to get me twelve ginseng roots. They must be one hundred years old."

He looked at the man blankly. He had been about to say, "Thank you for offering to come all this way," but now he stopped short, unsure of what to say.

"One hundred years old," said the man in the *hanbok*. "It's not easy to find, but it's not impossible if you go through an associa-tion. It costs about a hundred million *won* per root.[15] Our teach-er has his own unique method of manufacturing, distilling, and extracting it, you see. And you can pay for it separately . . ."

"Wouldn't that be too much of a burden? If our teacher looks for it, it's possible to find it for thirty million won," said the wom-an, who was fidgeting with her empty coffee cup. She was proba-bly a little over fifty and quite ordinary-looking, like women you could see all over town, but the two men called her Director Yoon in a respectful tone.

The man in the shirt shook his head. "No, no. It's better for you to find your own wild ginseng. And then there will be no chance of misunderstandings."

"Oh, I see . . ." Hee-sook's husband nodded ambiguously.

"We're well aware that this is not an easy decision to make. But you should let us know as soon as you can, so we can schedule you in."

A billion won ...[15] He had inherited some assets from his father, and although his business was small, it was stable enough to afford that much money. However, he couldn't make a decision, even after going over and over what the men had said. He called his siblings. Before he even finished talking, his younger sister said, "He's a con man, *Oppa.*"[16]

His younger brother was a little more cautious, asking, "Did she get any better?"

"The swelling seems to have gone down a little ... Anyway, she fell asleep. She had been tossing and turning all night ..." he said in a tentative voice. His brother asked again how he had found out about this person, told him to wait while he asked a friend who was a doctor of traditional Korean medicine, and hung up the phone.

When it was a little past eleven, his brother rang the doorbell. Even though he'd just gotten off the elevator, he was gasping for breath as if he'd run up the stairs. 'He needs to get more exercise,' Hee-sook's husband thought. His brother tiptoed into the bedroom and said, "She's become like a shadow in just a few days." He said it as if he were talking about someone suffering from the flu.

"Well, according to my friend, it's hard to say whether the wild ginseng is effective or not ..." He observed his brother's mood and was silent for a while. He was a warmhearted and thoughtful person. "I've been talking to him about her condition. He said that it's now in the final stages, which means that she's coming to the end, so the cancer cells will take all the nutrients she eats and it is very likely that her body won't be able to withstand treatment."

When his brother finished talking, he didn't say anything. Sitting side by side, they looked out the living room window.

"*Hyeong,*"[17] his brother said, "shouldn't you call your younger one in the States? Even if *Hyeongsoo* says not to, I think you should call that kid."

---

15 Approximately a hundred thousand dollars.
16 The familiar term usually used by a younger sister for an older brother.
17 The familiar term usually used by a younger sister for an older brother.

Something rose in his throat. His son who had no idea about his mother's sickness—the impact it would have to see his mother's changed face and gaunt body, and the pain his wife would feel when she had to face her son's eyes—it all weighed on him so heavily. He rubbed his chest as if trying to soothe it. The light from the illuminated cross on top of the church across the road bathed the window in red.

8. What Grows out of Sadness

He was afraid of that forgotten truth, that the human body was mysterious. About two weeks after she had been moved into the hospice ward, it looked like her body had hit its limit. Five minutes after sipping water she would vomit it all up along with dark green bile, the fluids and vital energy leaving her body. As soon as she heard the words, "Today you ate quite a bit of rice porridge," her face turned yellow and her arms stretched toward a spitting jar. It seemed that the pain left her body now by the power of morphine, but instead she sank into an endless sleep. 'Would it be today? Or tonight?' The days, guarded nervously by her husband and sons, kept going, but she was still alive. After a month had gone by, her husband went to see her primary care doctor again.

"Doctor . . ." He had nothing else to say.

"It's hard to say," her doctor's stiff face twitched a little and something like a smile appeared. "She's strong by nature . . . Seeing her endure this much when we're unable to do anything. Maybe a miracle will occur."

"We don't expect any miracle," he swallowed the words. He just couldn't stand that his wife was still alive, going through such pain. "She's suffering too much. I mean, isn't there some technique, or can we start a new treatment?"

"Well, as we've already told you, the treatment is meaningless at this point. The cancer has spread throughout her body, you can even feel it on her skin . . . You know all that. You know what the chemotherapy does. Her body can't withstand it. This thing, this treatment, it's only for the consolation of the living."

He was looking at the doctor absentmindedly. This was the person who had said that the cancer cells seemed to be drying up, that he had turned things around in the beginning, and then that there was nothing they could do—all these things had been spoken by the same person. He wanted to get out of there immediately. He regretted having come.

"Well, what can we do? Other than watch her . . ." He stood up and the doctor awkwardly stood up as well.

The same night, her primary care doctor made a statement. "Tonight may be the end. You should be ready." Her husband called his siblings on his mobile phone. Soon her brother-in-law, sisters-in-law, and brother-in-law's wife showed up. Although her consciousness and senses were gone and all the energy had escaped her body, she was still breathing. It was an unstable and heavy breath; the middle of her chest would rise suddenly and then abruptly fall again. They silently watched the movement, its rising and falling, like a bellows filling with air. The evening dragged on, and her sisters-in-law, drying their eyes from time to time, began to grow tired. "She's probably not ready to go yet," one of them said. What could she be clinging to?

"She is sad. Your sister can't go because she is sad," her husband murmured.

"You know *Hyeongsoo* is not the kind of person to show her sadness. She's very strong-willed." Her brother-in-law remained calm.

She was sad but couldn't show her sadness . . . There must have been so much, the sadness that had built up . . . Unable to ponder the depth of the sadness his wife had endured, he stopped. He felt as if there were a plug in the middle of his chest. He started to cry, holding onto her bed. He let out a long, long wail. "*Yeobo, Yeobo, Yeobo* . . ."

"Mom, Mom . . ." their sons cried out.

"*Unni,*[18] *Unni,*" her sisters-in-law followed.

18 The familiar term usually used by younger females for older siblings, friends, or in-laws.

She heard their cries in her dreams. The tears of her husband, sons, and sisters soaked her clothes and her body. The sadness was rising like water inside her heart. Like a river, her consciousness flowed slowly beyond the darkness.

Dad's Private Life

1. The First Day: When I Feel Like I'm Going to Lose Myself

At fourteen years old I was already a grown-up. It was something a character in a novel had said. I wasn't a grown-up yet when I read that novel, but I looked like one. Five foot five—really, I was just a kid who happened to be tall. Being tall was useful in several ways. Getting into R-rated movies, dating high school or even college boys, stealing Mom's clothes . . . My face looked like my mom's, a typical Southern face, average really, but people easily mistook me for a real beauty, probably because of my height. After my first year of junior high, I grew even more and reached five foot seven, but my mom kept insisting that I was shorter. Mom had a theory that people, especially men, don't like women who are taller than five foot seven. Since she was a willful person, she just kept believing what she believed.

My height came purely from my dad's genes. The prominent nose set in his pale face, the clean-cut eyebrows, the deep eyes, and the beard that covered his entire face if he skipped shaving even one day. Looking at my dad, I was convinced that one of my grandfathers' grandfathers' fathers must have been a European. Of course, my dad strongly denied that. When we went out, Dad used to enjoy acting as though I were a young friend or girlfriend, and when people were surprised—"No way. You have a daughter this grown-up?"—he would break into a boyish smile, which suited his handsome face well. Hanging around cafés, movie theaters, restaurants, and bars with Dad, I was happy to pretend I was his young girlfriend, and Dad, looking at me like that, enjoyed it. With Dad, I could easily get used to hiding my real age and identity. He said that life was like a play and that I could change the expression of my eyes, my facial expression, and my mind when the stage changed, as if taking on a different role.

That was the year before last, when I failed my college entrance exam. The role I'm playing now, well, is something like a private detective. The client is me, and my assignment . . .

The captain announces our landing, "This is your captain speaking . . ." That sleepy voice that sounds like the person has just woken up, and crudely accented English. Do they all take the same class at the same training center or something? Otherwise, how could they possibly all sound the same? The plane feels as though it's whirling down and the buildings appear in miniature beneath us. Touching the U-shaped window, I look down. The place, which is small enough to be hidden by my palm, is Hong Kong.

"There. Your dad is getting out," Mina whispers, leaning in to me. Dad is standing in the middle of the aisle in the line of people headed toward the exit. In his black sunglasses and plaid shirt, he looks a little tired. He must be nervous. Hiding myself in the seat, my eyes are fixed on him.

"Lady Unidentified just got up, too. Two people ahead."

Mina's voice reveals her excitement. Having picked up some ideas from who knows where, Mina dubbed her Lady Unidentified and made a solemn face, saying, "Doesn't this feel like a detective novel?" We found her name, So-hee Han, by rummaging through Dad's mail, but we still insisted on "Lady Unidentified." So-hee Han suggests—how can I put it—too much decency and feminine modesty. Our Lady Unidentified, wearing a purple scarf, opens the overhead container and tugs on her luggage. Dad stretches out his long arms to help her.

"Oh, thank you," is all she says, her voice audible as far back as we are. Dad and Lady Unidentified stand next to each other in line, waiting to deplane as if they are strangers. They have yet to take up their roles as lovers.

"They're exiting the plane now. OK, they're out."

Mina swiftly stands up and picks up our luggage, saying, "Oh, I almost forgot." She means the stickers she collects with phrases like "Do Not Disturb" and "Please Wake at Mealtime." Mina has a longstanding habit of collecting trivial objects and things that look like trash wherever she goes. She enjoys decorating her projects with them. We're majoring in sculpture, making form out of everything we see, hear, touch, and feel. Mina entered the department last year and I joined her this year. Before that, we spent six years playing, running, drawing, and handling clay at an art school. Fifteen minutes later, when two-thirds of the passengers have gone, Mina gets out of her seat.

"I assume the targets are in the front of the line. That means there's no way they'd see us now."

Mina and I get our hats and sunglasses and head to the inspection counter. The crowd smells like unfamiliar food and the strong scent of herbs. I feel nauseous, like I do when I drink. Of course I don't feel good. For your information, my limit is a glass of beer.

Although there are many people around, I immediately find Dad at the front of the line of foreigners. It's because he's tall. My dad, in no condition to be anonymous, stands side by side with Lady Unidentified, talking. Lady Unidentified keeps smiling.

"Hey, stop staring like that. A stare can be felt from far away," Mina warns me and I quietly drop my head. She is already experienced from when she tailed her dad's mistress, so in this arena she is the teacher.

"Don't be so uptight. Just think about enjoying yourself. We're on a trip, too."

"I don't like trips. It's not in my nature." My voice sounds blunt. The thought, 'Am I doing the right thing?' keeps coming back to me.

"That is your fatal weakness. Since ancient times every artist has needed to know how to enjoy traveling."

Ever since I consulted with Mina about my dad's affair, she's been acting like an older sister. Before, that used to be my role. She drags me through the line. Dad and Lady Unidentified are receding in the distance. They pass through the gate and head towards the escalator.

"No more following. We know their schedule. Let's go to our hotel first."

I stare at Dad's back fading into the distance. If he turned around, he'd be able to see me. Not sure if he'd recognize me though. I'm wearing a long brown wig. Like most men, Dad can't recognize women when their hair style changes. The two of them look natural and comfortable holding hands. They seem like a couple, old and gray, who still care for one another. Oh boy, what am I thinking?

"You seem like you're going to cry. I told you not to get carried away." She holds my arm.

"I'm not going to freak out. It's just, I feel so . . . crappy."

"What did you say when I told you about my dad's girlfriend? You said, 'Why don't you try being a grown-up? Your dad has a right to enjoy a love life, doesn't he?'"

I looked at her dubiously. Mina's dad is divorced, an available single man who does well as a fund manager. And it's obvious just from looking at Mina that her dad is good-looking. It would be strange for him not to have a girlfriend.

"Dads become nice when they are seeing someone. They hardly get angry about anything." Mina's face looks pretty serious.

There should be some reward for my playing detective. But my dad is nice by nature. He hardly ever gets angry anyway.

"Why don't you talk about yourself for a little while, about something other than your dad? You always listen to my troubles." Mina's long fingers grip my shoulder. Even without her words, I feel like playing the baby.

"I feel like a child. How do you say it, I feel like, all of a sudden, there's nothing and no one that I really know in this world."

Mina laughs, making a funny sound. "That's my line, my friend."

She has unburdened herself to me before, asking my opinion about many things that have happened to her. When she was accepted to three different colleges, when her parents got divorced, the day she was introduced to her mom's boyfriend, and when her little brother, a middle school student, was involved in a robbery. Since elementary school, Mina and I have been friends, and all the things that have happened to her have kept us as close as morning dew to the grass. It was natural that Mina would be the person I'd tell that my dad was seeing someone—or that I at least had a feeling he was seeing someone.

2. Ten Days Ago: At Three O'clock, When the Sunlight Is Rolling around Like Mercury

"Did you read it?" Mina asked me. What I had seen was a text message on my dad's mobile phone. I had slept late after staying up late working, and was just getting up. *Vrrr.* The phone vibrated under a newspaper on the corner of the dining room table. He probably forgot it when he went out. That was rare, since Dad used to sleep with it next to him. "Did you get some rest yesterday?" It was a simple sentence, but what I felt when I read it wasn't simple. I searched the inbox, checking the messages sent from that number. Dad wasn't very scrupulous, so there were several messages. "Might be a little late"; "Wait for me"; "Trying to get there soon"; and "Today is not good . . ." The messages were short and clear. I kept feeling like I was getting closer to the truth as I moved down the list of messages, one by one, like I was watching a fire spread throughout a house. I tend to respect other people's privacy in their love lives, and I'm not a strong supporter of monogamy. Nor do I think one should get excessively involved in people's personal lives just because they're family members. Still, this was different. At three o'clock in the afternoon, peeping at my dad's private life in the living room lit up by the sunlight slanting in from the veranda, it felt unreal.

"Isn't your dad a gentleman?" Mina had seemed surprised when she found out. Gentleness could be said to be Dad's motto. People usually think poets are cranky, but Dad was always a pretty ordinary person. He woke up early, drank a glass of skim milk, went to school, came home after his lectures, and went for a walk on the path behind our house. He became relaxed when he began to break a sweat, and then he came back home and read quietly in his study. Even when he was just hanging around the house in sweatpants, he was consciously stylish. The whole neighborhood, including all the apartment residents, and even the dry cleaner and the woman at the grocery store, knew Dad's occupation. Since it was rare to have a dad who was a professor and a poet, he was invited to my school from time to time as a guest lecturer. He was friendly to the kids, like a big brother or uncle, showing up in a white shirt and jeans. "Your dad is awesome." "He's so good-looking." The kids were jealous of me. As far as my dad was concerned, I had always felt lucky. A warm-hearted, diligent, and stylish professor. Except for the fact that he was too submissive to Grandfather, looking like a sad child, he seemed perfect to me. Until I found out about Lady Unidentified.

"All men are the same, though. Why don't you try and think of your dad as a man? Then you might feel better," Mina said, like an adult. But it didn't make me feel any better. That night I read Dad's emails. It was Mina's suggestion.

Dad's ID was poet94. 1994 was the year his first book of poems came out. When my grandfather got the book he said, "I guess you really are a poet." Dad, with an expression that seemed to say, 'Thank you for finally noticing,' responded with the proper etiquette to Grandfather's recognition. The problem was the password, but this was taken care of by trying several zeroes before and after Dad's birthday. Good to know it was worth listening to the advice to come up with a unique password. I checked his inbox first. Who says people don't read poetry these days? Think again. People didn't just read Dad's poetry. There were several emails from various IDs with excerpts of his poems and some silly, crude ideas. Some people seemed to consider it cute to quote lines of his poems to him, such as "Where the salt flat is, I am forty, Sitting on a flat bench in late autumn, Putting pressure softly on the edge of the path to the sea ..." (The lines are from "The Salt Warehouse"); or to ask him where it took place (That was my dad's hometown, *Kumdan-myun, Kimpo-gun*. The person was so serious about the question that I almost sent a reply. But I didn't want to risk getting caught). But there were also outright threats, saying, "I'll wait for you at such and such time and date on such and such place. If you don't show up, I'll come look for you at your school," causing me to wonder if they could sleep at night after sending something like that, even if it was anonymous. There were also some emails servilely begging him to do them the honor of reading their work . . . Being a poet was, indeed, a wearying occupation. Feeling relieved that I didn't have to read all these, I skipped over them. I finished searching the rest, including his sent box, and picked out three IDs among the ones I'd written down. MermaidL, soul99, and murder801. They were the ones who sent the most frequent emails. After comparing them with the dates of the text messages, MermaidL was left.

Dad and the mermaid had gone to Karaoke. Dad sang, "Love, about That Loneliness" in a sad tone. Dad and the mermaid went out for drinks (three different times). Dad saw the dead-drunk mermaid home (The mermaid wrote that he was a true gentleman, making sure she got home, and she really appreciated it). Once (I couldn't tell if they were with other people) they had gone to *Jeongdongjin* together. It was a cloudy day, so they couldn't see the sunrise. Dad and the mermaid saw the movie *The Island* together. The mermaid was a pharmacist. She sent some supplements to help Dad with a problem he was having, or that was threatening to come on. Dad received it. (I couldn't tell whether or not he took them.) The mermaid was about forty. She lived in *Boondang* . . .Well, it was a truly amazing result from such a small effort. There were only two possibilities. One was that they weren't really that close to one another. If that was the case, there would be no reason to destroy the emails. The other was that they were generally suspicious but careless in destroying the evidence. Whichever it was, it was clear that the computer was a dangerous thing. I logged into a music site and clicked on "Love, about That Loneliness." After the maudlin opening theme, a woman's voice started in, just as gloomily. *Could I ever meet someone and fall in love again . . .* The song was so unlike Dad's taste. Dad, who was slightly tone deaf, preferred singing songs that had a quick beat, so you couldn't really hear his tone clearly. It didn't fit his look, which made people like it even more. And how about *The Island* . . . Dad couldn't stand more than an hour of the stuffy air in movie theaters because of his sensitive respiratory system. He was a person who downloaded romantic, lyrical, and stylish movies and watched them in his study. Drinking Earl Grey, which he made himself. They had known each other for about five months, and the evidence that they were doing more than drinking tea or going to bars together was nowhere to be found. *To love someone is such a lonely thing* . . . The song ended and a lonesome silence followed. Taking Mina's advice, I kept fastidious records of everything I found.

3. The Second Day: Squatting and Looking, Endlessly

Mina and I are sitting on a couch in the corner of the hotel lobby where my dad is staying. Mina reads a book and I read a newspaper . . . no, hold a newspaper. I'm not so into TV dramas, but seeing myself copying them, I wonder if human beings have the instinct to follow. According to their schedule, Dad and Lady Unidentified were supposed to have the breakfast buffet from seven to nine a.m. The cafeteria is crowded with people holding dishes, but those two haven't shown up yet. They're probably sleeping in.

"Didn't you say they booked separate rooms? Could it be a cover?" Mina asked me. I don't know either—maybe, late at night, Dad knocked on her door, or perhaps they have adjoining rooms with a door between them. The confirmation email from the hotel says two rooms for three days.

"Those people are so noisy, aren't they?" Raising her sunglasses a little, Mina looks around inside the cafeteria. Around Chinese New Year, mainland Chinese people go on vacation in droves and are extremely boisterous. It's not the right season for a romantic trip, but then again, maybe it is. On the way back to the hotel, there were people swarming all over like bees.

"Hey, there she comes. Isn't that her?" The woman walking from the elevator—Lady Unidentified, in white pants and a black trench coat—looks noticeably more chic than yesterday. Hiding behind my newspaper, I watch her. A moderately built body, average height, with a black shoulder bag, Loewe sunglasses, and three-inch heels . . . Amidst the flat and round middle-aged Chinese women, her stylish outfit easily stands out. The man walking beside her is my dad. I retreat further behind my newspaper.

"Oh no, they're going outside. Hey, get up. I might lose them." Mina jumps up and is heading towards the turnstile. I follow her, pushing my hat down.

Dad and Lady Unidentified are getting into a taxi. We stop a taxi several cars behind them.

"Please follow that car."

The taxi driver looks at us suspiciously and asks, "What's going on?"

"They're my parents. I just want to surprise them." Mina's answer is as natural as if she'd prepared it. Her English is perfect. During every break from school she studied English abroad. The taxi driver keeps looking back at us with his suspicious eyes, as if to ask, "Is that true?" but he manages to keep up with the car. The taxi drives along a highway overpass, overlooking tiny, dark streets and busy avenues filled with cars.

"It was Ocean Park after the buffet, but . . . did they find a better restaurant?"

Although the driver wouldn't be able to understand Korean, Mina still whispers. It's not like Dad to make a reservation for a restaurant, but now I'm starting to get confused about this person I call Dad. After about twenty minutes, the taxi stops in front of a shabby restaurant. There is a signboard in Chinese characters that I can't read. The restaurant has a long line out front, and waiters holding menus are going through the line taking orders. Dad and Lady Unidentified, having exited the taxi, calmly approach the end of the line. We get out of our taxi about half a block down the street. "Good luck," the driver says cheerfully. The ugly wax figurines on the sidewalk provide us cover.

"That looks like at least a thirty-minute wait. Wow, *my* dad never goes to a restaurant where you have to wait. He gets cranky when his food is even a little late."

For that matter, my dad isn't that different, but I just say, "It's Hong Kong. Let's eat something, too. I'm about to fall over from hunger."

Since we boarded the plane I haven't been able to eat anything. The food on the plane smelled like dust or fungus, and the room service at the hotel is even worse. My eyes start swimming. I drag Mina into a small restaurant down an alley. A delicious smell is coming from a huge steaming pot. Suddenly, a rabid appetite comes over me. I feel like I could swallow everything in that pot.

The place seems to be a noodle and dim sum shop. I recognize *Hakka Hut* and *Siu Mei* on the menu, but that's about it. Glancing sideways at the next table, Mina and I ask the waiter what they are eating and what is in it, but unfortunately, the waiter doesn't speak any English. Finally, we choose three dishes and five minutes later the waiter bangs down two bamboo steamers dripping water and a wooden bowl filled with rice porridge. Taking a bite, I spit it out, thunderstruck. The searing hot meat juice had shot out of the dumpling skin. We swallow the food noisily. The dumplings and rice porridge are amazing.

"Look at that. They're still waiting."

When we have emptied the steamers and rice bowl and drunk all the tea, Mina pushes her digital camera toward me. I see Dad and Lady Unidentified. The two seem, at long last, to have reached the entrance.

"That place is a noodle specialty store called *Between Wu and Yue*. It's such a famous place that they say the wait is usually an hour to get in. What's written on the signboard means *Owolji-gan*,[19] well, you know, it's something about the Wu and Yue Dynasties."

19 The Korean translation of the phrase Between Wu and Yue.

It was a lot of information for having just strolled by the door for a few minutes.

"You look like a real professional, collecting evidence step by step. You could get a part-time job doing this." I'm not joking or being sarcastic, either. I mean it. A tiny camera that fits in her palm, a recorder the size of a pencil, sunglasses, a hat pushed far down, a long-haired wig . . . This is totally like being a spy.

"Most people walk around here with a camera anyway. You know, in the movies, Hong Kong is full of drugs, smugglers, gangsters, and stuff. I don't think anything would look weird here."

"I still feel a little weird about it all. About what my dad is doing. And what I'm doing . . ." I mean it, too.

We have to take a double-decker bus to get to Ocean Park. After making sure that my dad and Lady Unidentified are on the upper deck, we get on the bus. It's too bad, but to remain incognito we sit on the lower deck.

"Wow, hey, look at that. That escalator, that's the one from *Chungking Express*, isn't it?" Mina points across the street. She's still whispering. She wants to remain careful, just in case. In one corner of the narrow, sloped alley, there is a long escalator. The escalator is covered by a glass roof and walls and is full of people.

"Let's check it out later. I heard it's connected to the Soho streets. I finally feel like I'm in Hong Kong."

Both Mina and my dad are huge Wong Kar-Wai fans. Mina's ringtone is "California Dreamin'" and my dad's is "Quizás, quizás, quizás." It seems a bit too obvious to everyone. Because of them I saw *Chungking Express* three times, but due to what they call the hand-held technique or whatever, all I remember are some dizzy, shaky scenes. I at least remember the girl sneaking into the man's apartment, cleaning up his place, and falling asleep on his sofa, and the weird line when he's mopping up the water from the broken faucet and says, "My apartment cries." My dad cried when he saw *Comrades: Almost a Love Story.* The scene where Maggie Chung is sitting in a car and sees Leon Lai but doesn't have the courage to talk to him, then follows him and ends up putting her head down on the wheel. The horn honks so loudly that Leon Lai turns and looks at her ... Dad also cried when he saw *In the Mood for Love*. On the bus, the song from *In the Mood for Love* plays, a woman sings with a girlish voice. The bus, which has been driving for about an hour, passing forests of high-rise buildings on the highway, finally slows down. I see lines of tour buses and people. An uncomfortable feeling rises in my stomach. I don't like crowded places. As far as I know, neither does Dad.

"This is at least a two-hour wait," Mina murmurs, standing in the long line. We don't see any sign of Dad and Lady Unidentified. It seems impossible to find them in the swarm of people. A warm wind blows. Riding a cable car to the top, watching a dolphin show, riding a roller coaster, getting in line to buy fast food ... I nod my head unconsciously. This is really freaking me out.

"Did your dad do the same thing when he had an affair? He couldn't have possibly gone to an amusement park and ridden a cable car, could he?"

"Not an amusement park, but he did go to an ice-skating rink. It's the same thing, isn't it?" Mina snickered. Her dad's mistress was a young woman. "That weekend, I said to my dad, 'Dad, let's go ice skating. It's been a while.' Dad said, 'What? Ice skating?' He acted bored and did a good job pretending."

"That sounds familiar. It's like my Dad saying there was a poetry reading in Hong Kong."

"Did your mom say anything?"

"Yeah, she asked whether the universities were even open during the holidays. And then Dad said it seemed like they had scheduled it that way on purpose because they had a tradition during reading poetry on New Year's Day. He was very convincing."

My mom, who had been suffering through the New Year preparations at my grandfather's house, made a face that said, "Well, that's good. I can get some rest." On New Year's Day, twenty relatives and about thirty guests gathered at my grandfather's house. The middle-aged men solemnly bowed to Grandfather and, with a kind look, he passed out white envelopes. Everyone filled three rooms, eating *tteokguk*[20] and fruit, drinking *shikhye*,[21] and play-

---

20 A traditional Korean New Year's Day soup made with rice cake in a stock, usually made from beef bones.

21 A sweet dessert drink made of slightly fermented rice, malt, and sugar.

ing *hwatu*[22] with the money in the envelope. Being head daughter-in-law for twenty years had made my mom sick of it.

"Anyway, your mom is still nice to your dad. They dated for a long time."

Twenty-three-year-old Dad and twenty-four-year-old Mom. Dad, who was student teaching, had met Mom, who had recently started teaching. Mom was lively and generous. She helped unskilled Dad with things and filled in when he was late. Little by little, he fell for her. He believed she would love him like all the other women had. After his month of training was over, they didn't see each other. But he couldn't forget her voice, friendly smile, and the smell of warm citron tea she handed to him on the day he had to stay late to practice for the children's hymn-singing contest. One evening, he called her. He told her he wanted to treat her to a meal to thank her for all her help, but she told him she was busy. He called again the next day, but she still had somewhere to be and the next day she said the same thing. It was the first time he'd been in this situation and he felt embarrassed and annoyed. Somehow he found out where she lived, waited on her street and met her when she came home from work. For him this was an unusual experience.

"Why are you doing this?" Dad grumbled, and Mom smiled like a good-natured older sister. At that moment, he realized, "She's the one." He was grateful he'd gone through the teacher training, even though he'd initially only done it so that if worse came to worst he wouldn't have to inherit his father's work.

"Of course your dad was popular. He's good-looking, comes from a rich family, and he also studied abroad."

"My grandfather sent him to study abroad later. He was freaked out when my dad said he wanted to be a middle-school teacher. My grandpa thought Dad should have at least become a college professor. My dad's side is all well-off. Prosecutor . . . Doctor . . . Judge."

"Come to think of it, your dad must have been stressed. I heard my dad was the same. He almost got kicked out because he didn't study for the bar."

---

22 Korean playing cards. They are much smaller than Western cards and have colorful pictures on them.

Elders are all like that. They all want a sure thing, something to be proud of, something everyone else will see and say, "Oh, wow."

"So, your dad was a geek?"

"I think so. My grandpa is no joke. When you do something wrong, you're dead."

We talked about this and that. The line was long and we had nothing but time. It would be the same for Dad and Lady Unidentified.

The afternoon at Ocean Park was boring. Our turn finally comes and we take the cable car, but by then I'm thinking, 'What are people making such a big deal about?' As we float through the air, the sea beneath us and the yachts floating quietly on the bay are beautiful, like a picture. The cable car carries us upwards, making swooshing sounds at the end of its rope, and takes so long that I keep thinking, 'Aren't we there yet?' What happened between those two when they were left alone? Did my dad reach out and hold her hand?

"What a hand does is look for another hand. A left hand is always in search of a right hand, and my two hands search for others." It's a line from one of my dad's poems. His poems are as orderly as he looks. It's strange. Each new hillside reminds me of his poems. I didn't think I'd paid that much attention to them.

The chaos on the mountaintop where the cable car deposits us ... People, people, and even more people ... We see a special New Year's Day show, which ends up being a loud and boorish melodrama, we search the long line for the aquarium, go and check at the dolphin show, even though I'm sure they're not there, and pass by an enormous old roller coaster that looks like a movie set, but we can't find any evidence of Dad and Lady Unidentified. It's hot, noisy, and smelly ... I can't stand it anymore and say, "Let's go. Why don't we just go ride that Mid-Central escalator or something today?"

"Okay, let's do that. We can go back to their hotel later." Feeling tired as well, Mina meekly agrees. We leave the line of people, pass through the maze of streets, and find our way back. There is a long escalator going down.

"Chinese people have such a sense of scale, don't they? How long is this thing?" Even Mina, who hardly ever gets surprised, is impressed. She answers herself, "Once you go up, you might as well come back down." I am about to faint from exhaustion. I'm tired of everything: Dad, Lady Unidentified, following them, their affair. I am irritated and about to explode. Giving up on looking good, I sit down on the steps of the escalator.

"Hey, there they are." My hat had been hanging around my neck, and Mina suddenly pulls it over my head. Over there, down there, are Dad and Lady Unidentified. The distance between us is only about thirty feet. Close enough that our eyes would meet if they looked up. Suddenly I wake up from my daze. I watch them warily from behind Mina's waist. Lady Unidentified is in a yellow short-sleeve shirt, probably having taken off her black jacket, and looks cute, unlike she had this morning. I murmur, "What a chameleon." Dad is smiling. Lady Unidentified is smiling, too. What are they holding in their hands? It's ice cream. Dad, whose gums are weak, doesn't like sour or cold food. Of course, that means ice cream. The pink color in the cone is vibrant even from a distance. A bite after looking at one another, another bite after talking to one another, another bite after smiling, another bite after looking at one another again . . . It seems like this ice cream will never run out. It also seems like their gazing into each other's eyes will never end. The escalator moves down very, very slowly, as though it were endless.

On the way back to the hotel, Mina and I doze off. I feel like all the energy has left my body. How could I expect that seeing Dad eating ice cream would be so shocking? At least they hadn't been skipping down the stairs, playing rock, paper, scissors. Mina, who goes into the bathroom first, screams and says, "Hey, come here." The sluggish thing at her feet looks like a centipede. Even with its many legs it doesn't move, as if it were more surprised than Mina.

"What's the big deal? You've worked with insects before."

"That's what I'm saying. It reminds me of running around carrying an insect net with you."

Putting a dragonfly and a butterfly in a matchbox-like case,

Mina had also fashioned a girl about the same size and put her in the box. It was her entry for the high-school art competition her junior year. The idea of a girl kept penned up like that made us all sad. Mina picks up the centipede with a tissue. Only then does the bug twist its ugly body.

"They say this hotel has a history and even the bugs are old-fashioned. Look at this one. It has several different layers of color."

Her eyes, looking at the bug, sparkle as if she's found a toy. I snatch the clump of tissue from her hand and throw it in the toilet. "Whoa, whoa, whoa," says Mina, watching the clump of tissue disintegrating with an extremely sad face. If I had left it, she would definitely have tried to preserve it. Until she could use it for something.

"Your dad, I think, is not going to be easy." Mina says, lying on the bed.

"I agree." I have nothing else to say.

"In my opinion, your dad and Lady Unidentified are not just casually involved."

"I agree."

"In fact, this is more dangerous."

"I agree."

"That woman looked so cute today."

"I agree."

"Hey!" Mina yells at me suddenly. "Why the hell do you just keep saying, 'I agree'? We have to think of something."

"That's what I'm saying."

"Let's think about it. If—just if—your dad and she really like each other . . . What do you think they'll do?"

"Well . . ." I can't finish my sentence. Dad is a timid and moral person.

"There's no way he can ask for a divorce, right?"

"Well . . . I don't think he would. He's the kind of person who doesn't like change." I said it, but I didn't feel confident about it. If he said he wanted a divorce, my grandpa would eat him alive.

"If they don't get a divorce and he just keeps seeing her . . . What would you think about that?"

I had never thought about that.

"There are many people like that. More than you think. My dad was probably one of them. Even before he divorced my mom. Even among my friends, there are quite a few dating married men."

It sounds like we're shooting an educational drama for married couples. My mind goes blank. All I know is that I truly hate the idea of Dad being with another woman, eating ice cream.

"If he asks for a divorce, it would be so unfair to your mom. She quit teaching, huh?"

She's right. For my mom, who just became a full-time housewife and has thinning hair and sunken cheeks, divorce would be an awful thing. Even when I asked my mom what she'd do if Dad met another woman, she seemed not to care. She just said, "Since he's a poet, it's possible that he could have a girlfriend. But would he have the courage?"

"So, we should plan something. Something that would surprise your dad or make him run. Is there anything like that?"

Mina is serious. For some strange reason, I have no interest in her idea. In my blank mind, I keep seeing Dad eating ice cream and smiling with droopy eyes. I can't stand that image, but what is this feeling? I feel a little sorry for him. How weird.

"Actually, my dad is a chicken. He hates bugs—loathes them."

"What? Bugs?" Mina pouts.

"There are a lot of bugs in our house. He has a phobia about them. He freaks out like a little baby."

"Hmm," Mina says and then becomes silent. She's probably half asleep. My body feels heavy like wet cotton, but sleep doesn't come. It would have been better not to know. I should have ignored the text message. I shouldn't have cared whether they emailed each other or not . . . but it's too late. Something happened and I can't keep my hands off it. Should I put a bunch of centipedes in their luggage? How about spiders? What would be the worst kind of bug? I could probably find that kind of thing on the black market. Because this is Hong Kong. I turn on my computer and log on to the internet. I type "insects" in the search engine. A long list of items pops up.

Dad is afraid of insects. I'm not just talking about disgusting-looking insects like thumb-sized cockroaches and centipedes. He's afraid of beetles, crickets, grasshoppers, and even butterflies. When I caught a grasshopper as a little girl and kept it for a few months, Dad, who went out on the veranda to smoke, sneaked past the grasshopper's box like it was a savage dog, and stood smoking in a corner of the veranda. It was before he quit smoking—he who had always smoked, despite being treated like a pariah by his family because of it—which was around the time he was brought to the emergency room for asthma (but I know that the real reason he quit was that I had been secretly stealing and smoking his cigarettes). If by chance a spider appeared, he would call me over in a serious voice, "Ji-yeon, Ji-yeon, there's a bug . . ." Although we never skipped the monthly extermination, the house still had insects, and he required my help more frequently. "We should really move, or we might even start to get mice," Dad whined, but Mom was undaunted. The reconstruction was just around the corner, so we were staying put.

When did the sign go up celebrating the founding of the apartment reconstruction association? My mom was happier that day than the day I was accepted to college. She is our building representative in the association. She's so passionate about her association work that she even gave up her part-time teaching job, which she'd been doing ever since she retired. Although it was small and shabby compared to Grandfather's house or Dad's siblings' houses, the apartment was the symbol of her pride. Buying a lottery apartment from the Teachers Union, renting it out, building up savings, and getting a loan . . . this long process made the apartment possible. It was during the national economic crisis, so the price was ridiculously low. Having considered the future, the atmosphere, and the neighborhood, Mom chose this town, *Banpo*. Most of the tenants in the building had lived here since it was built. They were traditional middle class, frugal but not lacking for anything, polite with good jobs. Twenty years should have been enough time for the insects, who had been making their homes in the walls and pipes, to have gotten used to us.

4. The Third Day: You Can Get There but There's No Way Back

The Star Ferry terminal was crowded with Chinese people waiting for a ferry to *Tsim Sha Tsui*. It's the day when there is, supposedly, the biggest fireworks display in the world. We get on the ferry at last, avoiding Dad and Lady Unidentified. They're in white shirts and jeans, the perfect couple look. To the best of my ability, I'm controlling my desire to suddenly appear in front of them. What if I were to ask, "Hey, Dad, how did the poetry reading go?" I would take my wig off in front of him and he would be bewildered. What kind of face would he make? Lady Unidentified, standing on the deck of the ferry, turns her head towards Dad and speaks to him. Dad says something back, pointing in the direction of the convention center. The sunlight reflecting off the side of the huge glass building burns my eyes. Looking at the sea, I stealthily capture them with the small camera in my hand.

"Not bad. You're a natural." Mina giggles. "Wait here. I'll go take a look," Mina says and is already walking toward the two of them. She has come to my house a few times, but there's almost no chance that Dad would recognize her. This tall friend of mine with light brown hair, like an ordinary tourist, skulks around the side of the ferry with a combination of curiosity and fatigue, and then little by little, so they'd never notice, she closes the distance between them. As the boat rolls around in the waves my eyes begin to sway. Two men next to me take out steamed rice wrapped in lotus leaves and begin to eat it. Who ever said Hong Kong is a nice-smelling harbor city? The filthy odor from the boat floor mixed with the smell of rice makes me nauseous. Mina, passing by another couple taking pictures and a man standing alone, finally stands back to back with our couple. I get nervous. I would like her to hear and bring back every word of what they talk about, but at the same time, I don't want her to know about it. I would like it if their conversation were something like, "We're lucky to have such good weather, aren't we?" Mina, having returned to her seat behind the rough, vinyl-like veil, says in a mocking nasal voice, "Didn't you say she's a pharmacist?"

"I think so."

"It seems that she writes poems, too. They were talking about something like, 'That poem you sent me . . .'"

"It's a good idea. Approaching a poet with a poem."

"It's also sneaky."

"Nothing else?"

"No. She said, 'The wine we had yesterday was good, even though I'm not much of a wine drinker.'"

"My dad is a wine fiend. Maybe he got a decent bottle from the duty free store."

"Drinking wine and talking about poetry. It's so sophisticated. Their relationship might be more decent than we thought."

"Decent? Three days and four nights in Hong Kong?" My voice sounds a little shrill. I feel revolted and nauseous.

"Don't you remember screaming your lungs out, saying, 'Just because two people spend the night together doesn't mean something is going to happen'?"

She's talking about my ex-boyfriend, whom I broke up with. That boy and I spent exactly ten hours together on our own, but nothing like "something" ever happened. He just blinked his big, goldfish eyes, listening to me talking, and then fell asleep on the couch. We were at his house at the end of my senior year in high school.

"In all honesty, weren't you a little disappointed at the time?" Mina snickers.

"Disappointed? He was just a boy, not a man."

"Isn't your dad kind of like that, too? He has a tendency to act like an adolescent."

"I think you're right . . ." I do think she's right, but my dad is forty-seven and he's a healthy man who still quietly locks his bedroom door once in a while.

"Is that all?"

"Well, her voice was so quiet. It sounded like she was whispering, so it was hard to hear. Hey, they're moving to this side. Maybe they want to come inside."

"I'm watching."

As time passes, I'm becoming blunt . . . I'm getting so angry . . .

with somebody—I don't know who—that I can barely control myself.

Having walked around the *Tsim Sha Tsui* walkway all afternoon, all I can think of is finding a bathroom. I roam around looking for a restroom, see one and run to it, huffing and puffing, and throw up everything in my stomach. The nice stores with their goods standing in rows, the merchants handing out colorful balloons; none of it soothes my stomach. "You're going to be seriously sick this time. Let's get back to the hotel," Mina says several times. All I can do is nod. The world sways in front of me like a Wong Kar-Wai movie and I keep following Dad and Lady Unidentified, who are walking like an old couple in a movie. I don't think about gathering evidence anymore. Dad and Lady Unidentified go into a store, opening the glass door. Her trying on shoes and him cocking his head and commenting.

"Those wedge heels don't look good on her," Mina says, hiding behind a column by the door. "Should I go in and tell her?"

I am growing sour, "That sounds like fun."

Just for the heck of it, Mina adds, "Wow, those shoes are a pretty penny." Checking the price in the window, Mina tells me they cost 390 Hong Kong dollars. Not a small price for shoes.

"Oh boy, your Dad's taking out his credit card."

"I have eyes, too, you know."

Unlike Mina, I don't get that excited. My dad's action, signing and retrieving his card, seems too natural. Lady Unidentified is rewarding him with a grateful smile. "This is nothing," Dad's face seems to say. A cool guy, a man showing his position as a player, this man is completely foreign to me now.

After leaving the gigantic shopping mall at Harbor City, Dad and the woman tirelessly weave their way through the cluster of boutiques in the back streets. Every time they leave a store, Dad has more bags in his hands. These are shops displaying high-end goods in unique arrangements. How in the world did they find out about this place? Every time Dad comes out of a new store, we, holding up sunglasses or busily trying on earrings, end up with several bags in our hands, too.

"Come to think of it, this woman is starting to seem like a gold digger. These are very unusual shops. There's no way your dad would have searched for them on the Internet, so the woman must have planned all this."

Dad seems to be enjoying it. No matter who planned it.

"Are you okay? You don't look so good."

I'm not okay, but I say, "Of course, I have endurance. Throwing up and walking all day, you'd think I was on a diet." Just as I'm playing the cool daughter of a cool father, a guy interrupts.

"Excuse me, do you know where the Hard Rock Café is?"

It's not because I'm incapable of listening that I don't understand him. It's because this blond guy is just so good-looking.

"We're strangers here, too," Mina answers.

The guy, who looks like Leonardo DiCaprio, says something else.

"What's he saying?" His eyes are so blue that I can't hide my curiosity.

"He says it's a cool place and wants to know if we want to go find it together. He's with a friend of his." Behind the guy is another blond. He has a swimmer's body with broad shoulders.

"We saw that place in the guidebook yesterday. It says it's famous."

"What are you up to?" Mina whispers to me. "I know that. It should be around here someplace. But they're hitting on us. Why are you acting so innocent?"

"That's good. I'm not feeling so good, so why don't we wrap it up here and join them for dinner?"

She stares at me as if to say, "Do you mean it?" As Mina is signaling OK to the guys, Dad and Lady Unidentified walk in our direction. We step back, moving in between the two guys.

"Isn't it a place for young people?" Lady Unidentified is saying.

"It's not going to be like the *Hongdae*[23] area. Let's see the place first."

It's the first time I've heard Dad's voice in days. They turn a corner, heading somewhere, and I see that the street sign says Canton Road.

---

23 The word is short for Hongik University; the surrounding area is famous for art, cultural events, night clubs, live music, cafes, bars, restaurants, and so on, being particularly crowded by younger people.

"That's where we're headed as well . . ."

Mina's face falls. We follow after the couple with the two puzzled guys. I can see the flashing neon sign of the café, which features an electric guitar hanging in the air, from far away. The streets, lined with small bars and pubs, are still empty. Just as I'm thinking, 'This is a little dangerous,' Mina groans. Dad and Lady Unidentified open the door of the Hard Rock Café and walk in. Out of all those bars.

There's a line of people all headed to the same place. On the streets, a feeling of excitement is in the air. It feels like the moment just before a war. The taxis, with their headlights and their drivers with unreadable faces, brush past us. We wave our hands and go so far as to almost get run over, but they won't pick us up. Mina, wondering what's going on, approaches a traffic officer.

"We should hurry. He says this street will be closed soon. And the subway will stop running."

We are told that once the fireworks start, we'll be stuck here with no way out until eleven o'clock. There won't be any ferry service, either. People pass us, trying to get the best seats, close to the water, for the world's biggest fireworks display. They look serious and determined, as if this weren't something fun. I can't believe my dad is going to be joining them. Dad's voice will mix into the crowd's cheers every time a firework explodes.

"Whoa, this is kind of scary," Mina mumbles. I follow her through the streets. To the subway, the only way out of here.

5. And the Last Day: Empty Hands Are the Heaviest Burden

I fall asleep before the plane takes off and don't wake up until after we've landed. Mina, having roused me from sleep, is scolding me, tut tut.

"Are we there? Already? Did my dad get off?"

Mina taps my head. "Uh, yeah. It's been quite a while since we landed. Come back to your senses."

Dragging my luggage out of the terminal, I feel like I'm returning to reality. It feels like I've been dreaming for days.

"Let's get something to eat before we leave. It's going to look weird for you to get home at the same time as your dad."

Mina is scrupulous. On the way to the cafeteria in the corner of the airport, I see Lady Unidentified pulling a suitcase with wheels. She looks exhausted.

"My dad seems like a professional. Look how he left before her."

"This isn't Hong Kong. And there's another reason." Mina smiles as she looks at me. I am starting to get suspicious.

"What . . . what the hell did you do?" Suddenly I'm scared.

"Let's go. I'll tell you on the way. I'm hungry."

Her expression is noncommittal. She buys noodles and *kimbap* and I sort through the questions in my head. Mina speaks first.

"You slept like a corpse last night."

"So, you did something while I was sleeping."

"Well, I just stopped by somewhere."

"Where? At the fireworks?"

"You think I'm crazy enough to go there?"

"Then where? My dad's hotel room?"

Mina nods.

"So you went there and met him?"

"No, it was before the fireworks were over."

"Well, what then? You . . . couldn't possibly get into his room?"

She nods again.

"How? How did you get the key? These Hong Kong hotels must be full of crooks!"

"Hey, hey. Don't get worked up. I tricked them a little. I gave them your name and passport. I also gave them some Hong Kong dollars."

This is too much for me. It's my own fault for not realizing how corrupt—no, how professional, she was.

"So, what did you find in his empty room? Did you leave a letter or something?"

No, no. Mina shakes her index finger. I start to feel chilled.

"Do you remember the things from the airplane? I left some of those gray stickers. One on your Dad's suitcase and one on a page of the book he was reading. Also, one inside his jacket. 'Do not disturb,' 'Wake at mealtime' . . . I left all of them for him. It probably freaked him out, but I don't think he'd complain to the hotel, because he'd have to identify himself."

I look silently at Mina. "Why did you do that?" I want to ask, but I can't and don't. Now Dad would empty his inbox and erase any text messages right away. When he's alone in a room, he might suddenly feel like he's being watched. Worrying about being bugged, he might even check the potted plants in the house. Poor Dad . . . it was too cruel a price to pay for a few days' sin. My feelings are so conflicted that I can't speak. Would a fisherman who caught a huge fish with a casually thrown net feel this way? Would a hunter who caught a bear in a rabbit snare feel this way? It was too heavy a burden for me to carry, and I could never put it down . . .

"Don't get serious on me. Your dad will be careful now that he's scared. You might think this is too much, but I don't think so. There's nothing free in this world. That's life."

Mina was callous. I turn my eyes away from her. Through the glass wall I see a plane taxiing down the runway. "That's life . . ." Mina had said, like an adult.

"Are you crying?" she asks me. I don't answer. I don't try not to cry. I realize that the days of telling Mina everything are over. I would also have to play at being an adult, like Mina. The days of playing my dad's young girlfriend are over, too. I succeeded in tracking Dad, but when a wall comes down, everything becomes a wall. My eyes feel cold, my heart feels cold, my whole soul feels cold. Days like an open field with no barrier or milestone lay ahead of me.

The airplane, slowly moving down the runway, takes off and

abruptly rises upward. The object eventually disappears from my line of sight. Without shaking its wings, infinitely distant.[24]

24 Author's note: The poems that were excerpted in this story are "The Salt Warehouse" and "A Hand Looks for Another Hand" by Moon-Jae Lee, and the story was also inspired by images taken from about ten different poems of his, such as "Water's Zazen," "Sansevieria," "I Planted a Tree in the Desert," and "Empire Hotel." I appreciate the poet Moon-Jae Lee's generosity and understanding.

A Good Family

1. Before Noon

When the woman was ready to leave and came out, her son was still "playing games."

"It's been more than thirty minutes."

The child stopped her hand as it reached out to a palm-size machine.

"But I'm 'studying' now."

Following the machine's instructions, the child spelled and pronounced the English words. *Do you understand what I mean?* The screen changed and the next word popped up. "What? Only twenty points?" the child complained, moving the plastic button and clicking through to the next screen. A white puppy appeared on one side of the screen, its tongue darting out. "You failed," the red letters said.

"Gee, Mom. I lost to the puppy."

"I told you to stop." Her face twitched, which meant she was reaching the end of her rope. The child stared wide-eyed at her. It was hard to believe those innocent eyes belonged to a seventeen-year-old adolescent boy.

"I'm studying for the listening evaluation. We have a competition tomorrow."

Her son's voice was courteous. Whether it was a computer or a gaming device, any conversation with the child while he was in front of a machine tested the woman's patience. In trying to convince him, she always ended up raising her voice, and she had to assert her authority as a mother to wrap up the situation every time. Both she and the child knew that her so-called authority had run out like the air from a leaking balloon, and that there wasn't much of it left now.

"You don't understand. There're tons of kids in my class who do nothing but play games all day long."

He even smiled at her, as if he felt sorry that she didn't know that she should be happy to have a son like him. Going to school, going to an institute,[25] doing homework, working with a private tutor, doing homework, working on exercise sheets, doing homework … There was nothing she could say to him, since he was dealing with such a packed schedule. Even her nagging wasted his time.

"Well, thanks, my son. Would you like me to bow to you or something?"

She let it drop there. She had gotten him the Japanese game system last winter, just before his final exams were over. The child, who had been losing sleep at night from his eager desire for a game system that seemed more suited to an elementary school student, barely met the condition she had set, which was to be ranked in the top five percent of his class. To afford a more expensive system, he cut his own expenses and added the entirety of his *sebetdon*.[26] He was good-natured and docile. Apart from having fallen in with some worrisome friends, he left nothing to be desired.

"I'm going over to see Jae-min in a little while. You know that, right?"

Nodding his head, her child quietly stood up and went to his room. It would be a while before he could hold his head up again. She pitied the boy but didn't console him, because this was an incident that required self-examination. Her mobile phone made a weird sound, alerting her that it was ten o'clock. With a thick wool scarf tightly wrapped around her neck, she left the apartment. She adjusted her clothes again, looking at herself in the mirror hanging on the wall of the elevator. It was her daughter's old fake-fur coat, fuzzy with lint. The plain, warm clothes seemed to match her plain, un-made-up face. Looking in the mirror, she made a pitiful expression. A face untidy from lack of sleep, anxious eyes and narrow shoulders in a loose coat. Perfect. The woman caught a glimpse of a camera in the corner of the elevator and momentarily felt embarrassed, but this wasn't the time for that. Just as she started to feel the tears threatening to form in her eyes,

---

25 An academic institute for additional instruction. It is common in Korea nowadays for students to receive extra instruction after school at one or more private academic institutes.

26 Money customarily given by older relatives as a gift on New Year's Day morning.

the elevator stopped, and with a clear *Ding-Dong*, its door slid gently open.

"Hey, Ji-woo's mom. Where are you headed?"

The woman stepping in seemed delighted to see her. She was the mother of a *banjang*[27] from another classroom at the same school her son attended. She was a lively and involved mother, who helped with things like searching for private tutors, distributing information about the institute, and getting rid of clumsy teachers and uncooperative kids. Suddenly, a shadow crossed her face. Even though she showed adequate courtesy to the dean, the principal, his homeroom teacher, and any other teachers who might know about it and tried to downplay it as much as she could, it was possible that this woman might have heard the rumor. Reeling, she made a quick decision: cautious honesty was best.

"Oh my goodness, I'm in such an uncomfortable situation. I feel awful."

"What's going on? I had a feeling. Since you're wearing that . . ."

The woman had a smile in her eyes. Could she really not know? Even if she didn't yet, she surely would soon. Bad rumors always seemed to spread like the wind.

"My son, Ji-woo, got into trouble in a karaoke room with his friends, you know."

"A karaoke room? When? He has time to do that?" The woman asked, wide-eyed.

"They went there on the day they finished final exams. They seem to have gotten into a fight about something while they were there."

"Oh dear, did anyone get hurt? It wasn't Ji-woo, was it?"

"No, not him, but another child . . . The child's parents went crazy. They said they would sue all the children. Ji-woo didn't even know what was going on, since he had been sipping from the beer that the children were passing around and got tipsy. I'm on my way now to the child's house to beg."

"Oh my god, what in the world . . . oh dear . . . oh boy . . ."

---

27 A classroom representative.

The woman said in an exaggerated tone, clicking her tongue. "You must be really upset. But … well, try not to worry too much. All the teachers know Ji-woo is a good student. He's such a good kid."

Those words were not very comforting. She always felt unhappy to have "a good kid," the description always given to her son. Because of his good nature, because of his good disposition, he was suggestible and sensitive. He wasn't good, he was even pretty bad, at doing the little things that would help him get ahead, like reading a book during break time, refusing a small favor to a friend, or keeping his carefully compiled list of incorrectly answered exam questions to himself. She had been drilling this into him since elementary school—no, pre-school—but he never changed. Those little things kept him from reaching the very top ranks of his class. She was envious of parents whose kids exploded when they blew an exam, while her son just looked contrite. The elevator stopped and the cold air swept in.

"Good luck." The *banjang*'s mom lightly patted her on the shoulder. The security guard in uniform looked at the woman with a puzzled face and then bowed, saying, "Oh, *Samonim*."[28] She nodded at him and escaped the lobby with a few hurried steps.

After walking for about twenty minutes, her face and hands were cold and tingled like they were about to go numb, even though she was wearing quilted pants and gloves. It was a cold day, and her white puffs of breath seemed to freeze in mid-air. She could have driven to Jae-min's house, but she didn't. In her mind, she figured that Jae-min's mother might be more generous if she arrived frozen. Exchanging a greeting with the other three mothers she had talked with on the phone several times, who were now lined up in front of the blue gate, she quickly organized her thoughts.

"We should beg for forgiveness no matter what, saying that we're sorry and that it's our fault we didn't teach our kids right."

It was what she had already said several times to these shaggy-haired and fallen-faced women, but it was difficult for her to

---

28 A noun used to respectfully address a married woman, one's teacher's wife, or one's boss's wife.

shake her fear that they might stray from this message. Anger suddenly rose in her, wondering how in the world her son got involved with the sort of sons these women raised, and where she had been while it was happening.

"But we already apologized, and Jae-min's mother is still seething with anger. When I called her this morning, it was clear she was still holding a grudge."

Although she had advised against it repeatedly, that woman seemed to have called again. The son of that woman, who seemed to pout even when talking on the phone, complaining the whole time, had been the mastermind of this whole incident.

"What did you say? I explained to you that calling them again and again would be counterproductive."

The woman spoke in a low voice, "Well, I mean, you know, boys can get into a fight and when they fight . . ."

"Kyung-tae's mother!" She cut off the woman's words. The mother of Kyung-tae looked at her with eyes full of anger. She continued to speak in a wheedling way. Her words came out in broken pieces, the cold air freezing her mouth. "Didn't I tell you? The more we talk, the worse things are for us. We found out that Jae-min's father is a policeman."

If she made a few calls, she could find someone to handle a single police officer, but she didn't want to keep talking about this any longer.

"Think about it from her position. The scar on the kid's face . . . it's terrible." She spoke to the woman in a low tone, as if she were soothing a child, but she still seemed upset.

"Really, boys can exchange blows and get into fights, and in the process they might get hurt, but who would try to do that on purpose? I'm just saying that they're being treated like they're some kind of gangsters."

Is there such a thing as a gangster-in-training? Harassing a kid, forcing him into a karaoke room, and ganging up on him . . . they were really no different from gangsters. How in the world did Ji-woo get involved with the son of a woman like this? Another sigh escaped her lips, but she quickly pulled herself together. Thankfully, another mother settled the situation for everyone.

"Whatever the case, we can't let our kids have marks on their school records. Can't we just bow our heads and beg?"

It was a woman who ran a coffee shop in the city. 'She knows a little better than the others, having a job instead of staying at home.' Her sense of being offended by the woman's too-bright red coat diminished a little.

"Let's go inside. I'm freezing to death."

The other mother, who had made such a bad impression on the phone and even now seemed to be saying, "What have I done?" made a fuss, thumping her shoes. The woman, looking over the other mothers, as if controlling unruly children, pushed the doorbell next to the metal gate.

2. The Afternoon

The frozen blue sky, still and crisp, as though it might crack apart with a clink, was slowly growing cloudy. The wind died down and the air was thick with moisture. "Is it going to snow?" The woman picked up the phone, pressed three buttons, and checked the recorded forecast. They were predicting a half inch of snow. If it was only a half inch it would melt from the car fumes and people's breathing, disappearing before it piled up. Wearing a black woolen coat, she opened the shoe closet. The neatly organized black shoes were sitting quietly like they were waiting to be chosen. She picked up the plain four-inch heels. Listening to the sound of her own heels on the way to the elevator, she walked slowly. Having spent the morning on her knees, kowtowing like she would do anything for forgiveness, her walk looked a little unsteady as though the heels were too much for her, but she didn't give up. A sophisticated, respectable, elegant, and moderate woman; she needed a perfect image of all that at this particular moment. Having made a few trips back and forth along the marbled hallway, walking like a model with perfect posture, she restored her serene and masterful steps. The woman, whose height had suddenly increased with the heels, and who even had entirely different eyes from the middle-aged woman in the old coat this morning, pushed the button for the elevator with an elegant hand gesture.

After driving for thirty minutes on the highway, through a tunnel, and then on city streets for about ten blocks, she reached the front of the high-rise building downtown. She drove down to the fifth floor of the underground parking garage, along a passage that was as winding as a snail, ignoring the dizziness, and stopped the car, following the directions of a young man waving a fluorescent stick. She turned on the light and applied gloss to her cracked lips. After checking fastidiously if her mascara was smudged or her eye liner drawn too long, the woman spread out her arms and then folded them, several times in succession. The movement, *jangpung*,[29] which sent out a wind from her palms, was her way of relaxing the tension in her body. She applied a drop of Coco Chanel perfume to each of her earlobes, took a deep breath, and opened the car door. She walked slowly across the parking lot, which was filled with heavy air and exhaust fumes, then stepped into one of the five elevators.

On the twenty-first floor, there was a hallway with dark reddish-purple carpet, flooded with bright fluorescent light. Turning a corner, she found herself facing a large glass door and stepped towards it. On one side of the glass door was a tiny machine with a red light the size of a pea. The door could be opened by flashing her husband's ID card. Entering boldly, throwing open the office door, staring at the man at his desk, and ... Although that was what she had imagined doing, she couldn't bring herself to do it, and instead flipped open her phone and called the office.

"The director is not currently available to talk on the phone. He's in a meeting," a woman with a soft voice kindly informed her, but she didn't give up.

"I'm right in front of the office now. I really need to see him."

"Who am I speaking to, please? I'll take a message for you. He's in a very important meeting. I cannot connect you." The re-

---

29 A martial arts move, which sends out energy like a tremendous wind from a person's hand.

ceptionist spoke politely. It was the reaction she had expected.

She took a deep breath and said, "As I just told you, I am right in front of your office now. If you don't connect me to him this minute, it could get a little noisy." She spoke in the most calm, cold, and callous voice she could muster, which felt a bit frightening even to her.

The receptionist seemed slightly dismayed. "May I ask who this is? I was told not to connect any calls . . ."

She cut her short, saying, "Oh, I'm sorry. This is Director Mahn-bohk Kim's wife."

The other end of the line was quiet. After about three minutes the woman said, "Please wait just a moment," and came out, opening the office door. "I was told to bring you inside. The director said he'll be with you shortly."

Dozens of eyes peered out from behind the partition that the woman walked along. Holding her head up and straightening her back, she walked slowly, looking straight ahead. She thought she heard voices from somewhere, but she wasn't bothered by them. Passing through a long hallway between the partitions and entering the office, with the receptionist leading the way, she held her breath as she opened a glass door covered with blinds. It looked like it was about ninety-some square feet and seemed a little bigger than her husband's office. There was a mahogany desk, a black leather chair, and a neat, grey couch. Her eyes brushed over the nameplate engraved with the name "Director Sung-jin Koo."

"May I get you something to drink? We have green tea and coffee. We also have regular tea," the receptionist asked with a smile. She had a sweet face.

"I'll have a cup of coffee. Black, please."

Tap, tap, tap. The woman's shoes made a sound as she went out and returned with the clatter of cups.

"It's been a long time, and you still look the same. I visited your house when I first entered the company. You probably don't remember me, but I'm Representative Jeong, Representative Ji-young Jeong."

When her husband was department manager, she had invited his co-workers to her home several times and prepared them dinner. Even though her husband tried to dissuade her, saying, "Why bother with all that?" she wasn't bothered at all and prepared a meal for thirty people, steaming shrimp, marinating skate, and making salad with pickled salmon.

"Oh, that's right. I'm sorry I didn't recognize you." And she added quietly, "I heard you got married and have children; I can't believe you're still in such a good shape."

"Your husband . . . I heard he's gone to Africa. Is he still there?"

The woman nodded her head absently. Representative Jeong, who seemed like she was about to say something else, closed her mouth. A man was standing in the open door. The man stood there holding the door knob, silently looking at the woman and Representative Jeong. The woman stood up from her seat and took a step back towards the couch. Representative Jeong stood up quickly, went out of the room and closed the door.

'So that's Sung-jin Koo,' the woman thought as she observed the owner of the room. She looked him over slowly, like an interviewer who was grading him: glossy, carefully trimmed hair that looked waxed, white shirt, blue striped tie, shiny brown pants, black shoes with slightly crude heels, a generally sophisticated style, firm-looking arms, and French cuffs with glittering cuff links on his shirt sleeves.

"I apologize for my unexpected visit. As you were told, I'm Director Kim's wife." The woman was the first to speak. She sounded polite, but not particularly apologetic.

"Not at all. I am sorry for making you wait."

Director Sung-jin Koo was gentle and courteous. He wasn't overly polite, nor did he seem pretentious. His voice was low but powerful. Behind the light-brown horn-rims, his eyes were smiling. It was a smile of a person who was accustomed to politeness and manners. Thinking of all the stories she had heard from her husband, the atrocities he had committed last year, it was unexpected, but then again, it felt somehow fitting. She looked straight into his eyes. He didn't avoid hers. His eyes were dark brown. You could say that there was almost nothing one could read in those eyes. She kept her mouth closed for quite a while. In the meantime, his mobile phone rang twice and then fell silent.

"Don't you want to answer your phone?" She wanted to show that she was calm.

"That's alright. They'll call back."

Blinking his keen eyes, he looked at her. Even though she had been thinking all night about how to start talking and what her first words should be, she changed her mind now. She began to think that he might be a more difficult opponent than she had expected. 'Let's do it simple and clear,' she thought. Her decision was made.

"I was told that my husband is planning on submitting his resignation."

"Oh, is he?"

Slight wrinkles appeared on his forehead and then disappeared. The action looked natural, as though it were rehearsed.

"Are you telling me you didn't know?"

"I guess he probably talked to the President. I haven't been informed of it yet."

It was an appropriate reaction following an appropriate pause. He was a person who knew how to handle a conversation.

"Even if you didn't know about his plan to resign, you are aware of the reason for it, aren't you?"

He only twisted his lips faintly and said nothing.

"According to him, it will take about a month for it to be accepted."

"Under normal conditions, that would be the case. It requires a settlement from company headquarters and a reassignment of the work."

The perfunctory question-and-answer procedure ended there.

"So I would like to tell you . . ." She continued after a short pause, "That during that month my husband intends to prove that his resignation is unfair."

She held her back straight and shifted her legs. During high school, she had led a protest with some of her friends. A classmate killed herself after being physically punished for a minor infraction. She wasn't close to the student; however, she was the class *banjang*. In her opinion, the teacher had gone too far and the punishment had been inhumane. The teacher, who would often attack people's character, came into class after the suicide looking shameless and unrepentant, and showed how unstable he was by striking the lectern with the attendance chart. She and her friends drew up a written appeal, made calls, and held several meetings; their plan spread to all the students who, on the day of the gospel-singing contest, gathered together in a hall. The students refused to attend class and demanded the dismissal of the teacher. After this situation, which took several weeks to resolve, she and her friends were put on probation; as a punishment, the leaders of the protest, who were good students and always on the honor roll, had to organize books at the school library for a week. Teachers often visited them at the library and lectured them solemnly and seriously, making them stand until their feet grew numb. Some of the students needed to stretch their bodies and hands, but she didn't. If necessary, she could remain standing in one position for two, even three hours.

"No one insisted on his resignation, as far as I know. I don't know what to tell you."

A perfect poker face: that was what Director Sung-jin Koo had.

"I didn't come here to ask your opinion. It was my husband who decided to resign. It is his will. However, what he finds problematic is the decision that created this situation. He says he's going to pursue a case against the company. I'm sure that you're well aware of how he'll proceed. He'll do it exactly the same way you did."

He looked at her, leaning back in his seat.

"He is only a moral person. He never thinks of himself." She watched his hand push up his glasses and his fingers sweep over his cheek, playing with his chin. He seemed more nervous than before.

"Director Kim . . . Are you saying that he has confirmed it? That he's going to sue the company?" His stiff facial features betrayed his tension.

"My husband is gentle in most ways, but once he gets angry,

he never lets up. He believes that this is what the company needs; he's not doing it for himself." She wanted to ask, "Don't you already know all this?" but she kept it to herself.

His face suddenly froze. "As I told you, no one forced him to resign. When it's his own decision, is it still possible to sue?"

She smiled calmly. Now was the moment to clinch the deal.

"There seems to be a misunderstanding; my husband is not trying to withdraw his resignation. He is saying that it was unfair to reappoint you."

". . ." He scowled again.

"He thinks it's important to openly discuss the confusion this situation has caused the employees—hiring back the person who created so much trouble for the company. He's going to prove that the poor judgment of the head office is causing a serious problem for the company."

Sung-jin Koo was looking at her, blinking his eyes. 'He doesn't believe me,' she thought. He coughed, huh-um, clearing his throat and opened his mouth.

"I find it hard to believe that Director Kim has made such a decision. It's not going to be easy to inquire into the legitimacy of the head office's decision. Why would he put himself through such a stressful process? He's a logical man. Why would he want to do such a thing, regardless of what happens to the company, when he plans on leaving?"

She smiled faintly.

"That's the difference between you and my husband. He's the kind of person who would never say 'regardless of what happens to the company.' He is a person who acts with determination and responsibility."

A look of embarrassment appeared on his face as if he were thinking, 'Damn it. I should have seen that coming.' The man burned with determination; she had been right about everything she said. Her husband was deeply connected to Sung-jin Koo's dismissal and reinstatement, the incident, and the long lawsuit and trial.

"Oh, and I don't think you need to worry about how he's going to proceed with the lawsuit. He has learned a lot from you."

Having finished what she had to say, the woman faced Sung-jin Koo with determined eyes. Um-hum, hut-hum-um, clearing his throat again, he said, "Excuse me. I seem to be coming down with a cold." The dry, warm air hung in the room, as though the thermostat were set a little too high. He raised his arm and swept his hair back. His mobile phone rang again, but he didn't answer it. He definitely looked nervous. Springing up from his seat, he asked, holding the handset of the phone in his hand, "Would you like her to get you something more to drink? I'm a little thirsty."

He sat down again and waited, looking at her with narrow eyes, until an assistant came in with a glass of water. He seemed to be trying to determine how far she and her husband would go with this and how much it would affect him.

"If you're a plant under glass, I'm a weed. Even if you died and came back to life, you'd never be able to understand a person like me ..." That was what he had said to her husband. As he said himself, he was like a weed, so he didn't expect to lose this fight; nevertheless, he had just finished a tough battle. Even if he won, whether he was a weed or a plant, this situation would leave him withered and depleted.

"Well, let's clear things up." Taking a sip of water, he continued, "You're saying that Director Kim is planning on suing the company and that he will make the case that the employees suffered material and psychological harm from the reappointment of a person who previously caused trouble for the company. Am I right?"

"I think you have a good understanding of what I said."

"And I am the person who caused trouble for the company, right?"

She nodded her head.

"As you must know, a system does not so easily change a decision once it has been made. As you may also know, the original case took over a year in court. Whatever Director Kim thinks, it doesn't look like he has a very good chance of success."

She quietly smiled. The more questions, the simpler and more succinct her answers should be. When it came to conversational techniques, she was confident as well.

"As you're aware, didn't the company—the system, as you call it—already reverse its decision regarding your dismissal? It will probably be the same type of case. Boring and exhausting."

"So ..." Director Sung-jin Koo massaged his cramped hands and cracked his fingers, making a loud sound. "You're saying that the purpose of Director Kim's lawsuit is to cancel my reappointment."

"I suppose so."

"Then ..." He took a deep breath and continued to talk. "Could I ask you why you came here to tell me all this? I assume that Director Kim is unaware of you meeting with me like this."

"Of course he is unaware. He has gone on vacation. If he found out, he'd be very upset."

"Mrs. Kim, since you've come all the way here, I gather that you might have a different opinion than that of your husband."

As she had thought, there was something sharp about him. This was the moment she had been waiting for. She continued to speak calmly.

"I'm well aware of the details of the situation so far. I mean, the incidents with Chief Cho and Representative Kim, your dismissal and reappointment, and the proceedings of the trial. My husband consulted me throughout the whole thing. It was he who made the choice of whether to submit a resignation or to undergo proceedings. In fact, I don't agree with him, but I also don't think there's any decisive reason to stop him. My husband's heart has already left the company. He couldn't stand to just quit and leave behind this kind of situation. I understand him well enough. But if I were him, I wouldn't do it this way. If I were in his shoes, I would prefer to watch you every day from nine to five, tracking your every move, until the day you left the company. However, he is different from me."

She stopped talking then. She felt she had talked too long.

"So it seems that, in the end, you agree with him. If that's the case ... Could you tell me why you've come to see me today? You haven't answered that question yet."

"Ah, that's simple," she drew out a soft voice. "I just wanted to see you in person once. I wanted to see for myself what kind of person, what kind of character would make my husband go through such a difficult time."

His hand, heading towards the water cup on the table, pulled back. The cup was empty.

"So then . . . According to what you've been telling me so far, there is almost no chance that Director Kim will change his mind. Is that right?"

"Probably not."

"Then . . ." Rubbing his palms together and shaking them off, he raised himself from the seat. "Now that you have informed me of his decision and seen me in person, you've accomplished your purpose. I think we're finished here. I'll show you to the elevator."

Opening the door and courteously taking a step back, he let her go out first. She left the way she had come and walked toward the entrance. Six o'clock. It was nearly closing time, but there seemed to be no one preparing to take off. The office was filled with tension. She liked the tension produced by her appearance there. Now Sung-jin Koo, the President, and the head office would be busy. They would have to have several meetings a day, exchange many emails, and answer the phone at all hours of the day and night. The thought of being involved in the whirlwind of another lawsuit would make the president of the head office sick to his stomach. It was their own fault if they thought they could push him out after more than ten years of service—after all the time he had spent there, a person who was good-hearted and sincere—without paying some price. Just as when she entered, watched from all directions, she held herself very straight. She hoped that she would never had to come back to this place again.

While they waited for the elevator, Director Sung-jin Koo stood looking at the wall and never glanced at her. He must have been running through several different scenarios in his head. Ding. With a lifting sound the elevator door opened. Having nodded at him and entered the elevator, she turned around and looked straight at him. Bloodshot eyes looked back at her. It must have been a rough afternoon for him as well. She thought that it was too easy for him to live like a weed around men. Now he would realize how tiring it was to play games with a woman — not like the diffident subordinates he was used to, but a woman just as smart, cowardly, and cunning as he was. Just as the door was closing, Sung-jin Koo's hand stopped it.

"I would like to meet with you outside the office soon. I'll contact you."

He looked at her so intensely that it seemed she would be devoured whole. She didn't answer him. The elevator door closed silently.

3. Evening

"I would like to meet with you outside the office . . ." The low, strong voice echoed in her ears. She drove slowly in bumper-to-bumper rush-hour traffic. The traffic was so thick that it took ten minutes just to get through an intersection. *Drrr.* Her mobile phone was vibrating.

"Mom, I might not be able to come home tonight."

It was her daughter. She said she was at the site of the fire at *Namdaemun*, the South Gate.[30] Having been moved to tears while watching the scenes on the news last night, her daughter had left home at sunrise to join the candlelight vigil for the victims.

"It's outrageous. How could such a thing happen? I don't think I can sleep at all after watching that. I'll stay here a little longer, get some work done at school, and then sleep a little in the lounge."

Her daughter said she even became teary-eyed when hearing the national anthem. She was as pure-hearted as her father — maybe even more.

"Honey, it's too cold. What are you going to do? You already have a cold. Did you have dinner? Do you want me to bring you something warm?"

---

30 The South Gate, Namdaemun, is one of the four ancient gateways located in the center of Seoul. It was partially destroyed by an arsonist in 2008, and it has since been in the process of restoration.

"No, please don't. Everyone here is cold as well. I'm fine."

Her daughter hung up the phone. Having passed a huge sign reading "Rice Porridge" at a crossroads, she turned her car around. It seemed like appropriate food to bring to her daughter, standing with a candle, coughing. Her day was becoming a very long one because of her good son, good husband, and too-good daughter. Picking up three different kinds of rice porridge, she headed toward downtown, going back the way she had come. She wondered, if he called and wanted to see her, what would he say and what kind of suggestion would he make? "It's a good day for a picnic . . ." "No matter what, I'm not going to give up on you . . ." "Someday you'll have to give in to me . . ." The words from the text messages Sung-jin Koo had sent to Representative Kim and Chief Cho floated through her mind. It was impossible to believe that those were the actions and words of a man who seemed so canny. After doing such awful things, he was dismissed from the company, but with skill and tenacity he was able to get that decision reversed. "He's a nutcase," her husband said, getting upset. Even though her husband was right, he had only seen one side of Sung-jin Koo. The craftiness, selfishness, the extreme ambition, the blind passion that didn't know how to surrender, and the violent fighting spirit . . . There seemed to be no way to fully describe Sung-jin Koo.

Moodaeppo:[31] from the moment Sung-jin Koo entered the company, her husband called him that. It was always, "You'll never believe what *Moodaeppo* did," or, "Earlier today, that *Moodaeppo* . . ." He had pulled some strings, so to speak, to be appointed Director of Sales out of nowhere. He soon gained attention not only for his achievements in the Sales department, but also because an executive at the company, the one who had recommended him, turned out to be friends with the chairman of the head office. From the moment Sung-jin Koo entered the scene, the company started changing: the man, who had a distinguished background, was guaranteed a director position, a million-dollar salary, and a Lexus, and was appointed as executive of the Tokyo head office, but not of the Seoul branch. He disapproved of the familial, casual

---

31 A slang word for a person who is stubbornly self-centered and reckless.

atmosphere of the Tokyo office, which he saw as mere laziness. Under his influence the company became more systematic. Things that used to be communicated verbally were now documented in writing, and all of the employees' time, actions, and attitude were assessed in formal evaluations. Sales rose steeply, and even employees who had previously complained had to accept the success of his tactics. Around that time, a rumor circulated that he was unofficially next in line to become President. It was unprecedented. The company had branches in Korea, Singapore, Hong Kong, China, the United States, and even Europe, but the presidents of all those branches were Japanese. "What if he really becomes President? I don't want to work under the supervision of someone so much younger than me." Although her husband made a long and serious speech about his concerns, she initially thought he was just complaining and exaggerating. She considered it childish to call someone who was only a year younger "so much younger." The trouble started soon after, one day in autumn.

"Honey, why don't you have a seat? I have something to tell you."

Her husband's tone was unusual. "Chief Cho came to me today and said that Director Koo asked her to sleep with him after they had dinner last week."

"Out of the blue? Was he drunk?"

"Well, he was kind of tipsy, but not drunk enough to make such a mistake."

"Huh, well. Chief Cho's married."

"Right. She even has a kid. He knows all that and did it anyway. He grabbed her by the wrist and started dragging her off, so the bartenders had to get him under control, then they sent her off in a cab."

"Is that all? She wouldn't have mentioned it if it was just that . . ."

According to her husband, all the workers in the company, especially the Sales employees, hung on Sung-jin Koo's every word, expression, and even his slightest glance. He said that they never relaxed in their efforts to please him or remain in his favor.

"They also say that something similar happened when he was on a business trip in Japan, on the way back from dinner with the head employees there."

"What a creep."

A man who tried to force himself on women: he was out of his senses. Exploiting his position as their boss was shameless and dirty.

"Chief Cho's smart. She meant for me to be informed as a General Director, but not to tell the President. She probably thinks it's impossible to accuse the competent Sales Director of doing such a thing."

She was thinking the same thing. "What are you going to do?"

"Honestly . . . I'm not sure. This is totally unprecedented, you know."

As she expected, he asked her opinion. She guessed that he was a chronic offender. There had probably been many previous attempts, only it had never become a problem for him before. "I think Chief Cho needs to see Director Koo and set things straight. Tell her to meet with him in a bright, crowded place and make herself clear. Tell her to tell him, 'I don't want to sleep with you. Don't ever make such a demand of me. If there's another incident like it, I'll report you to the President.' And ask her to tell you what happens afterwards."

"That sounds like a good plan." Her husband gave her a satisfied smile. "Whenever I talk to you the answer appears right away," he said.

"Tell her to keep a record of where they meet and the details of the conversation. If possible, she should record it. And I think you should report it to the President. It'll definitely happen again. People like that don't just stop. If something happens later, it's going to be your responsibility."

"But she asked me not to tell anyone, so how can I . . ." He looked uncomfortable.

The incident seemed to pass by just like that. "I see. If you don't like it, I don't like it, either. But don't think I have given up." They could let Director Koo's silly answer go as just a joke.

Sales increased day after day and the company continued to grow. New workers rolled in and the branch in Korea became the leading benchmark. It was only natural that his position within the company became more secure. One day, her husband called across the apartment to her: "Hey, come here. I have something to tell you."

Director Koo's new target was Representative Kim, a twenty-nine-year-old single woman. Representative Kim made copies of everything Director Koo had said, the text messages and emails that he had sent, and brought them to her husband. Having read those embarrassing, childish papers, her husband asked Representative Kim, "What would you like me to do?"

"She asked me to report it to the superiors. She says she can't work with such a person."

She didn't say, "What did I say? Didn't I say it was going to happen again?" Nor did she say, "It would've been better to deal with it the first time." Director Koo was no longer an easy opponent, but the case was now very serious.

"Go ahead and report it to the President. And include what happened earlier to Chief Cho."

"It's going to be a big issue . . . It might only end with someone's termination . . ."

"Of course, he has to go. It wouldn't be right if he comes out unscathed from this. Sexual harassment is such a horrible thing. These days, people fear getting a reputation for sexual harassment or alcoholism more than anything."

"You're right, but . . . I'm worried that someone's going to get hurt. I doubt Director Koo will just admit it and resign peacefully."

"Just report it to the President and leave it to him. Don't confront Koo yourself. You said he's already started to become wary of you."

"The President is . . . well, you know how Japanese people are. They are extremely reluctant to report such things to their superior and go through the investigation and all that, so there's no one but me to take care of it."

It was true, and at the same time, it wasn't. Director Koo was an executive in a different division of the company from her husband, and Chief Cho and Representative Kim were also in separate branches. Just because the women had consulted him didn't automatically make him responsible for handling the issue. "I'm the only one . . ." His response wasn't unusual. The disposition of a Boy Scout: her husband had a nature that was primed for justice. It was the source of his strength. Even though he knew that this sense of justice made his life painful and lonely, he even seemed to enjoy that.

A long, tiresome battle ensued. Director Koo said he had just been joking. He tried to show how casual it all was by saying he would be willing to apologize if she felt uncomfortable. The vice president who had been dispatched from the head office to investigate was a faithful servant to the President from the beginning. He wanted to end the situation by having Director Koo apologize and penalizing him with a temporary salary reduction; however, when Representative Kim, in a fit of rage, said that she was going to the union board, they had to come up with something new. In the end, the head office decided to dismiss Director Koo, but he refused to accept the decision. He filed with the union board to have his dismissal cancelled. The head office had to hire an attorney. Until the District Union Board and the Central Union Board made a decision, Director Koo kept trying to enter his office, even though his desk had been removed. The company had to hire private security guards.

One day, when everything seemed to be over, her husband was on his way to work, and ran into Director Koo, who was lurking in the hallway. Her husband tried to be friendly to him, out of compassion, saying: "I have no personal grudge against you; I merely had to act according to my duty in this situation. You're a capable person, you'll always get a job somewhere, and I was told that the Chairman of the head office, where they made the decision, really regrets having to fire such a competent person as you . . ." He had said that Director Koo stood listening to him with an absent-minded and exhausted expression. Her husband did not realize what repercussions that encounter would have.

The following day, Director Koo sent an email to the President of the head office. It was simple and to the point. "I intend to file a lawsuit against you . . ." The short, threatening sentence turned the head office upside down. Until then, Director Koo had claimed that he was framed and that the leader of the conspiracy was Director Mahn-bohk Kim; he even seemed to believe it himself. Up to this point, he had foolishly persisted in his lawsuit because he believed the Chairman of the head office had not been involved in the decision. Maybe Koo was really mad, or perhaps he simply thought his appeal would clear everything up—whichever it was, the head office ended up reversing their decision, to the outrage of many. Standing on his previous record, Koo accepted the company's offer on the condition that he receive a new position, a salary increase, and the newest Lexus model. Rumors flew back and forth: one of the stories was based on the economic principle that it doesn't matter if a cat is black or white, as long as it can catch a mouse; another was that the Chairman of the head office had a pathological fear of trials, and that Director Koo had some dirt on him. Director Koo made a splendid reentry. He wasn't hurt at all by the whole affair. Representative Kim left the company, saying that she couldn't work for a company that operated like that. Her husband, Director Kim, also left.

He went on a two-week trip. It was a long and magnificent trip through Africa, starting in Morocco, which would have been unthinkable while he was working at the company. She wasn't going to tell him that she had met Sung-jin Koo while he was away. She knew that when her husband had said, "I'll be forced to file a lawsuit too," he had just been making a passing comment because it was expected of him. Fight, hate, disparage, and win . . . He was a person who was disgusted by all those things. As the left arrow signaled green and she turned the wheel towards *Namdaemun*, her mobile phone rang.

"*Hyeong-nim,*[32] are you busy?"

It was her sister-in-law.

"Oh, hi. What happened?" She always answered the phone tenderly when it was her sister-in-law. Her mother suffered from

---

[32] The name used for an older sister-in-law.

dementia and her sister-in-law had been quietly taking care of her for eight years.

"It happened again, and I need to clean her up, but it's hard for me to take care of it on my own now. Hee-chul's father said he couldn't come over now. I was wondering if you could help me."

"I'm on my way. Wait for me."

A parade of swaying candles, shivering people in front of a fire, and the demolished palace came into view. As she was driving slowly, looking for her daughter, she heard honking from behind her. She had to give up the search.

Washing her mother was difficult. She wondered where the hell this skinny seventy-seven-year-old woman hid that kind of strength; her mother, afraid of falling down, held onto the steel chair even after she was done washing.

"Mom, we're done washing. Let's go to your room and eat, okay?" She tried to gently calm her down, but her mother didn't respond.

"Mom, I brought pine nut rice porridge. It's your favorite."

As she opened the plastic container and showed it to her mother, the fragrance of pine nuts wafted through the air. A bright smile appeared on the old lady's face. The rice porridge was still warm.

One spoon at a time, she slowly fed her mother the rice porridge. Her mother was enjoying it, half of it getting into her mouth and the other half dripping down her chin. The way she opened her mouth every time she held up the spoon reminded her of a baby swallow.

"Hey, you became a baby, Mom."

Her mother smiled like a baby in response to her comment. She raised the empty bowl to show her mother.

"You ate it all. Wow, that was a lot. Aren't you full now, mom?"

Nodding her head like a baby, her mother stretched out her hand towards the woman. She held her mother's dry hand. "Mom . . ." She missed her mother terribly at that moment: her mother who had raised two daughters and three sons and was so brave and high-spirited, who had suddenly let it all go and entered a different world.

"Mom, today, you know, I've been all over . . ."

Holding her mother's hand, she started talking about the events of the morning, the afternoon, and the rest of the long day she had had. "So, you see . . . That man was . . . I really didn't want to go there, but I couldn't help it. My husband is really a good person . . . My feet hurt so much because I'm not used to wearing heels like that . . . The kid's mom got angry and, oh, my goodness, she tried to slap me on the cheek . . . What could Ji-woo possibly have done . . . He's an honest kid . . ." Her mother, who was half listening and half dozing off, was suddenly startled and jerked her head up.

"What is it, Mom? What do you need?"

Holding her head up and looking around, her mother's eyes stopped at the side of the bed. There was the empty bowl, and the squash rice porridge and the abalone rice porridge were getting cold in the other two containers. Her mother raised her hand and pointed at the rice porridge containers.

"You want some more? Would you like the abalone one this time?"

Obsession with food is a common symptom for Alzheimer patients. If her sister-in-law found out, she would be upset, but she picked up the container and opened the lid. The rice porridge was still a little warm.

When she stuck out a spoonful of the rice porridge, her mother swung her hands around wildly.

"What? You don't want it?"

"Gee, you changed you mind quick," she mumbled, putting the bowl down. But her mother stopped her, grabbing her arm and bending it slowly upwards, bringing the head of the spoon up towards her daughter's mouth. And she motioned to her, saying, "Come on, eat this, aren't you hungry, come on, eat, dig in . . ." Her mother's mouth twitched as the garbled words came out.

Not taking her eyes off her mother, she slowly ate the cold rice porridge.

Where Is Everyone Going?

M was, by nature, insolent. Not many people were aware of this because his insolence always seemed quite natural. Even though he appeared to listen carefully to people's stories, he usually ignored them and gave inconsiderate answers. Whenever patients said things like, "I have a headache," or "I have a pain in my chest," he would respond with something like, "Then we should probably fix that." Most patients' questions were similar. "Why did this happen? Nothing unusual or stressful has happened to me lately." They were disheartened by M, who stared blankly into their faces as if to say, "Why are you asking me?" Of all the patients who babbled on about their daily lives, the ones who heard, "Maybe there's a problem with the flow of blood to your head," received the kindest treatment they could expect. Most of the time he didn't tell his patients much, practically nothing, but they still looked at him politely, humbly asked him to fix their circulation problems, and hesitatingly stood up to leave afterwards. Sometimes he had more demanding patients, and he had to elaborate for them by saying something like, "All the problems in our body arise from circulation issues. The circulation of our blood and energy must be smooth. We need to check for problems in the kidneys, gall bladder, and liver." But as soon as the patient left the room, he would look at the closing door and prescribe whatever he had in mind: usually digestive medicines.

He toned down his brusqueness a little when he had very young or very old patients. He would wait for them to say what they wanted to say and ask their questions, and then he would say, "I understand—you need acupuncture," or "I'll give you some medicine for that—you'll feel better soon," before receiving the next patient. One could say that kindness and arrogance passed over his face in waves during those moments, but they never appeared together at the same time. Although the people who pointed out his arrogance, like his wife or his friend K, threw around theatrical phrases like, "Is there anything you don't know?" or "Your arrogance will be the death of you one day," most people mistook his insolence for coolness and seemed to expect it, considering his profession.

Being arrogant with every inch of his being, he despised his colleagues who forgot his wise words about a particular issue, or those who knocked back shots as if they didn't have to work the next day, while toying with a waitress's breasts, getting complete-ly wasted, and having to call substitute drivers[33] to drive their cars home. He reproached the doctors who ran the Korean medical clinics that claimed they could help with college prep, obesity, in-fertility, and menopause, and he felt sorry for fools who boasted of losing weight by taking traditional medicine.

He himself was naturally healthy, so much so that he could wake up with a clear head after drinking three times as much as his colleagues, and was even sober enough to drive himself home. Since he thought drunk-driving was foolishly irresponsible and was reluctant to call substitute drivers, he usually called women, such as S, R, or O, who responded to his call quickly. Those women knew that was their role.

1. Coincidence

It was after midnight, and the woman he called that night was P. Even though he found her personality and appearance annoying, suited as they were to her job as a *hakseupji*[34] tutor and instruc-tor at an academic institute, he found it comforting that she act-ed like an airhead sometimes, so he kept things shuffling along with her. While P, who looked like she had just rolled out of bed, gripped the wheel and started driving, he reclined the passenger seat, stretched out his body, and closed his eyes. A sharp pain in

---

33 A driver who works for an agency providing transport for people who are too drunk to drive their own cars home. The substitute driver drives the customer's car for him or her.

34 Hakseupji is study material delivered to the home from a private academic institute. A hakseupji tutor helps students study that additional material.

his back had been ruining his mood for a few days. P was talking about something, but as usual he wasn't really paying attention, so she just rambled on carelessly for a while.

"Listen, where did you get the wine you brought last time? My mom loved it. I told you my mom has low blood pressure, right, so she drinks a glass of wine from time to time. I kept the bottle, you see. Tell me where you got it when we get to my place, OK?"

Since he didn't answer her, she asked, a bit embarrassed, "You forgot about my mom's low blood pressure, didn't you?"

Just as she leaned toward him saying, "What's wrong? Do you have an upset stomach? Do you want me to stop the car?" there was a loud clanging sound and a heavy impact.

"Oh, oh, oh . . ." She slammed on the brakes too late.

"What is it? What happened?" M asked.

"I guess it was a red light. I hit the car in front of us. What should I do?" Her face suddenly became pale. While pushing the button to raise the passenger seat, the sharp pain, forgotten till now, rose up his back. 'What is this? What is this feeling?' He opened the car door, but as he stepped out of the car, he screamed and crumpled on the ground. The pain was suffocating.

"Get out of here. Go home!" M yelled, but P couldn't make out the words that barely escaped his mouth.

Just as the tow truck, which came so fast it seemed like it must have been on standby, was loading his car onto its bed, an ambulance arrived with its sirens blaring. M was leaning against a tree trunk, assessing the scene. He was close to fainting, and the pain blurred his vision.

"Are you okay, sir? Can you walk?" A man in an orange vest asked.

"No, I can't." M's voice was solemn.

When he opened his eyes he saw the usual hospital scene. The IV stuck in his arm, someone groaning, rushed footsteps, and the loud snoring coming from behind a curtain.

"Are you awake?" He was a bit shocked to realize that the person talking was his wife.

"Oh, you're here." M's voice was calm.

"You gave me a scare. Dr. Yi says it's unusual to faint after hitting a stationary car. That made me worried. But now I wonder if you were just drunk?" As usual, she was relaxed.

"I called Dr. Yi a little while ago. He should have arrived by now . . ." She turned and walked toward the emergency room entrance.

P was standing there looking lonely. He didn't know what to think. 'Should I signal to her to leave, to hide her from my wife? What'll I do if she comes over and asks if I'm feeling okay with a weepy face? She couldn't possibly do that, could she?' As he was thinking this, P hesitantly approached him. 'Go away, go away,' he thought.

From behind P, who had stopped a few steps away from him, he heard, "Dude, what the hell are you doing here in the middle of the night? You're fine . . . no sign of bleeding." The stout body of Dr. Yi bounced toward him. "Why bother coming in for a mere fender bender?"

Shaking hands with the arm attached to the IV, M greeted his friend in a very different way than usual.

"Is this someone you know? Oh, was she your substitute driver tonight? Well, now, what was the cause of all this, Miss? Was he getting out of hand or something?" His quick-witted friend burst into laughter at his own joke.

The crisis of the day seemed to have passed, since P disappeared at some point. Although it wouldn't be a big problem even if his wife discovered P, he would have to explain it all and sit through a scolding . . . He didn't want to go through that. On top of everything, P meant nothing to him. Maybe P was feeling hurt, but she had caused the accident, with her careless personality and her inconsiderate actions, and M soon dismissed her from his mind.

The real problem was discovered by chance.

"Doesn't this look a little off?" Even from a cursory glance, it was obvious that M's spinal column looked weird in the X-ray Dr. Yi brought over. Four white masses that looked like snowballs, about two inches in diameter, surrounded his spinal column. Dr. Yi's lips quivered and his face turned slightly pale.

"In my opinion . . ." M spoke first, "It looks like a sarcoma."

"Well . . ." Dr. Yi's tone was cautious. "At this size, there's a good chance they could be cystomas, though . . . Have you been feeling any pain so far? Look at this. One of these is completely embedded in the spinal column."

His eyes were fixed on the X-ray. The gently curved backbone and the white circles the size of ping-pong balls; it looked like an abstract painting. It was like a picture that someone had deliberately fabricated. His back problems were chronic. A long time ago, he had postponed joining the army due to a problem with a cervical vertebrae disk, and he ended up being exempted from duty completely.

"How is it that you're a doctor yet you care so little about your body . . ." M didn't hear Dr. Yi's jab. He was absorbed in looking at the white circles in the dark picture. 'It is definitely a sarcoma. This didn't start in the last few days. This is malignant . . .' His experience and knowledge told him that.

"What is it, honey?" His wife was approaching him, rubbing her hands like she was coming back from the restroom. She was a lively woman by nature. This increased when she was around other people.

Dr. Yi whispered to him, furtively hiding the X-ray, "I'll get back to you after I talk to my brother-in-law tomorrow."

It was likely that his brother-in-law would be booked solid for the next couple of months, but M didn't say anything. Dr. Yi's brother-in-law was an expert in town. He was the best one to accurately analyze the situation and inform him of a provisional plan. 'If it is malignant . . .' He felt his mind grow blank. 'A year, maybe less . . .' He sank into the bed and closed his eyes.

2. On the Edge of a Cliff

He fell into delirium for a few days. "I'm sick. I'm suffering from a disease. I might die . . . No, I *will* die . . ." He talked to himself in the afternoon when there were few patients. A doctor who got sick; it was an extremely strange association. In his opinion, a disease, by its nature, was not something that could be understood by the patient. In Western medicine, when something exceeded the range of the normal, it was called a disease, and when something was within acceptable limits, it was not a disease; however, the Asian medicine that he had studied was different. The body didn't always exhibit pain when there was a disease; disease could be present even in the absence of pain. And the human body didn't always have to be diseased to have pain; it could feel pain even in the absence of disease. Still . . . it was hard for him to believe that the pain that had started only a few days ago could kill him. He had no choice but to believe it; he became despondent and felt empty, but gradually he calmed down. Three days later, when he received a call from Dr. Yi in the afternoon about their next scheduled meeting, his voice was tranquil, as usual.

The next day he met with the director of his bank and requested liquidation of his six overseas funds and two domestic reserve funds. He regained his leisurely manner enough to smile at the director as they discussed the tantalizing recent rise of the market. The cash he could ultimately secure by combining the redeemed value of his funds and the death benefit from his life insurance was about five hundred million won. That included the value of his apartment, which was assessed at two hundred million won following a wave of reconstruction, and a farmhouse in *Yicheon*. If it really did add up to that much, it would be enough for his wife and two children to live off of. Although his father-in-law wasn't the type of person to neglect his daughter and two grandchildren if M was gone, he still had his pride.

His wife . . . when he thought about her, he didn't know what to do. "How will you live without me?" Not having to say such a thing to her made him feel both grateful and lonely. A rich father, reliable siblings, and a devoted mother . . . His wife could be said to lack nothing. That would be even truer if he were an affectionate husband, but for now, she didn't have many complaints about him. A long time ago she had stopped asking, "How did I end up with a man like you?" When he asked if she wanted a separation since she was so unhappy with him, she said, "A divorce? Why bother?"

He agreed. She was a devoted mother and fulfilled her filial duty to his mother. As for him, he couldn't expect more and he didn't. His wife often went to stay with their child in the USA; and when she wasn't there, she slept in a separate room, spent time in different places, and ate dinner with other people. She told him, "There are many people who live like this — more than you think." He wasn't interested in how other people lived or thought. He believed that it was nothing to be proud of, but also nothing to be ashamed of.

M knocked on his wife's door that night. "I have something to tell you."

Glancing quickly at him, she said, "Why do you look so serious? You're scaring me."

Although she appeared to be indifferent, she was an intelligent woman. After all, they had been living under the same roof for many years now, so he told her the truth plainly. Even when he told her about his scheduled appointment tomorrow, she was unable to speak.

"Dr. Yi's brother-in-law is a tumor specialist, you know. I'll have an exam ... and I suppose they'll have some things to tell me. There's nothing to worry about for now." His wife looked at him with vacant eyes and flew into a rage.

"What kind of person are you? How can you not know there are tumors growing inside you? What kind of fool are you? How could you have done this ..." Glaring at him angrily, her eyes turned red and filled with tears. Her face was flushed and blotchy, and she couldn't stop crying.

"They could just be cysts. The human body is weird like that — sometimes it just grows cysts," M hesitated, and then approached her. It was his duty to console her. He softly caressed her back, which shook from the force of her sobs. He began to think that his wife might have a hard time going on without him. That consoled him, but at the same time it left him feeling empty.

The next day, he was taken in for a CT scan and an MRI. His wife went along with him from room to room.

"You look funny like that," she said, looking at him in a patient's gown. "Your dress looks ridiculous, but your face is serious. Why don't you relax? You're acting like the head doctor instead of a patient," she teased.

"Let's schedule your operation for three weeks from now—that's the earliest I can do it." Dr. Yi's brother-in-law was a prudent and polite person. When he and M had spent sleepless nights in school together working in different labs, M used to call him *Hyeong* and often invited himself over for dinner at his student lodging house.

"The CTs and MRIs don't really tell us anything right now . . ." He didn't even show M the results of the scans.

'Has it gotten worse?' M's heart grew heavy.

"It's still early in the week . . . Can't we do it before the weekend?" his wife asked with a disappointed face.

"Let me see. Even if I push back all my other patients, I'll still have to check with the other doctors," he said, explaining that it was an operation that required doctors from five different departments, including Orthopedic Surgery, Neurosurgery, Anesthesia, and Plastic Surgery.

M's wife asked again why they needed a plastic surgeon.

"I'll explain in due time. Just try to stay calm now. Nothing's going to happen in the meantime. Don't worry too much. And get some rest. You might not be able to completely shut down your office, but you can probably make an excuse and only come in during the mornings. Don't get nervous, and consider this a chance to get some rest." Dr. Yi's brother-in-law was excessively kind.

"What? The exams didn't tell him anything? Is he really an expert?" his wife muttered as they left the room. She trudged along with a look on her face that seemed to say, "The next person I meet is going to get it."

"What do they need a plastic surgeon for?" she asked as they walked.

"The tumors are quite large. After they remove them, there will be some empty spots, so they have to fill them in with something." The X-rays he had seen in the emergency room crossed his mind. He couldn't tell if the tumor on the spinal column was removable and if the spinal cord would be affected. He might never be able to stand up straight again.

"How can you act as if this were happening to someone else? How can you?" his wife asked with a truly curious face.

That night, like every night, the couple went to sleep in their separate rooms, but it wasn't easy for them to fall asleep. He tossed and turned, his imagination running wild, and she tossed and turned, thinking about him. 'Why is this happening? He's serious and quiet, and he used to be as healthy as a horse . . . He used to be capable of ridding himself of any kind of stress . . .' She kicked off the comforter and abruptly sat up. As she still didn't know what to do and what was going to happen, she just felt terrified. She remained awake in the dark for a while, staring at the walls.

When he awoke at dawn after sleeping for only a short while, sunlight was streaming through the window deep into the room. Ever since he had opened his practice at twenty-seven, right after completing his internship, he had never taken a single day off. He didn't come in late or leave early. He quickly got dressed and left home. The door was locked and the sound of the electric lock opening, beep, woke up his wife. Her husband was going to work as he always did; it wasn't that she didn't expect him to, but just because it was familiar didn't mean it didn't feel strange.

Pushing M's door open a little wider, she stood there and looked inside. The untidy blanket on his bed, the pillow thrown aside, and the pajamas laid on top of it. She heard the hum of his computer on his desk. She carefully entered the room as if someone were watching her. The room was strange, and she was a stranger in it. The room didn't need her attention because it was cleaned by a housekeeper and organized by him. She gently touched the pajama pants he had taken off. They smelled like him, but that was also strange. How long had they been sleeping in separate rooms? Five, even ten years? Maybe, she thought, it had been longer than that.

Little things added up over time. For example, early in their marriage she would say to him on a Sunday morning, as she was heading to the public bathhouse, "Why don't you come with me? Let's get some exercise, swim, enjoy a sauna, and have blowfish soup."

He would smile at her and say, "You go ahead and do that on your own, and let's go out for blowfish when our schedules match up." Once he said that, there was no changing his mind. The days of harmonious and happy living in an apartment—a bedroom, kitchen, and bathroom—that was only 530 square feet, which was the size of her bedroom before she got married, didn't last long. They clashed with each other again and again: when they went grocery shopping, when they went out, when they went to see her mother-in-law, and especially when they went to see her parents . . . Often, they would have small arguments followed by silence, and occasionally they ended in yelling and dirty looks. This happened even though M gave in to her most of the time. When they moved to a new place and got a new car, he said, "Whatever you like," but he never drove the new car and he acted like a guest in their new house.

"It's because he grew up poor. You should understand." Even without M's mother's comment, she believed that she understood him. But understanding didn't mean she liked it. It was probably a bit naive of her to have fallen in love with a man who was difficult, callous, indifferent, and insolent. There was even a time when she wondered whether he might be descended from a forgotten royal family because of his steely stare, noble forehead, and formal speech. She hadn't come to hate him all at once. One day, they had been arguing about something and she said to M, "Why are you making a big deal out of this? You're being childish . . ." It had just been an off-hand comment, but he didn't see it that way. If he had blown up at her, she could have apologized. She also could have accepted it if he had scolded her. But he didn't do either. He simply turned around, went into his room, and closed the door quietly. When they argued, each person's expressions and emotions, crossing and colliding with each other, egged the other one on. In this back and forth of hurt and hurting, she grew tired first. One evening, she suggested several ideas to him. They could keep living under the same roof, but they would not interfere in one another's business. They would fulfill their basic duties to their children and their extended family. They would remain polite in order to avoid rumors.

"I'm alright with it, but are you sure you can do it?" M had asked her.

She said, "You think I'm still reckless, huh? I've learned a lot from living with you." That was how their separation started.

She took up his limp pajamas and blanket and left the room. She filled the bathtub with water, put in plenty of detergent, and dropped in the whole blanket.

The housekeeper, who had just come in, looked at her with eyes as wide as a rabbit's. "You just need to separate them. They fit in the washing machine. I can do it."

M's wife pushed the hovering housekeeper out and closed the bathroom door. She took off her clothes and got in the bathtub, slippery with suds. She worked up a lather, stepping on the blanket. The warm air came up; soon her body grew hot and her forehead oozed with sweat. She realized, of course, that sooner or later every married couple faces a crisis. She didn't seem to think that the crisis of their married life or their way of dealing with it was anything unusual. She thought that it was uncomfortable but bearable, and had a vague expectation that they might eventually reconcile. Although she wouldn't lay out his clothes, make soup, or cook his favorite bean noodles for him, she imagined they would have meals together and care for each other again . . . Maybe that was the sort of reconciliation she had hoped for. She didn't wholeheartedly detest her husband, and she seemed to have felt that if she had wanted to see him, his door was open to her.

She was so confused. His illness was horrible and caused her great sorrow, but whether she was feeling that for him, or for the children, or for herself . . . Surprised and disappointed in herself for being calculating about possibilities she couldn't even imagine . . . Unexpectedly, like a dam breaking, tears began to flow. The pain was so strong it felt like her nerves were being severed. She felt so sorry for him. Never before had she felt so clearly that he was another human being. He, who was smart and capable and lived as if he didn't need anybody's help; she couldn't stand it, but she hated herself for not having held his hand, empathized with him, consoled him, or even cried for him. Despair welled up in her as she realized that she would never be able to bridge this gap, and she sank into the sudsy water, sobbing.

3. People

The news spread quickly from M's wife to his father-in-law, from one friend to other friends, and from them to the other doctors they knew. The first person who asked to see M was his father-in-law. They met in a hotel in the downtown area where the fitness club that his wife and in-laws frequented was located.

"Mr. Chairman is already here." A pretty woman with her hair up in two separate knots, like a Chinese girl, guided him. He walked down the hallway, the sound of his feet swallowed by the thick red carpet. As he opened the door, his father-in-law, smoking a cigar, quickly got up.

"You need to tell me the truth," the short-tempered father-in-law demanded as soon as the waiter left. "I heard the news from my daughter, but . . . You know, she can be a little flaky." The idea that his daughter, whom he had had in his mid-forties and doted on like a doll, could be a widow had shaken him.

"As you know, they found some tumors on my spine. As for what kind they are . . . they will know that after the surgery."

Tut-tut. The father-in-law clicked his tongue for a while. His daughter had declined numerous men he recommended, polite men from respectable families, full of promise like a well-paved road, to marry this man: a man brought up without a father, with many siblings who depended on him, and his daughter's mother-in-law had spent all her life as a *kimbap* seller in a market place . . .

On top of all these things, he detested M's callous personality; the man didn't seem to know how to answer any question with more than two sentences. He couldn't forget M's eyes when M had first visited his house, his arrogant eyes that looked like they were saying, "What can you do when your daughter loves me?"

"I was told the surgery will happen in three weeks . . . But isn't there a way to find out anything before that? I mean, you're a doctor. Don't you have a lot of doctor friends? Can't they open you up tomorrow and see what's inside? If it's difficult for you, what if I ask someone?" He couldn't stop talking even though he knew he shouldn't behave like this when M was sick. He was so angry that he thought he might lose control of himself. His heart was racing and he felt like he was going insane.

"Father," M interrupted him.

"What?" he blurted out, recoiling in shock at M.

"Father . . ."

Only when M said it again did he stammer, "Yes, yes. I'm sorry. I was surprised . . . I was surprised to hear the news and . . . I was just surprised . . ." M had always called him the strictly polite title, *Jangineoreun.* He had always been disappointed by his taciturn, inexpressive, overly polite son-in-law, but at the same time he never felt relaxed around him either.

After knocking on the door, a waiter came in carrying a huge tray. "Excuse me. I have the *buldojang.*[35] It's hot." The waiter, smiling at them, put the small covered pots down on the table in front of M and him and then uncovered them in order.

"Have some. I ordered it for you." M's father-in-law took up the spoon first. He slurped as he ate. The hot broth slid down his throat and he felt like his heartburn was coming on. His son-in-law was silently lifting the spoon to his mouth. Only then did he notice M's conspicuously haggard face. Perhaps because the father-in-law was expecting it, M's waist and back also looked bent over. Just as the *buldojang* was finished, the next dishes were brought out one by one: a five-item cold dish, shark's fin, and fragrant *bok choy.* They ate in silence as if they were arguing.

"If . . . I say *if.* If by any chance the results aren't good . . . I

---

35 A Chinese delicacy whose name literally translates to "Buddha Jumps over the Wall."

have a favor to ask of you," said the son-in-law to break the silence. He waited until the desserts were served after the meal.

"It's not the time to talk about things like that. Right now, what we need to worry about is your condition . . ." His brow furrowed because he had a piece of pineapple stuck in his teeth.

"Well, we need to see the results of the operation, but as far as I'm concerned, this isn't just ordinary tissue. If we assume it's malignant, about a year . . ." The son-in-law stopped talking and calmed himself down before continuing. "I think that's about how long we'd have. Being in and out of hospital and on medication . . . I don't know how long I would be myself."

"Whoa, look, Min-*Seobang*."[36] The father-in-law put his fork down and had a sip of jasmine tea. His hand trembled as he wiped his mouth with a napkin.

"Please let me finish, Father." Although M's tone was tranquil and calm, his face was pale.

"Are you in pain? Are you feeling all right?"

"I took some painkillers, so I should be fine. As you know, my wife is not very aware of affairs at home . . . I'm talking about Ji-won. He has been planning to study in the US for three more years, so . . ."

The moment he heard his grandchild's name, he felt a twinge in his heart. Even as a toddler, the boy could read and absorb information with no effort; it was because of this child that he finally approved of his youngest daughter's marriage.

"Ji-won's studies cost about thirty thousand a year, and I've already arranged that money separately."

"But, look. I don't think it will come to this, but if you were gone, I'll support him for as long as he wants."

"No, Father. I will cover it." His son-in-law's tone was decisive. "When he thinks of me . . . Even if I left too soon, I would still like to be remembered as a father who, at least, helped with my child's studies . . ."

Looking at M, he rubbed his face with his dry hands. This was his son-in-law, the brat, the thought of whom had always provoked him—M, who was so cold-hearted and callous that they

---

36 "Min" is the character's last name, and "seobang" means "son-in-law."

had never gotten along. He had been annoyed when his son had talked him into inviting his son-in-law into the company like his other children, and had tried to convince him that M was quick-witted and hardworking, only to be rebuffed by M. Now, for the first time, his son-in-law was telling him a long story. M was actually asking for a favor, talking on and on as if he were reading a report. Occasionally, he interrupted the monologue by mumbling, "Hey, look. No, listen . . ."

Finally, he exploded with rage, "Stop. That's enough!" His voice trembled. "They are my grandson and my daughter. Are you . . . Are you stupid?" Even though his son-in-law said he was sorry, he did not put his head down or stop talking. Crazy brat. Stupid fool . . . His chest felt as though a massive weight was sitting on it.

"You . . . As you're well aware I have always been unhappy with you. With my temper, and the way you are . . ." He stopped himself. He couldn't find the right words.

"I know you haven't been satisfied with me."

Tut-tut. The father-in-law clicked his tongue again. "When I found out about the two of you living like strangers . . . I even told her to get a divorce." Although he regretted it as soon as he said it, his son-in-law's face was undisturbed.

"My wife told me that you had said so."

"I didn't say it because I hate you. I said it out of frustration." Did he hate M? He probably did and didn't at the same time. The new apartment, the expensive memberships, and the sleek, shiny car . . . The crossed wires and missed connections . . . He came to realize that he had hated, detested, and finally ignored his son-in-law, who never seemed appeased or humble in front of him.

"Above all else, you must take care of yourself." He wished he could say something else. He wanted to show sympathy as a father-in-law, something suitable to a sick son-in-law, to the man who sat there with a gloomy face, as if he knew this was coming, and to the insolent man who tried to sit up straight even while propping up his torso with his hands.

He lit the leftover cigar.

"I am a person with no fear," he stopped again. He was irritated that he kept pausing, but he was even more irritated that he couldn't find the right words. He had lived his life undaunted in everything, directly facing everything. That was how he had set up and organized his company and managed his wife and five children. He felt he had come through countless distressing, absurd, and inescapable situations . . . but now, at the age of eighty, he thought for the first time that he had lived too long.

He managed to continue talking. "I . . . found it hard . . . to get along with you." He looked at his son-in-law and then calmly lowered his eyes.

"So did I, Father." M's voice was too low to be heard. They looked at one another. The two men sat for a long time in the room filled with strong cigar smoke and soft music.

4. An Evening Spent Eating Dumplings

"What brings you here when you're so busy?" His mother greeted him in a confused rush. "Strangely, the dumplings run out fast these days." She gave him an uncomfortable look as she wiped the flour off her hands onto her apron. The smell of *kimchi* and pickled peppers filled the small house.

"It's because your dumplings are so good. Do you have any steamed ones? I'm hungry." He walked toward the table that sat along one wall, and she opened a pot. Soon a bowl of steaming dumpling soup was placed in front of him.

"It's a little spicy, isn't it? The peppers I pickled this time were a little spicy, and some people liked them that way." She had some long-time customers. She had been selling in the market for thirty years, and they came to her for dumplings, sliced rice cakes, blood sausages, and *tteokbokki*[37] mixed with sticky red sauce. For holidays, she would make the stuffing for the dumplings, enough

---

37 A dish eaten as a snack or a light meal made with rice cake, spicy red pepper paste sauce, fish cake, vegetables, and other ingredients.

to fill a large bowl the size of a baby's bathtub, while he rolled the dough; then his mother and two siblings would spend all night making the dumplings. Until all three of her children had graduated from college, she rose at dawn and would only lay her sore back down after midnight. Even though all her children told her to take it easy, she never listened.

He looked at his mother's tiny face in front of him. His mother, who had raised three children—a doctor, a teacher, and a reporter—was a legend in the market.

"Isn't the lease for this place up next month?" He mumbled as he chewed on the dumplings.

"The lease? Why are you asking about that?"

"I mean, why don't you move? Don't you ever get sick of this place?"

She carefully studied his face. "Did your wife say something? I know she doesn't like to come here, but . . ." Indeed, it wasn't the kind of place for a woman in a Fendi dress with a Louis Vuitton bag. During one visit, his wife had discovered a deep scratch on the side of their sleek silver Mercedes and flew into a rage. He had said, "It was probably just some kids," to which she responded, "I'm more afraid of bitter poor people, adults or children, than anything else."

"I do what I do regardless of what she says. There's no elevator, and I'm worried about your legs. Have you seen the new apartment building next door? I'll check with them about a similar size." He didn't tell her that he had already signed a contract in his mother's name for a nine-hundred-square-foot apartment with southern exposure on the eighth floor in the new building. When his father had passed away after three years of illness, his mother was thirty-seven years old. His mother, whose straight back had become bent and whose pale face had grown age spots—how could a small apartment repay her for thirty years . . . His heart was breaking, but it was all he could do for now.

"Are you feeling okay? You don't look so well." Just as M got up to leave, his mother placed a hand on him. "Just wait for a minute," she said and opened the refrigerator, taking out a plastic bag. "This is red ginseng extract. *Maknae*[38] brought it for me the day before yesterday. It hasn't been that long since I had some herbal medicine. It's really our own fault as old people for constantly depending on medicine." She smiled as if she were frowning. "Don't pay too much attention to the house or me. I know how you feel. Take care of yourself, instead. Of course, you would, though, since you're a doctor." Her tone was cautious.

"I'm going," he said, pushing the door open before turning around and hugging his mother tightly. The plastic bag hanging in his hand fell with a thud. "My child, what's . . ." she said and gently patted his back. As their embrace relaxed, there was an awkward silence. His mother didn't ask, "My child, what's going on?" He didn't say, "Something's wrong, mother." The reticent mother looked at his face, as sorrow, anger, and remorse passed in waves over her sad eyes. After a short while, something close to a smile appeared on his face. Her heart pounded. Just as his eyes seemed about to tear up, her son winked at her and closed the door.

5. Pain

The surgery was over too quickly. When M opened his eyes in the recovery room, the wall clock read ten. Two hours; it was a short operation that hadn't taken even half the time it was supposed to. "They couldn't touch it . . . They just left it and closed it up again . . ." he thought dimly. "It's over now . . ." A pale hand came near and tapped him on his shoulder.

"You're awake. They said it went well." It was his classmate who had attended the operation as an assistant doctor. M looked deep into his eyes. Even in his weakened condition, M wanted to read his mind.

"They removed the tissue, and a sample was probably brought in for a culture, and then the results will come back in a few days."

It was just as M had thought. The tumors had not been re-

---

38 A name for the youngest children in the family.

moved. Perhaps he would have to go through several more operations. He wanted to ask, "Were they hard or soft, white or red?" but he couldn't open his mouth. He shivered, feeling a chill.

Five days later, with a scar shaped like a *giyeok*,[39] M was discharged from the hospital.

"In about three or four days you can come back for the results. You'll find all this resting boring." His primary doctor's tone was light, as if he was treating a patient who had just had an appendectomy. M's wife was delighted at first. Having grown pale in the course of a few days, she looked seriously ill herself. While the caretaker was packing, M's wife opened her mobile phone and made some calls. Not even five minutes had passed when two stout men in suits stepped into his room. One of them removed the orchid pots tightly crowding the window and threw away the baskets of wilted flowers. The other man came in pushing a wheelchair and politely bowed at him.

"Shall we go?"

"No, I'll walk," M politely refused.

Even though everybody phoned him—all the people who had suddenly become kind to him—M barely saw anybody for the two days following his discharge. Nor did he read any books or watch TV. Instead, he sat all day doing nothing, thinking about the weakness and resilience of his organs. While fighting the lingering pain and trying to trace its roots, his body and mind, the mental and physical, kept uniting and pulling apart. He didn't take the painkillers that his wife offered him. The pain radiated through his whole body, from the scar and the tumors that remained, but he wanted to understand it on a more fundamental level. He couldn't know what kind of faulty genes or bad blood were circulating throughout his body. At any time, they could become vulnerable. One moment he felt like he understood everything, the next he was afraid he would never unpack the secrets of his life.

During this time, M's mother and younger sister and brother came to visit him. His wife, who couldn't argue with him in the

39 The first consonant of the Korean alphabet: ㄱ

hospital, had called them against his wishes. M's mother shed tears, thinking of his last visit.

"I've been having bad dreams for days," she said, trembling. "I'll move and wrap up my business. I'll do whatever you say from now on."

His sister wiped the tears running down their mother's wrinkled face. "Mom, he said the surgery went well. *Oppa* says he's okay," his sister said, her eyes full of tears.

"*Hyeong,* how could you do this to us? When are you going to let your family help you? Have you thought about how hard it's been for *Hyeongsoo?*" *Maknae* grumbled at him.

"Well, I'm just . . ." standing behind him, M's wife looked restless. "You know how your brother is. Being sick didn't change him." Sulking and pursing her lips, she had finally spoken her mind.

M thought, 'That's just who she is.' He felt relieved. His wife's face, which had been contracted from playing her role as a prudent and calm wife since the onset of his disease, looked cheerful once again. His mother, siblings, wife, and children . . . M quietly watched them sitting next to each other and drinking tea. It was painful to realize that he was connected to all of them. That he was alive and together with them and that he had spent so much time living in pain and hiding it from them . . . He felt the aching deep in his heart. The fact that he still belonged to their world made him happy, and this feeling of happiness threw him into an altogether new pain.

Although he felt terrible, he acted as if he were peaceful, so his wife went out occasionally, leaving him at home alone. One afternoon while he was alone at home, M made a phone call. He wrote down the number and stood frozen for a while before picking up the phone again. He didn't believe that he could turn back time, just as water never runs backwards. Nor was he interested in returning to an earlier time. He pressed the numbers slow and hard, one by one. He thought, 'Sickness does something bad to a person,' but his heart was still pounding violently.

6. And the Place Where the Water Runs

The woman was still living in the town where he had been born and raised. When she heard his voice, she said, "Oh."

Slowly, he said, "I'm sorry for calling you out of the blue. I'd like to see you if it's alright with you . . ." He didn't tell her that he wanted to see her no matter what. The woman he remembered was prudent and quite shy. M had to make up a story to get through to her. *I came here to attend a conference. I heard you were around. I'm not far away. Could we meet for tea?* While he was speaking, he felt like he was choking. He had even wanted to look up her address and stand under her window if she refused. He felt like he had no choice.

"K," he called out her name. He heard a long sigh from the other end of the line. A deep sigh escaped from his lips as well. Between their sighs, he felt as though she were near enough that he could reach out and touch her.

"I'll be done with patients by six o'clock. I could see you for about one, maybe two hours after that." And she added, "Let's have dinner."

He would have to hurry to get there by six. M applied another layer of bandages over his scar, which he had just finished dressing. As he changed clothes, got his painkillers, and walked out the door, he looked at himself in the mirror hanging on the wall. He rubbed his beard, which he hadn't had time to shave. He felt like he smelled stale. M couldn't remember when the last time he had seen K was. If she felt disappointed with his changed looks, he couldn't help it. Just as he had changed, she would have as well.

As soon as he got on the highway, M drove fast, changing lanes rapidly. Scattered traffic cameras caught his car a couple of times. After passing by a dam, the road entered a rural area, following a river. As he crossed the border of the province, the geographical features began to change and he could see the mountains from the winding road. Opening the window, M drove against the wind. Once, back when they commuted to school togeth-er by train, K had said, "Listen to this," and had put one of her earphones to his ear. It was Beethoven. Listening to a piano so-nata for the first time; it had been an event. So was the fact that they were connected by earphones, huddled around a small cas-sette player. Once he knew "Moonlight Sonata," K had recorded "Appassionata" for him. It was also K who had introduced Rach-maninoff, whose music made him imagine delicate finger move-ments, and lively Mozart, to which he read Hesse and Goethe. M remembered one afternoon when K was covered with mud, step-ping in puddles and wet grass on her way home.

Maybe K only existed as a fantasy, not as a real person. May-be she was the same as all the other women he had known, like R or S or O. He didn't remember when K had faded from his mem-ory and become a fantasy and he didn't remember when or why he had left her.

Like two boats riding the waves, they had turned around and around and finally drifted apart. He had never expected to see her again. K, from whom he had drifted apart, was forgotten and dis-appeared from M's memory. No, that wasn't true. M's memory, his body and all of his senses were running back to the past. He drove almost unconsciously, turning the wheel, hitting the brake, and controlling his speed mindlessly.

In the afternoon, school girls walked past his office window—her face rose before his eyes as he watched the white school uniforms glittering in the sunlight, two or three of them, or sometimes, a solitary one . . . A woman with long hair hailing a taxi on the crowded streets late at night . . . The low voice he heard when his steps were halted in front of the speakers by a familiar melody . . . He felt like K had never left him even for one single moment.

Could one call that eternity? M believed that he had forgot-ten her only by exerting a superhuman effort again and again and then eventually he had even forgotten the fact of his forgetting. K's existence, which despite his efforts remained preserved in-side him—he who did everything exactly as he wanted or as he thought he wanted—was wondrous but also meaningless. What would he say when he saw her, and what difference would it make if he saw her . . . He didn't know. He didn't even know what he wanted. He thought about what had happened to him in the last few weeks. Being scared, sad, and angry . . . And he thought about the pain that lingered where all those missing things had been. The rays of the sinking sun stung his eyes through the window. "Let's take it as it comes," M quietly persuaded himself. Like a negative gradually exposing its silhouettes to the developer, he felt that something was slowly emerging.

Just as he entered the city, M's mobile phone rang. It was his doctor.

"The results just came back. The tumor's benign. Congratulations!" he said.

Vacantly listening to him, M asked, "Didn't you say the results wouldn't be back until tomorrow?"

"Well, the tissue grew faster than we expected. Everyone's shocked because the chances that it was going to be benign were close to zero. In fact, I didn't tell you this, but I expected the worst." The more excited his doctor got, the calmer M grew.

"Let your wife know right away. Your father-in-law even seems to have been calling the director of the hospital."

"I see. Thank you," M said.

"Dude, you can't believe it, huh? I couldn't, either." The voice on the other end grew tender. "Come in tomorrow and see the results officially and then we'll schedule the treatment. Even though it's benign, it's still a tumor."

M parked his car on the shoulder. His body, which had been growing agitated, gradually lost tension and he became absentminded. He put his hand on his abdomen and felt the wound. He opened the door and walked out of the car. The tumors in his abdomen, according to this news, were something like water-balloons. He walked slowly against the wind. 'Where is everyone going?' M wondered.

The Interview

Manja was very excited that morning. She checked the clock on the wall seven times before leaving home at nine o'clock sharp. In between, she looked in the mirror on the living room wall, powdered her forehead and nose several times, and kept putting on and taking off her pink scarf. 'It looks elegant, but maybe also a little tacky?' According to the color testing she had done with her digital camera last night, it looked soft, but it wasn't easy to tell how it would look on TV. In the end, she decided to keep the scarf in her bag so she could wear it if she felt like it. Mir, her dog, wagged its tail and stared at Manja as if it could sense something was out of the ordinary.

It was a typical autumn day, with a gentle breeze and clear sky. She saw a cloud that she thought looked just like a horse and carriage, and she hummed a nursery rhyme, "I'm Riding Along in a Carriage," which she had picked up who knows where, while walking out to the main road.

"Hello, Manja. Where are you headed?" A woman in shabby black sweatpants standing on the street corner seemed delighted to see her. It was Mina's mother from the apartment building across from hers. Manja pouted. When Manja had told Mina's mother that she had taken a beautiful pen name, Hye-young Yi, Mina's mother burst out laughing, saying, "You're Hye-young Yi? You?" Since then, Mina's mother refused to call her In-young's mother, which she had called her for ten years, and started calling her Manja-*Ssi*[40] all the time. Mina's mother looked like she had just come from the dry cleaner, hauling several vinyl bags full of clothes over her shoulder, and her hair was unkempt.

"Hey, you look like a young lady in that outfit. What are you up to?"

---

[40] *Ssi* is a suffix that functions as a formal title, such as Mr. or Mrs., but without specifying gender.

Although Mina's mother approached her smiling, Manja just said, "I'll tell you later," and rushed off. Even though Manja would occasionally have tea with Mina's mother and chat about an unfashionable sweater or what shoes were in stock at the apartment complex's *yangpumjum*,[41] she felt like now even that would come to an end.

When her second collection of short stories had come out last month, and when an interview with a fairly large picture had run in the paper, she had waited eagerly to hear what Mina's mother would say, but Mina's mother pretended to know nothing about it. She did this even though it was in the best-selling newspaper in the country. Moreover, when Manja showed her the article, which she had carefully clipped out and neatly laminated, she said something like, "Oh, well, we only read the sports section." And then, as she turned around and walked away, she added as if she had just thought of it, "Oh, by the way, Manja-*Ssi*, why don't you help Mina with her writing? What day would be good for you?" But Manja didn't want to criticize Mina's mother. She was well aware that she was an uncultured person.

Although Manja had planned to arrive about five minutes late, on this particular day a cab appeared right away, the roads were empty, and the lights were all green so that the cab driver sped up, passing other cars as if he was enjoying it. She inadvertently arrived at the meeting place, in front of the county hall, ten minutes early. As she had expected, there was no one waiting to meet her. A few of the shuttle buses that no one ever seemed to get on or off of stopped in front of her and left, and the minutes passed. Tired of checking her watch, Manja took out her pocketbook and decided to review one last time. Question number one was too obvious: "What motivated you to become a writer?" It was such a cliché question, but she couldn't figure out how to deal with it . . . whether she should ask it in a serious or a casual tone. Just as it had for the last few days, seeing the list of questions in front of her made Manja worried again. Manja thought that what mattered most was the tone. Whether in a story or a human relation-

41 The name originally refers to a shop that sells Western-style clothing and accessories, but nowadays it refers to a small store that carries all kinds of miscellaneous goods, including apparel and accessories.

ship, she believed that tone determined everything. 'It might be better to start simply and lightheartedly.' She thought that would be more appropriate for someone like Yeon-sook Kim *Seonsaeng*,[42] who projected *seriousness* from every pore. She rearranged questions three and one. "In all your novels, including your latest one, none of your characters fall in love. Don't you believe in love?" She thought it was a little puerile but amusing. A person named something-Kim from the Art Committee said that Yeon-sook Kim *Seonsaeng* had personally chosen Manja as her interviewer. For Manja, who had only published two books and didn't know many people in literary circles, it was, in fact, an unexpected surprise. 'It's a web magazine uploading a video clip, so maybe they wanted a camera-friendly writer? How could they know that I have a sweet voice?' Feeling giddy, she couldn't calm herself down for several days.

"Aren't you Yi *Seonsaeng-nim*?[43] You're here early," said a dull voice. As she turned around, she unwittingly frowned. The guy, who must be something-Kim, looked scruffy, as if he had just awoken from a three-day nap. Reeking of nicotine, with disheveled hair and a wrinkled trench coat, the man smiled at her, squinting his baggy, bulging eyes.

"Oh, well . . . I live nearby." Manja smiled back at him, hoping to look natural as she raised the corners of her mouth.

"I was told that the TV crew is running late, so I guess that means more waiting for you." He lit a cigarette and put it between his lips without any sign of pity, and pulled out his business card, saying, "Oh." "THE COMMITTEE OF LITERATURE, HAK-SOOL[44] KIM" was written in letters as small as sesame seeds. Despite having an unusual name herself, worthy of days of stories, she couldn't think of anything to say except that the name was unique.

"The committee members, so . . . who are they?"

He looked confused in response to her question. Having just wanted to fill the silence, Manja wondered if this was something she shouldn't have asked and suddenly felt cautious.

---

42 *Seonsaeng* means teacher. It is a title placed after a person's name to show respect.
43 *Nim* is an honorific word to call a person.
44 Hak-sool is an unusual name because it means "academic."

He was excessively honest in his response. "Well, it's kind of a meaningless position that rotates around. If you are on the Art Committee and you go to the Department of Fine Arts, you become part of the Fine Arts Committee, and if you move to the Department of Literature, you become part of the Literature Committee."

She switched to that universal topic, the weather. "The weather . . . is really nice, isn't it?"

He responded with enthusiasm, "It really is. It must be beautiful in *Kangchon*."

"Shouldn't we head north first?" The man behind the steering wheel hesitated, gauging the direction. The man in charge of driving today didn't seem like he would belong on any Committee of Driving. As if avoiding the unnecessary, this man with the soldier's crew cut refused to meet Manja's eyes and spoke in a hard, clipped way like a military man.

"Take Olympic Road first and then in *Misari*, what is it again . . . turn in the direction of *Guri* and go right . . . No, no. You should've made a U-turn over there. Oh, we passed it." While bothering the driver in this way, Hak-sool Kim, sitting in the passenger seat, asked, "Yi *Seonsaeng-nim*, have you ever been to *Kangchon*? Do you know a shortcut, by any chance?"

"I would take the *Kangbyeon* North Road, and there's a detour coming up," Manja immediately answered from the backseat of the car. She thought she knew the roads pretty well, and could even get them to *Kangwon* province. She used to drive around on weekends, and sometimes even during the week, whenever she had some free time. That was how she thought a writer should live. Everything stimulated and awakened Manja's imagination: parking under a tree while driving on a strange road, the smell of the soil while walking through a field, tea she drank by herself in a hidden café, and the fantastic, lonesome sunset on the way back. During one of those trips, she fell in love with a fifteen-thousand-square-foot field with an old, crumbling cottage in *Hongcheon*, and felt that it was all she needed in the world. Whenever she thought of the land she had bought, about building a pretty wooden house, preparing a study, and writing novels in the sunlight someday, nothing but novels, Manja smiled even in her sleep.

Crammed into the backseat with two members of the TV crew, Manja felt a little nervous. When she had asked about transportation, they had said, "A member of the staff has a decent car. We'll drive you." Had she been wrong to expect a van with plenty of space? She was trying to adjust to the *decent* car, which turned out to be so old and small that she wondered if it would even make it. In order to bear the unidentifiable packages that littered the floor, the piles of used tissues carelessly left here and there, and the old stench of wet tobacco and dust permeating the car, Manja held her breath and carefully exhaled. One of the men from the TV crew talked on the phone the whole ride until they passed over *Banpo* Bridge and entered *Kangbyeon* North Road.

"No, no. I didn't mean that. How do you expect me to go to work? Do you really want to do that? Mom, is saving face that important?" According to what she could overhear, he seemed to be about to get married. The towns and regions, *Sanggye-dong, Junggye-dong,* and *Kwangmyeong,* flew by and disappeared. He was on the brink of turning a corner on the difficult path of life.

Manja had a sister who was putting off getting married with all her might. When Manja left her boyfriend of three years and entered an arranged marriage a month after meeting her husband, her sister had said, "Well, there's no law against marrying someone you haven't dated very long." But during the wedding she had given Manja a strange look. The man her sister was dating was a stage actor, just like the boyfriend Manja had left. Once in a while, Manja went to *Dongsung-dong* or *Shinchon* with complimentary tickets from her sister. She could say with confidence that she only went out of a feeling that she should attend cultural events, and with no ulterior motive. Her sister's man appeared on the stage in a number of roles, such as a second son who suffered from a lack of affection and lived in his older brother's shadow, an unreasonably intelligent *jajangmyeon*[45] deliveryman, a poet still

---

45 Noodles with black bean sauce, a common comfort food in Korea.

suffering from the scars of the Vietnam War, and others. He was terribly unsophisticated and single-minded even onstage. Manja often wondered why on earth her sister couldn't—or wouldn't—leave this man. How much time did she need to realize that he had been born clumsy and unrefined, and that it was a fate he could never escape? Her sister still didn't seem to understand that once she actually left him, she would realize that all her hesitations had been a waste of time. Although Manja sometimes ran into her ex-boyfriend by accident—and although she would even exchange awkward greetings with him, "Oh, hi, how are you doing?" and afterwards, on the way home, she would be surprised that he still had innocent eyes—it was nothing more than that. His eyes inspired in her a vague sadness and a longing for something unknown, and she thought that was enough of a role for him in her life. But she never completely rid herself of her feelings for him, which would have enabled her to see him again socially. What was the point? When she had left him, she had stored him away for later, expecting that a man so preserved might, from time to time, awaken excitement or the wound in her heart. It hadn't happened yet, but who knows? She hoped that he would remain single, keeping his artless ways and serious, sad eyes always available to her.

Fortunately, the riverside road was fairly quiet in the morning. The sunlight breaking on the river was utterly beautiful.

"Wow, the light is amazing right now," Hak-sool Kim exclaimed giddily, admiring the view. The driver seemed to enjoy speed, even though he wasn't good at directions, and the car kept pushing forward, passing other fast cars.

"Did you stay late the night before last?" Hak-sool Kim asked the driver.

"No, I left early, around one A.M.," the driver responded shortly.

"Well, that night in *Insa-dong* all these famous people came out. They seem to like hanging out all together as a big group. I prefer more intimate gatherings." Hak-sool Kim dropped the names of a poet, a writer, and a critic.

"Maybe they enjoy dragging nobodies along." It was another short reply.

"I was out late again last night. In fact, I'm still hungover."

Thinking, 'So, that's what it was. Working life is hard for everyone after all,' Manja looked at the back of Hak-sool Kim's head with a slight sadness in her eyes. The next moment, the driver, whose name she didn't know, said, "So am I." Manja's face turned pale.

Just as the car was approaching *Cheongdam* Bridge, she took out her phone. Then she remembered that she had forgotten to feed Mir that morning. She ran through the options in her head: texting *Maknae*, who always arrived home first, or reluctantly texting Mina's mother. Who else had the combination to the door? Deep in thought, Manja's eyes suddenly opened wide.

"Oh!" she cried out. But it was too late; they were already on *Cheongdam* Bridge. Even though she said, "Oh, no. This isn't the right way," the driver didn't slow down at all. He had to be really hungover. She tensed up and realized 'Now I absolutely have to remain alert.' There was a real chance that they wouldn't make it to *Kangchon* before sunset. She might not be able to meet Yeon-sook Kim *Seonsaeng*. 'I can't let that happen—I've been looking forward to this for so long.' Even in her wildest dreams, she never thought that such a small thing as this would get in the way, but she didn't lose her temper. She calmed herself down, thinking, 'I have to concentrate. Those two said they were still hungover. One way or another, the cameraman, his assistant, and I have to get to *Kangchon*, to Yeon-sook Kim *Seonsaeng*.'

The man who had been on the phone had fallen asleep, his head sinking down.

"If we keep going straight on this road, we will reach *Bundang*. There, we should take that exit." Manja's voice was calm as she directed the driver.

"Oh no, I really didn't want to come here," the driver spat out in self-pity when *Seongnam* appeared after the exit.

"Oh, your ex-girlfriend, huh? Why did you break up with her, anyway?" Hak-sool Kim asked.

"Why bother asking? You already know why." The driver and Hak-sool Kim seemed to be completely absorbed in thinking about that woman. Finally, they reached the crossroads of *Seong-nam* and *Garak-dong*.

"Um, which way are you planning to take here?" Manja interrupted, losing her patience.

"Oh, which way would you suggest? Maybe we should get off again, but we're going in the opposite direction now, right?" Hak-sool Kim asked. His voice was calm, as if nothing was wrong, even though they knew they were going the wrong way.

"Actually ... You should turn left, then go over to *Yang-jae* Bridge, pass *Garak-dong*, then go over the Olympic Bridge again ..."

While Manja repeatedly recited the directions to the men, the car suddenly slowed down, taking *Yangjae* Bridge. She continued, "Okay, through the underpass. No, go straight. Keep going straight. Take a left turn over there. Yes, left. Now move towards the right, not the first lane, the second lane. No, no, no ..." Finally, they succeeded in turning the car around to *Kangbyeon* Road North, almost losing their way a couple of times, including taking a wrong turn that would have put them back on Olympic Bridge headed toward the airport.

She wanted to ask, "Would you mind if I drive?" but the car was a stick shift and she had never driven one before.

Yeon-sook Kim *Seonsaeng* was wearing a bright purple suit. *Seonsaeng* approached the crew, her face radiant with joy. Her arms were outstretched, as if she were greeting a son returning from war or an estranged grandson. She shook hands with Hak-sool Kim and then took Manja's hand.

"Oh, Hye-young Yi *Jakga*.[46] It's very nice to meet you. I have always wanted to meet you. Was the traffic bad?" *Seonsaeng* looked at Manja with warm eyes and held her hand tightly. *Seonsaeng*'s hand was warm and soft, and a ripple of excitement passed through Manja's heart.

"Thank you for sending me your last book. I haven't finished

---

46 A writer. It can be used after a person's name to show that that person is a writer.

reading it yet though . . ." *Seonsaeng* said.

Manja blushed. She thought back to the postcard that Kim *Seonsaeng* had sent her shortly after she had sent her a copy of her book, the rush of emotions she felt from the fine handwriting and the hastily scrawled line, "I'll savor it."

"Isn't it nice here? The village chief seems to have gone out. I should've called him." Yeon-sook Kim *Seonsaeng* led them into the literature museum. It looked like one of those places that pay special tribute to local writers. A group of students was wandering around the museum. The man who seemed to be the teacher of these students, who were seriously examining the artifacts—a dead writer's manuscript displayed in a glass box, a commemorative picture of some chairperson from a literary society, an image from some writer's childhood, someone else's pencil sketch, and so on—suddenly rushed over to Yeon-sook Kim with a shocked look on his face.

"Aren't you Yeon-sook Kim *Seonsaeng-nim*? I knew you lived here, but I didn't expect to see you here . . . It's an honor, I, um, I met you briefly and introduced myself at the last Night of Literature. Do you remember me?" The man introduced himself as Mr. So-and-so "the poet" and called out to the students.

"Hey, kids. Look here." About twenty children raised their heads at the same time and looked at Yeon-sook Kim and Manja. "This is the novelist, Yeon-sook Kim *Seonsaeng-nim*. Do you remember the novel *The Time of Farewell* from your textbook? Why don't you come over and say hi?" Whispering to each other, the children approached Kim *Seonsaeng* one by one and bowed their heads.

A girl hesitantly held out a notebook. "Can I get your autograph? My mom is a huge fan of yours."

Kim *Seonsaeng* awkwardly took the pen, smiling. Soon, all of the children were lined up, paper in hand, and Kim *Seonsaeng* was occupied with them for a while.

"By the way . . . You look familiar. Are you a writer as well?" the teacher asked Manja. It was a familiar scene for her. People often asked her this kind of question at gatherings like award ceremonies, end of year parties, or book launches. "I'm sorry, but what's your name?"

"I'm Hye-young Yi, a novelist," she would reply. At that point, nine out of ten people mentioned her debut piece, "Oh, you're the one who wrote *Seokmodo*. It was such a good novel."

Although she had published twenty-two stories after *Seokmodo*, people only talked about *Seokmodo*. They talked about the style of *Seokmodo*, the structure of *Seokmodo*, the tragic destiny of the female protagonist who wandered about the seashore, and how the scenery was like a watercolor painting. She was disappointed, but she got used to hiding it. Sometimes it seemed to her that people might be too busy to read or remember her other work. How did the world become so materialistic?

"I'm Hye-young Yi. I write novels." Manja's answer was polite.

"Oh, so you are. I'm sorry I didn't recognize you." Thankfully, he didn't talk about *Seokmodo*.

"This is me," he handed her his business card filled with tiny little letters. Poet, Essayist, Head Teacher of Korean Language at Keumkang High School of Information Technology, Director of Higher Education, and Chairman of the *Kangseo* Branch of the *Bareuge Salgi*[47] Movement . . . She stopped reading there and put it in her pocket.

"By the way, you're beautiful. Do they select writers by looks nowadays?" he blurted out suddenly. Even though that attitude and even that comment weren't very surprising, Manja always felt a little uncomfortable when men were so frank. However, she managed to smile politely and he seemed to think that his compliment had pleased her.

The man's voice grew quiet. "My phone number is on my card. Please give me a call when you come to *Kangchon*. I'll introduce you to a nice place that could be helpful for writing. And that's my address, too. Please send me a copy of your new novel when it comes out. I'll send you mine as well. My last essay had a run of about twenty thousand. I'm kind of well-known around here. Quite a few writers from this area have been well-known. Poet

---

47 *Bareuge Salgi* means "Let's live rightly (or righteously)." In Korea there is a government council devoted to this movement, which aims at improving the minds and lifestyles of Korean people.

something, writer so-and-so . . ." The vague names floated past her ears.

"You know Sang-woo Yi, the novelist, right? He was my class-mate in high school." He was almost whispering now, as if he were letting her in on an important secret.

"Whenever we would go to literary competitions, I would win first place and he would come in as either second or lower, but somehow he made it big. You know he's being awarded the Korea Literature Award, right?"

All Manja could think about was this man's horrendous breath.

"Well, uh, what's your address?" The man, taking out his small notebook, pen poised, looked at Manja. She wasn't sure what to do as this was a new situation for her. As Manja debated whether or not to give him her address, Yeon-sook Kim *Seonsaeng* approached.

"Oh, Yi *Jakga*! Would you like to say hi to the students as well? They probably want to get an autograph from a rising star!"

Manja's face turned red. Some students, looking bored, turned to Manja.

"Now, shall we head to my office? Why don't you ride with me, Yi *Jakga*?" After leaving the museum, *Seonsaeng* walked towards the parking lot. The old black sedan was filled with the scent of the ocean.

"Your car is in great shape even though it seems like an old model," Manja exclaimed.

"Oh, I don't like to change things. This woman writer I met not too long ago, her name was . . . Oh, well. My memory is fad-ing these days. She came to pick me up for a seminar and she drove a shiny foreign-made car. Well, it's not that one car is right for all writers, but it just didn't feel right."

Manja kept her mouth shut. She drove a German car. It was three or four years old, and it still shined on a sunny day, even though she often took it out for long rides.

"Then again, maybe it's time for there to be a millionaire writer. Having one's stories made into TV dramas and movies, getting paid well for the rights ... I think it could be good for the field if there were more money in it. In my day, the middle-aged men coming to writer's gatherings were somewhat down-at-the-heels. Now I see young writers who are tall and good-looking."

Manja sifted through her memory but couldn't think of any tall, good-looking writers, so she changed the subject to TV drama.

"Your early novels, *The Time of Girls*? It was a trilogy, I think. I loved it."

"Oh, you even remember that? It must've been when you were little." Yeon-sook Kim *Seonsaeng* was delighted. Although it wasn't that Manja even remembered that, but more that she only remembered that, Manja smiled at her quietly. How could one not know that series? That series made her a name; her novels moved from the required-reading corner to the best-seller shelf.

"You know that the person who adapted it became a TV drama writer, right? Among my novels, that one had the simplest plot, but the adaptation must have been an ordeal. That writer still complains, 'Because of you, I didn't become a novelist.' That person had good prospects as an author."

"There must have been movie proposals as well. Aren't you interested in that kind of thing?" Manja was determined to build on Kim *Seonsaeng*'s palpable excitement.

"Well, there were some, but as you know, for the most part my novels are not heart-warming or cute stories. It's hard to find someone who can produce something like that, who can make that kind of emotion work on the screen."

Manja nodded. She was mostly right, but even if one was able to preserve the mood, Manja wondered if such a film would recoup its production costs. Nevertheless, *Seonsaeng*'s confidence swayed Manja. 'Isn't that the power of a renowned writer?' Her respect for Kim *Seonsaeng* grew a span in her heart.

The car gradually slowed down as it entered the city.

"So, your office is in the city. I thought it would be located somewhere on the outskirts, maybe in farmland ..." Manja remarked.

Kim *Seonsaeng* turned and looked at Manja. "Why? Do I seem a little old-fashioned?"

"No, I don't mean . . ." Manja mumbled.

"You seem to be envisioning a kind of idyllic atmosphere for some reason, something like a white wooden house with a swing hung on the front porch . . ."

"Well, that is . . ." She stuttered.

"I've actually been looking for a farmhouse with some land . . . Oh, by the way, where are you from, Yi *Jakga*? Any children, a kid in elementary school, for instance?" Kim *Seonsaeng* asked, changing the subject.

"Yes, I have one child in elementary school and one in middle school." Seeing the look of shock on Yeon-sook Kim *Seonsaeng*'s face, Manja stopped, not mentioning her high-school-aged child.

"It's so hard to tell how old you young people are these days. How could a baby face like yours have a child in junior high?" Baby face? That was the first time Manja had been called that. Dropping her eyes shyly, Manja blushed red like an infant.

"There," *Seonsaeng* pointed at a building with a glass exterior. The light reflected off the glass, shining in Manja's eyes. The empty parking lot smelled of wet cement.

"This is a new building. This area is sort of a new urban district in *Kangchon*. It's a little crowded, but when you go upstairs, it has a nice view," *Seonsaeng* said as they walked up the stairs. Some unfamiliar smell, which seemed to be a combination of paint, glue, and air freshener, pervaded the elevator and hallways. Maybe because of this, Manja felt a little dizzy.

"Wow," Hak-sool Kim exclaimed first. Along the walls, several thousand books were lined up in apple-pie order on bookshelves that seemed newly assembled.

"It really looks like a library," the camera director added. Indeed, the books, alphabetized by author, produced that effect. The books that had been received recently were neatly arranged on a table in the center of the room. Manja felt somehow hollow inside. She had expected to encounter the aroma of a writerly existence, even if it wasn't completely traditional—at least an old desk and piles of scattered books. But what she found instead was the smell of drying paint.

"How big is this place? I guess it's possible to have an office this size out here in *Kangchon*, right?" the camera director asked when Kim *Seonsaeng* disappeared, probably preparing tea.

"Well, wouldn't this kind of arrangement be possible in, say, an eighteen-hundred-square-foot apartment? If you use the living room or the master bedroom, you could create a space like this, couldn't you?" Hak-sool Kim commented.

"It would be difficult even with that much space," Manja interjected. She didn't mean to reproach his sense of space, but she wanted to correct his assumption, since she knew that this kind of room was impossible even with eighteen hundred square feet.

"Is that so? Then maybe twenty-eight hundred square feet?" the camera director asked. Manja wasn't foolish enough to tell them that she lived in an eighteen-hundred-square-foot apartment and didn't even have room for several hundred books, so the space discussion ended there.

"Oh, here's Yi *Seonsaeng-nim*'s book," said Hak-sool Kim, picking up a book from the table and holding it up. It was the book that Manja had sent to Kim *Seonsaeng*, about which she had said, "I'll savor it."

Hak-sool Kim continued: "Yes, I think I read it a while back. The cover photo is good. That background looks familiar. Where was it taken?" Manja stared at him dumbfounded. She wanted to say, "What do you mean 'a while back'? That book just came out last month," but of course, she bit her tongue.

"It was by *Kyeongbok-gung*," she said and Hak-sool Kim seemed delighted.

"Oh, right, at the literary café they have there, right? Somehow it seemed familiar to me. Producer Yi! Wasn't this the place where you filmed the poet Ji-sung Hwang *Seonsaeng*? Right? That day, Hwang *Seonsaeng* and, who was it . . . some baby writer . . . they seemed to be embroiled in a fight. Oh, my goodness. I'd never seen anything like it." Hak-sool Kim laughed and then stopped abruptly, realizing he had gone too far.

"Does Yeon-sook Kim *Seonsaeng* teach somewhere? There are so many papers," he remarked as he looked over the table.

"She's been tenured at Kangseo University for twenty years," Manja informed him, her voice low for fear that Kim *Seonsaeng* might hear.

"Ah. I see." Hak-sool Kim slowly nodded. The Committee of Literature must have their hands full with other matters.

Hak-sool Kim wasn't the only one making himself busy. The producer finished setting up the two cameras, closed the windows to correct the lighting conditions for recording, and completed all the other preparations, then said, "Let's get started." Just at that moment, Yeon-sook Kim *Seonsaeng*'s mobile phone rang.

"Excuse me," she said as she came back into the room and opened her phone. Her voice changed as she answered. "Well, well. *Seonsaeng-nim*." Kim *Seonsaeng*'s silvery voice chatted on for over ten minutes. "This is about the last trip to North Korea, right? Well, we should follow in the footsteps of that kind of person." Just as she ended her call and the story of the person whose footsteps we should follow was over, *Seonsaeng*'s phone rang again. "Oh, Kim *Gija*.[48] It's good that you called. You know, the meeting from last time. Don't you think it'd be better to set up a seminar supported by the province? I think that it would look better." Her voice was energetic again.

Manja thought, "Is this day just going to get crazier?" It could still end up being a fun day, though. She wanted to believe that. While she debated about whether to take the pink scarf out of the bag or not, Manja realized it had been a good decision not to wear it. Maybe wearing it would add to the chaos. Manja deliberated throughout the rest of Kim *Seonsaeng*'s phone call.

"It was a long period of time, but looking back I can see how that time was helpful to me." Yeon-sook Kim *Seonsaeng* was certainly logical. She had been asked about the ten years she had spent working at a pharmaceutical company after her debut. She had taken a position as the director of the department of public

---

48 A title used for journalists.

affairs, and after that had been unemployed for three years … Manja practically had her career memorized after having scoured the internet for days, carefully reading through the biographical dictionaries.

"That time allowed me to come to terms with my lack of talent," Kim *Seonsaeng* made a solemn face. Manja agreed that *Seonsaeng* was not a brilliantly talented writer. But regardless of whether her books were read, sold, or given awards, she kept writing. That was what Manja admired the most about her. At some point, her works had entered the spotlight, and she began receiving most of the literary awards. It was the model Manja most wanted to follow.

Manja judged that the mood had dipped. 'Should I try to brighten up the mood a little now?' Manja grinned and moved on to the fourth question.

"What do you think about, shall we say, the recent trend of easy-going, lively young writers? Do you read the popular internet novels, by any chance?"

"Oh, of course, I seek them out and read them—things like *Temptation of Foxes* or *The Wind Boy*." She was confident. The producer's eyes, behind the camera, opened wide and Hak-sool Kim, standing with his arms crossed, muttered "wow"; whether it was a groan or a compliment was unclear.

"Wait," The producer stopped Manja with his hand signal, "Hak-sool Kim *Seonsaeng-nim*'s voice was caught in the background a second ago. Can we just redo that part?"

"Can't you erase it later? It seems like technology can do anything these days," Yeon-sook Kim *Seonsaeng*'s face looked unpleasantly impatient.

"We still can't isolate the sounds out like that," the producer responded as he rewound the tape.

While the producer was spooling the tape, Hak-sool Kim interrupted, "*Seonsaeng-nim*, have you really read those novels?" Impressed, his eyes glittered with excitement.

"Why would I have lied? We should read all kinds of things. So we can have this kind of conversation and teach our children."

Why was *Seonsaeng* gazing at Manja, of all people? Manja blushed a little.

"Let's do it again," the producer joined his index finger and thumb to form a circle.

"It's been forty years since your debut, *Seonsaeng-nim*. What has driven you to keep writing and publishing novels all this time?" Manja asked, looking at her with the deepest respect. This was what Manja most wanted to know.

"Well, I don't know about other people, but I'm very aware of my complexes. I was full of them when I was young as well. You know those kids who are too shy to greet teachers, or who study hard but are never first, are never the pretty one, the good singer, or the most kind-hearted . . . I was always jealous of those little things." *Seonsaeng*'s face took on a childlike innocence. Manja had thought that *Seonsaeng* would have been like that as a little girl. Second, never first, and frustrated that she wasn't prettier.

"When I grew up, I no longer compared myself to others, but something like a fundamental solitude weighed down on me." *Seonsaeng* smiled, slanting her head like a young girl. It was a gentle smile, with a tinge of sadness.

"Solitude is in my nature. I have many siblings, and my childhood home was usually bustling with activity, but I was always solitary. I don't think that inclination is something that disappears." Her answer was not what Manja had expected. Manja had seen her several times before, and remembered that Yeonsook Kim *Seonsaeng* was always surrounded by young and old men. Whether speaking passionately or graciously accepting the drinks and compliments that followed, she was always majestic and graceful, like a queen.

"You have many students, colleagues, and followers . . ." Manja trailed off because she couldn't think of the right way to put it. "Is your life something like a crowded solitude?"

Seonsaeng smiled. "Isn't that a writer's destiny? A writer has a house inside herself. Even though one talks, laughs, and cries with the people who live in that house, one is basically a solitary being, and one should be alone." Her tone became sad.

Manja thought of *Seonsaeng*'s two marriages. Since, as a young woman, she had been a beauty of the literary world, she had been the subject of gossip. Manja supposed that it was generally known that her marriages had not been peaceful, and that there was much more that the public did not know.

"What do you do when you feel alone, besides writing?" Manja was determined to go a little further. It was a personal question, but *Seonsaeng* didn't evade it.

"Ah, gardening is my main hobby. It's also my specialty. My garden is about seven hundred square feet. You should come and visit some time. There's always some type of flower in season. Right now, the chrysanthemum is in full bloom. Growing flowers is similar to writing, that is to say . . . it's true labor. I often think that modern man's tragedy began when we lost the meaning of labor, when we stopped appreciating the depth of labor. While taking care of my garden, wearing a wide-brim hat and a pair of white gloves, squatting down low, I get all sweaty and begin to feel a blanket of peace spreading over everything in my life. I especially love small chrysanthemums; their fragrance is fantastic." Her eyes grew misty as she thought of the spacious work place, the open garden, and the small chrysanthemums . . .

Just as Manja started to imagine the garden, *Seonsaeng* asked, "How about you, Yi *Jakga*? What do you do when you feel alone?"

These interviews were structured as conversations, and Manja had prepared several stock answers; however, this particular question came as a surprise. Manja had hoped to get the chance to say, "Writing has always been my dream since I was small . . . I won the grand prize in a writing competition sponsored by a university newspaper when I was in high school. You were the judge. You might not remember, but you made a strong impression on me with your eyes. After the awards ceremony, you bought me *jajangmyeon* and I never forgot the taste of it . . . My favorite well-known writer would have to be Thomas Mann. I tend to prefer slightly boring writers. Their work somehow resembles 'life' more closely."

Manja had never thought very deeply about this, the solitude that was the so-called destiny of a writer. Realizing this, Manja felt that maybe she was not destined to be a writer and became a little depressed.

"I . . . Well, I don't know. I don't have a garden and . . ." Manja stuttered. She could have said that, as a matter of fact, she didn't have any time to feel solitary, between her three children in elementary, middle, and high school, her husband, finding time to work in her spare time, and the cultural outings that she felt she couldn't skip . . . however, she didn't want to give such a dispiriting answer.

"Indeed, aren't there just so many joyful things at your age? It's still a time when the world looks beautiful." Yeon-sook Kim *Seonsaeng* gently smiled.

Although Manja could have continued the conversation on the beauty of the world, it was not on the prepared list of questions, so, after courteously smiling at *Seonsaeng*, she skipped to the fifth question.

"It's the awards season now. You've received quite a few awards—which one of them has made you the happiest? Do you feel different after you receive an award?"

Yeon-sook Kim *Seonsaeng* listed all of the awards she had received, counting them in sequence on her fingers. 'She really has received a lot of awards,' Manja thought and was struck again with admiration for her idol.

When all five fingers of one hand had been folded and unfolded and there were only two fingers left, she said, "Honestly, I am happy when I receive awards. But I think that one shouldn't chase after awards. An award has to follow a writer. When a writer chases after awards, things become ugly. I've heard that some people even undertake some kind of campaign to receive an award, and I think that's foolish."

Manja expressed her agreement with *Seonsaeng*'s comment by nodding her head and smiling. How does one even organize a campaign for a particular award? Did awards allow themselves to be caught? Even if it seemed foolish, had anybody ever successfully chased down an award? Manja wanted to ask these things, but she kept her mouth shut because they didn't seem to fit the tone of the show.

Seonsaeng's answers had all been highly formal, but also extremely theoretical, and impeccably neat. Manja thought that her manner of speaking resembled her workplace.

"Are those your tools?" Manja pointed at the shelves. A typewriter, a defunct Rumo word processor, and two old PCs—a 286 and a 386—sat next to each other on the shelves.

"Oh, well, those became my tools after I had stopped writing my manuscripts in longhand. My generation underwent a huge change, not only socially and politically, but also in writing tools. When I first became a writer, I used to order paper with my name printed on the bottom corner of the page; it just felt so personal and friendly. I am sure that the effort of writing a novel hasn't changed much since then, but the feeling is different. It's like— how do I explain it?—the difference between wearing clothes that were sewn by hand and clothes that were made on a sewing machine. Even if I don't know my readers' names and never see their faces, if I come to them with a novel that feels handmade, it is perceived as something intimate and friendly . . ."

Manja, who had started off writing on a Pentium PC, had never known that side of things. Manja zeroed in on the word "friendly." Manja asked her in a very careful way, "But your novels tend not to be very kind to the reader. It's like you're saying, 'Follow me if you want to.' Do you think of your readers that way when you write?"

Seonsaeng laughed in a low tone. "I know my novels don't sell. Sometimes, I even feel sorry for the publishers. Nevertheless, as a writer, I believe that one should write for the next generation, rather than for the current one. When we write, we have to consider whether the stories that please us now are going to continue to be read in the future, and whether they will still be seen as valuable enough to be shared."

Even though Manja nodded her head, she didn't whole-heartedly agree. Who in the next generation would read a writer who wasn't even read in their time? It might have only been possible in the Analog Age. Every generation had one or two geniuses, Man-ja mused, and she knew for certain that she wasn't one of them herself. Was Yeon-sook Kim *Seonsaeng* one? Nobody could know; readers were capricious.

Manja replied, "Someone I know once told me, 'Don't be too earnest when you write novels. In fifty years, they will just be put into a museum.' I think he meant that literature has its own sunset. What's your view on that, *Seonsaeng-nim*?"

A smile suddenly broke out on Yeon-sook Kim *Seonsaeng*'s face. "My guess is that that person is also a writer. Am I right?"

Manja nodded. He was a poet whose two books of poetry hadn't sold.

Seonsaeng continued, "He has his reasons for thinking that. Traditional literature has come to be merely supplementary, like condiments. It's ceased to be mainstream. However, when was it ever truly mainstream? I think that literature may be destined to live on the periphery of society. It is only then that I feel comfortable being a writer, actually."

There was a sense of despondency in her words. Manja was a little discouraged because she had expected a more ambitious spirit from a writer at Yeon-sook Kim *Seonsaeng*'s level—a writer who doggedly wrote unpopular novels, no matter what it took, and supported herself entirely on her earnings as a writer. Manja knew that she had not become a writer in the hopes of one day having her handwritten manuscripts displayed in glass boxes, and the thought that there was no guarantee of remaining on display was a truly lonely one.

Manja forced herself to ask the last question, "Even so, do you have any words of encouragement for motivated young writers and prospective writers?"

"Literature, well, in fact . . . literature won't do anything for you. Some say that it's a means of redemption or a haven, but I don't agree. On the contrary, it is suffering. It neither feeds you nor helps you to live. I think that nothingness is the reason literature exists. Like unrequited love, it's something that never hopes for compensation, and even if there is never any reward, it is a labor that one can never give up . . ." Yeon-sook Kim *Seonsaeng's* final answer drove Manja into a deeper gloom, her low voice echoing throughout the pleasant, spacious study.

"Yi *Jakga*, why don't you have dinner with me before you go? Are you busy?" Yeon-sook Kim *Seonsaeng* called out to Manja from behind the producer and Hak-sool Kim, who were packing.

"Well, I came in the same car with them." Even as Manja answered, she was a little worried about enduring the drive back.

"You can take the train later. It has a unique spirit."

While Kim *Seonsaeng* disappeared into one of the other rooms to get changed, Manja examined the bookshelves and leafed through some of the books lying on the table. It was strange for her to see the names of all the writers she knew, all the magazines she knew, and a lot of published materials that she didn't know. 'To be a great writer, I guess you have to read all this.' Manja's heart felt sore from all the deep self-reflection.

"We'll be going then, *Seonsaeng-nim*. Thank you for your time." Hak-sool Kim waved good-bye and disappeared through the door, leaving only the slanting afternoon sunlight in the spacious room. Dust that she had not noticed before floated and bounced on the sunlight, making its way to where Manja was standing.

Glancing at the postcards, cards, and letters piled to one side of the desk, Manja turned on her mobile phone, which she had switched off earlier. The signal blinked as if it had been waiting for her.

"Mommy, where are you?" It was her *Maknae*.

Manja said in a soft and warm voice, "Mommy's busy now and I might not be home in time to make dinner for you tonight."

The child didn't seem upset by this; it wasn't her first time being left alone. "When are you coming home?" the child asked in a dull tone. Even when Manja had hung up, after carefully reminding her child about the schedule for the *hakseupji* work, the institute, and her violin lesson, Kim *Seonsaeng* hadn't showed up yet.

Manja thought, "She was sweating a little during the interview. Is she taking a shower or something?"

Manja was getting bored, and as she began to look at some postcards, she finally heard Kim *Seonsaeng*'s voice from inside. "Yi *Jakga*. I'll be out soon. This call is getting long."

Manja couldn't answer. A piece of paper had fallen out of the pile of postcards. *Hongcheon-gun Naechon-myeon* . . . There was a small cadastral map on the back of a copied form. A memo was scribbled: supervised area, semi-farmland. A diamond-shaped piece of land marked off with a red pen. Manja was stupefied. When she saw her name, Manja Yi, written in the space labeled "Owner," her confusion turned to shock. She had been receiving calls over the last few weeks asking if she wanted to sell the land, but they had seemed no different from other calls she had received earlier, and she had paid them no mind. The person who called had said, "There's someone who really needs it," but that wasn't unusual, either. The value of the land went up a little each time she answered the phone, but she had never given it much thought because she never considered selling.

Just as Manja had replaced the piece of paper and flipped open her phone, *Seonsaeng* showed up.

"Oh, I'm sorry, Yi *Jakga*. That person had so much to discuss and just went on and on. They wouldn't get off the phone." Yeon-sook Kim's tone was friendly.

"Um . . . *Seonsaeng-nim*," Manja said haltingly.

"Yes? Is there something going on? Are you leaving?" She looked at Manja with her deep, courteous, and kind eyes, smiling.

'I've been looking for a farmhouse with land . . .' As the conversation in the car returned to her mind and she tried to remember what she had thought at the time, Manja faltered. "My child, *Maknae*, is still young and keeps whining to me about being scared at home alone. I think I've got to go," she mumbled.

Leaving behind Yeon-sook Kim *Seonsaeng*, who was visibly disappointed, and walking down to the parking lot, Manja called Hak-sool Kim. When he answered, Hak-sool Kim told her that they were already out of the city and on the highway.

"Why? Did you forget something?" asked Hak-sool Kim.

"No, I just wanted to thank you for your good work. Be careful not to get lost." She heard his laughter. Manja said a gentle good-bye and hung up the phone. She walked slowly until she could no longer see the shining glass of the high-rise apartment. She took the *Cheongnyangni*-bound train at the *Kangchon* Station. The train ran slowly, *with its unique spirit*, its wheels clacking as they rolled along. Her mobile phone rang just before the train reached the last stop.

"It's me. How are you doing?" It was the man from her past, the man who still said simply, "It's me" and "How are you doing?" Nostalgia flooded her heart.

"I'm doing well. I'm on my way back from *Kangchon*. I had to interview someone," Manja answered sonorously.

"That far? You've gone a long way," he observed.

She did feel that she had gone a long way. 'Today has been strange. It's been chaos all day long,' she thought.

"I just called because the fallen leaves looked pretty." His breath sounded so close she could almost reach out and touch it. She hung up shortly after. It was getting harder to deal with this mess.

After getting home, Manja, out of habit, meticulously wrote down everything that had happened to her that day, from leaving that morning to walking back through her door. She didn't write about the documents she saw on *Seonsaeng*'s desk. She hoped that the confusing incident would disappear into the chaos. She wrote about how the interview with *Seonsaeng* had helped open her eyes to a lot of things, truly precious things. She wrote that she should learn from her extraordinary passion and perseverance. 'It's been a long day,' she thought. Because the joy didn't rise in her as she had hoped, she sat at her desk for a long while, even after she had finished writing.

Having already checked on her sleeping children and gone to bed, Manja got up again. She had some vague and undefined feeling of unrest. Coming out of her room and thinking, 'What did I forget?' she heard her dog, Mir, whining. Typically, Mir would have greeted Manja, wagging its tail when she came home, but she couldn't remember seeing Mir this evening.

"Mir, come here," she affectionately called to the dog. Mir stood motionless.

"What's wrong? Are you feeling sick?" Suddenly, Manja remembered and rushed to the kitchen.

"How in the world—I let you starve! Mommy's out of her mind." Sitting next to Mir, she petted the dog. "I'm sorry. Mommy was busy."

Basakbasak, the loud sound of Mir crunching the dog food between its teeth, echoed in the dark. It was a peaceful sound. 'Something was on my mind, and it was you.' Manja leaned against the wall and watched Mir drink water. Sleepiness rushed in like the tides.

Sugar or Salt

"H, do you remember me?" a man on the other end of the phone asked. His tone was cautious, as if he hoped I would remember him but didn't expect me to. The moment I recognized his voice it triggered something inside me. A memory, like the headlights of a car speeding towards me through a dark tunnel ... H ... I blocked my memory as if stopping the car with my whole body. My mind went blank in a flash of sharp light, but the light gradually dimmed and then disappeared.

"I heard yesterday that you happened to be here."

When he said that, I responded, "I'm sorry, but I don't know anyone by the name of H."

My tranquility had been restored; my voice was calm and my tone decisive. I heard his thin breath and long sigh. No matter what he said, I wasn't H. I could deny whatever story he came up with to try and bring H back. He was silent for a while. I felt like a snake was slithering, sneaking towards me along the electromagnetic wave. The feeling was exceedingly wicked.

"I'm near your hotel. Just a short visit would be enough," he said, finally breaking the silence, but I neither responded nor hung up. Keeping the phone close to my ear, I started removing the rollers from my hair. As I unrolled them with one hand, they tangled in my hair.

"I think you're mistaken. I am not H." I spoke in a neat and kind voice just as he was about to say more. When there were three rollers left, the man hung up the phone, apparently giving up.

The tight curls bounced up and there emerged in the mirror an aging woman who looked like she'd just left a hair salon. As I loosened the curls with a hair dryer, the woman's face started to look like a tired spinster. I called the front desk.

"Good evening." As soon as I heard the kind voice, speaking English, I instructed the staff not to connect any outside calls from now on.

"Anything wrong, Miss?" the staff member asked cautiously.

"Nothing wrong. I just want some rest."

I spoke bluntly, trying to control my rapidly rising temper. I put on some pink lipstick, beige-colored eye shadow, and peach blush. By the time I was done, a bit of vitality had appeared on the face of the woman in the mirror. After applying eye liner and mascara, plumping each lash with care, the expression of the eyes was revived and my heart started to pound. Just like it always did when I met K.

The name of the man on the phone hadn't even entered my mind until I was dressed and had left my room. Nor did the name he had called me, H. It was a name that had been thrown away and forgotten, one I had used a long time ago, back when I was in my twenties. All the names that once were mine—J, O, and E—passed through my mind one after another. Those names had all eventually been abandoned, as naturally as an insect leaves behind its cocoon. Although at times I had used several of the names simultaneously, I never got them confused. In terms of staying focused, I had always been number one, and my ability to keep things straight had always been one of my best weapons.

Click. The room door closed. I made sure the Do Not Disturb sign was hanging on the door handle. A maid approached me from the other end of the hall, pushing a cart filled with towels and bed sheets.

"Good evening, Madame." She smiled gently. She would pass by my room again today, tilting her head to listen. During my week-long stay my room hadn't been cleaned once, but it was as clean as the moment I stepped into it. Although the sheets hadn't been changed, they didn't have a single strand of hair on them and showed not one wrinkle. The towel, which I spread on the heater every night to dry, was as fluffy as new, and was lying neatly on a rack in the bathroom as it had been originally. In terms of

not leaving a trace, I knew what I was doing.

It was raining. It had been raining, raining, raining since I arrived without letting up for even a single day. The rain moistened the city quietly, making it seem like the city was eternally wet. "I'm sick and tired of the winter here. You feel like you never get warm, even with the heater on." That was what K had written on her wedding invitation to me. She had gotten married in a small Catholic church in this city where it rained all winter. The man, K's husband, was tall and thin. Fair-skinned K, in a white veil, had smiled and laughed through the whole ceremony, standing next to this man who looked somewhat melancholy with his long, thick eyelashes. K's father, who had flown in last-minute from Korea, had the same gloomy look. I couldn't understand this man; it almost felt offensive that he wasn't the least bit bothered by this sudden marriage of his daughter, whom he had sent abroad to study. K, who had always been at the top of her class. K, who was beautiful and smart. K, who had no one in the world to envy, and who was expected to take over as the president of a good university—a position that had been handed down from her grandmother to her father—after finishing her studies and returning home. I could not understand how K could give it all up for the son of immigrant dry cleaners, and all through the wedding I acted like an ill-tempered older sister who was marrying off her younger sister first. Smiling back at K's husband, who stretched out his hand while his thick eyebrows frowned slightly, something inside me welled up. I didn't know then how strong my hostility really was.

Outside, a woman with long hair was getting out of a car; it was K. She came straight up to me.

"Hi, there. It's really '*Long time no see.*' How long has it been? Let's greet in the American style," she said, hugging me. Her shoulders were so skinny I could feel them through her thick coat. Untangling myself from her embrace, I took a step back and looked at her.

"You look so thin."

For some reason my heart ached.

"Thin? I've grown a huge belly." She sounded like an *ajumma*,[49] which was something I had never heard from her. "And look who's talking. Everyone's going on about the 'Gold Miss'[50] these days, and that's just what you are. How can it be that you haven't aged a bit?" K's eyes were smiling kindly.

"So, you're the new transfer student." From the moment she had said that, extending her hand to me on the day we met, K had always been kind and sweet. The one time I had beaten her and been at the top of the entire class, she had still been overflowing with kindness, saying, "Hey, Congratulations!" and patting my back. Being so nice in every situation and having a natural face that showed everything—the existence of such a person was hard for me to comprehend.

Mother—not my birth mother, my father's wife—was not kind to me. But she was never kind to anybody, so it didn't especially hurt me. Everyone in my father's family always acted like they were angry about something. The conversation over the breakfast table every morning was simple and straightforward.

"I'm going to be late today. I have a club meeting after school," my oldest sister—half-sister—would say, while Mother silently nodded. And when she said to me, "Your midterm results came out yesterday. You did a little better this time," my second-oldest sister and Mother seemed not to care. A house from which neither loud noise nor laughter erupted. To my young eyes they sometimes looked like they were all acting. It wasn't easy to find my place, and I soon realized that nobody was particularly interested in me.

I remember once when Mother handed me a white dress and told me to put it on—it must have been for some special occasion. She said, "Brush your hair neatly and tie it up." The dress

---

49 Koreans divide humans into three genders: male, female, and ajumma. Women who are seen as less feminine than other women, or who are significantly older than the speaker, are sometimes referred to as ajumma. Ajumma originates from the word ajumeoni, which translates to aunt, housewife, or ma'am. Technically, the term means "Mrs." But it is often used in a condescending way and is considered by many young Korean women to be an insult.

50 In Korea, this phrase is used to refer to a single, college-educated female between the ages of 30 and 45 with an annual income of at least forty million won (around forty thousand dollars). Unlike old maids and spinsters, which most women dread becoming, the Korean "Gold Miss" has become an object of envy because of her freedom from both financial and family concerns. The phrase is a twist on "old Miss," which meant spinster.

was my sister's and had a black collar. Wearing that dress, with my hair up, I thought I looked like a maid at a fancy house or a waitress in a restaurant.

"I don't like it," I said after a while. Mother's hands froze. Her face expressed incredulity at what I was saying.

"I'll just wear my school uniform. I don't like that dress." Even though my heart was pounding, my tone was clear and respectful. Mother looked at me blankly.

"Do as you're told," Mother said, adding in a falsely sweet tone, "I don't want to hear you complain that I'm the kind of mother who won't even buy you a dress." Being young, I burned with anger because I didn't want to wear what I didn't like, because I didn't want her to think I was complaining that she never bought me clothes, and because I resented the fact that I had grown so tall over the summer that I couldn't fit into any of the pants I had brought with me without showing my ankles.

"That's not my style. Look at the things I chose for myself." I opened the closet and drawers and started taking out my own clothes. I pulled out light pink, ivory, and lilac pants, jeans with cute little pockets, and several white shirts. A kind saleswoman in a department store had helped me choose these clothes; Mom — my biological mother — had taken me there. They made me look like a little prince, like the only son from a noble family. When I had chosen each of the items, the saleswoman had seemed so pleased, and Mom's face lit up when she saw me in them.

Mother didn't seem to understand. I bit my tongue to keep from crying, but my lips began to twitch and the tears poured out. Mom never taught me how to hold back my tears. She always sensed what I wanted before I wanted it, and being a polite child I knew what was good for me to want and what wasn't. It wasn't something anybody had taught me. While I was still young I had realized that Mom and Dad had an unusual relationship, and it almost seemed like I had known about it since birth. Mom read children's books to me and sang me my favorite songs. When she sang, she used to look at me with affection, wrapping her hands around my shoulders playfully. Mom said that as a young child I hardly cried, and that I was like that before I even learned how to speak.

"You were strange. As a baby it seemed like you thought it childish to cry just because you were hungry or had a wet diaper." When she said that, Mom looked slightly uncomfortable. She always looked like that when she talked about my childhood. The stories she would tell always sounded fabricated, like I wasn't a child she had carried inside her womb, a child she had seen, touched, and raised, but instead had arrived one day as a fully developed child.

Did I wear my school uniform that day? I don't remember. But after that day, Mother never forced me to do anything. I said what I wanted without holding back, and Mother compromised on almost everything, unless it was something really impossible. Her face, whenever that happened, seemed to say, "I just want to avoid trouble." My three sisters thought I was strange, acting like that, but they didn't complain about it. They were people who never expressed what they felt . . . they were entirely different from Mom. That spring, summer, and autumn had been a terrible time for a thirteen-year-old girl who was passing from one world to another, but I knew that it was something I couldn't escape. To survive, to become myself, I had to make it through those days.

"Let's go eat somewhere. Aren't you hungry? Do you want Korean food?" K asked, getting into her car.

"No, it doesn't have to be Korean." In fact, I wasn't hungry at all. Had my internal organs been thrown off by the time change too? Since my arrival in this city, I didn't seem to ever feel hungry. K drove through the chaos of rush hour. A blue vein rose up in her pale fingers as she gripped the steering wheel.

"So, you said this was a business trip, huh? Are you done with your work? When do you leave?"

She speedily cut through the traffic, talking about this and that.

"Do you mind going a little further out?" K asked, "There are too many Koreans in this town," she added in a tone that sounded falsely casual. I understood her perfectly. There had been a huge crowd at her wedding, so her divorce must have been a hot topic here as well.

"By the way, didn't you say you came here on publishing business? Do you still work at the same place?"

I didn't tell her that "the same place" was long gone. I had been an editor at a place that mostly published collections of proverbs and fables. During the unrest of the end of the century, while people rolled their eyes ironically and seemed to only care about finding good deals on stocks and apartments, they still liked to carry around stories about good people. Back then I would often see people reading the books I had edited on the subway. But the good times didn't last long. One autumn morning, as a rumor was going around the office that profits had gotten high enough to allow for a new building and the launch of a magazine, the director of the press ran off to Canada with only the clothes on her back and her handbag. When her husband discovered her absence and showed up looking like an innocent fool, the office she had abandoned was a chaos of rumors regarding money and lust. No one realized that they were about to file for divorce, or that it all resulted from an email somebody had sent her husband that revealed her long-standing affair with a mysterious man. When her husband was at the office, I looked straight into his blank face for a long time. I felt no pity. I detested people who couldn't see the truth when it was right under their noses, and people who couldn't let go, even when their fate was clear. It was only right that such people should face misfortune.

K parked her car next to a pier. Where the parking lot ended, the ocean stretched out towards the horizon. The restaurant looked like somebody had picked up an Indian village and plunked it down here.

"Do you like the view? Just to let you know, the food here isn't that great." Sitting down at our table in the restaurant, K made a cheeky face.

The waitress greeted us in a clear voice, lighting the candles on the table. "*Good evening, young ladies.*"

K's face brightened.

"The fried oysters are okay here. You like oysters, don't you? Um . . . and . . . Let's get some drinks. Do you want some wine?" Holding the menu and asking me these questions seriously, K suddenly lowered her voice. "It seems they can never tell an Asian woman's age. They even check my ID when I order drinks. They check to make sure I'm not underage and then act surprised. In Korea, you know, who would ever consider an *ajumma* approaching her forties to be a young woman?"

She smiled sweetly. It was probably the flickering candlelight, but the thirty-seven-year-old, long-haired K really did look like a young woman. Wine and beer were served and the food appeared.

"Let me propose a toast. It's so good to see you. Thank you for coming." K's wine glass clinked into my beer glass. The dark beer tasted strong and bitter. When had I last shared a drink with K? In our college years, K had been quite a drinker, something unexpected from such a skinny person. While her drinking partners succumbed to drinking, tears, or fights K kept filling her glass with a sober face, wiped their tears, sent them home in a cab, opened her wallet, and paid the bill. A thin bracelet tinkled on K's wrist as she tilted the glass. She was still graceful and beautiful.

"When I talked to Mom on the phone yesterday, I told her about you . . . She said, 'She's better than you.'"

I wondered if her mother had mentioned that I had called her from the airport before I boarded my flight, but it wasn't that.

"It turned out that I didn't know anything. You know my mom. She doesn't give me the details on anything. It was only when I told her you were coming that she started telling me about this and that, about all that had been happening . . . . Well, you know the old lady." She said it as sarcastically as she could, but K's mom was not the kind of person one would call an old lady.

"To be honest, I have so many complexes related to my mom. That coy voice of hers, at her age . . . Ugh, it gives me goose bumps." Pretending to shiver, she giggled, "Hee hee," like a little girl.

When I first visited her house we were in our first year of junior high. Watching K's long, slender legs under her baggy skirt as I followed with my short steps up the high hill, we arrived at her house. K's mom was studying abroad then. That detail was far more surprising to me than the splendid garden with dense pines, her elegant grandmother, or the big black dog that looked straight out of a movie. At that time, when traveling out of the country was still somewhat uncommon, how could a mother, a woman with three children who had filial obligations to her mother-in-law, leave to go study abroad … K's mother, whom I met not long after that, was slender, beautiful, and intelligent, which seemed to fit with this audacity.

"My mom was good at school, studied abroad, became a professor soon after she returned, and you know what else? Even though she started playing golf just to keep my father company, guess how good she is at it now! How on earth does such a person exist?"

"You were good at school, too. And it seemed like you just weren't interested in becoming a professor. Why don't you start playing golf as well? I bet you'd be really good at it," I said, trying to cheer her up. "In fact, I play pretty well myself."

K, silently smiling, opened her eyes wide. "That's not all. Did you know my mom sculpts?"

Although I had attended the openings of both of her exhibitions, carrying flowers in my arms, I kept it to myself. Throughout the openings K's mother kept me by her side, and when somebody asked her about me she said, "Oh, she's my daughter," winking at me.

"She said she just started it as a hobby, you know, to prepare for retirement. But then I heard she won some competitions and was featured in some newspaper. Whenever I go back home to Seoul there are always sculptures everywhere in the garden, a female nude or a woman hoisting a water jug."

There were no nudes, but I listened like I didn't know anything about it. K's mother only sculpted women. Her women, wearing *jeogori*[51] or simple peasant clothes, had an air of inno-

---

51 A traditional woman's garment worn on the upper body.

cence and warmth about them. It might have been when I visited K's house on New Year's Day that those women looked so beautiful to me, standing between the bare trees and the pines, covered with snow from the previous day.

"Her children are even well-off. Of my two siblings, one is a professor and the other is a doctor ... It's almost perfect. What kind of person ... I never really felt close to her."

K's eyes sparkled. I couldn't tell if it was from longing or hatred. K must have known that her younger sibling, who was now a professor, would soon become president of the university. If she had wanted, she could have had that life.

"So ..." A deep sigh escaped K's lips. "To my mom ... I'm probably her only flaw."

"That's not true," I said. "I've never gotten that impression from your mom. She was always so proud of what you were doing."

"That's what I mean!" K said loudly. A man next to us turned around. She nodded and smiled at him. He smiled back at us. Quietly, she said, "I'm saying that I don't like that. What kind of mom, when her daughter wants a divorce, only asks 'Why?' and 'I see ...' and that's it. Doesn't she have to, at least, pretend to stop me? You see, my mom has absolutely no idea how I could possibly separate from the person I married out of love. She just thinks, 'How can love change?' That's what it is. What I do, counseling Southeast Asian women, the homeless, and victims of domestic violence, I mean, how great can my work be if she only asks about it when I bring it up. I know that she worries like hell if I go out with a white guy here, but she never opens her mouth about it, you know."

Was it her divorce that had brought her to this? This was the first time I had seen K so agitated. She never spoke ill of people.

"I doubt that two glasses of wine would make you drunk ... Things seem to be going alright here for you."

"Well ..." she said and called over the waitress who was passing by, asking her for a glass of iced water.

"There was no one I could talk to about this and I had decided not to. It's just . . . I'm happy to see you and it just came out. Anyway . . . I learned to play guitar here. I even played in a group recital. I thought I was surpassing her this time, but then she announces that she's sculpting. So . . . I gave up. I said, 'Oh well, I don't know. I can only be myself.'"

The waitress, eclipsing K's lonely face, put down the water glass. K slowly emptied the glass of water like she was swallowing bitter medicine.

"There's no such thing here as substitute drivers like in Seoul. One glass of wine per hour is the limit . . . if you don't want to get caught."

I asked her how she managed when she had more than two glasses of wine.

"I call a friend or something."

"A friend? A man?"

She chuckled.

"You're curious, too, huh? Would a woman who has been divorced for five years have a boyfriend, and if so, who would that be . . . But hey, you're still so patient. How come you waited this long to ask me?"

K's expression, her eyes, and her hair blowing in the breeze . . . Why hadn't it occurred to me until now that there was someone who caressed and gazed at her? I straightened up in my seat and pulled myself together. Tension rose in my throat. I felt like I was about to start hyperventilating.

"He's from here, isn't he?" I asked.

"How did you know?" K's eyes danced playfully.

"Are you likely to find your equal among Korean men? It was already hard to find one in Korea."

K burst out laughing. So it was true, but she didn't talk about it anymore. Was he blond or African-American? Maybe Hispanic. Even though it seemed reasonable for her to socialize with local men, the tension in my body wouldn't go away.

"I've been talking about myself the whole time. How about you? Is your mother doing well? Doesn't she nag you to get married?"

I looked at K without speaking. The pain in my heart seemed unavoidable.

"She passed away last winter."

Panic flashed across K's face. I told her about the breast cancer, which had recurred after surgery. The second time around, Mother had refused treatment. Neither my sisters nor I could stop her, and my father, who was in an Alzheimer's ward, only laughed loudly, staring blankly at Mother. And as for my biological mother ... Since I had left home, I hadn't heard a thing about her, but I believed she had died. The thought that she might be alive somewhere, with someone else, tortured me. If she hadn't died ... She had been so expressive and full of life. The idea that she could disappear from my life for such a long time was unthinkable; it was impossible.

"I had no idea ..."

K's face showed her sorrow. Mother closed her eyes for the last time at dawn on a cold day, as if falling asleep. I was with her, alone, when she died. Mother's dead face looked as solemn as it had been when she was alive. I wiped her face with a warm, wet towel after she had stopped breathing. I wiped her two hands and feet. After I cleaned her up, she looked more comfortable. I felt relief at the early death of the woman who had accepted me as a little girl and taught me how not to cry. I was happy for Mother that she no longer had to see her husband, who, in his blind pursuit of a son, had women everywhere he went, and even in the hospital often exposed himself out of habit. I folded my legs under me and settled down, preparing to call my sisters.

"Everybody dies. She went comfortably."

"The way you talk ... it's still the same." K looked at me out of the corner of her eye. "Sometimes I used to wonder. How could she have been so aloof? You were so mature. What people call 'cool' these days, that was you."

I wondered what kind of face K would make if I said to her, "It was because of you, because of your kindness." But I didn't say that.

"You know it's just the way I am, bad at expressing myself."

"I know you're bad at reacting, but not at expressing." K's eyes sparkled, as if she had just thought, 'Yes, that's it.' "You seem like you express yourself with your face and your eyes instead of words. When you finally speak the words, it sounds so nice," K said, her bright expression that I remembered from the old days returning to her face.

If reacting meant showing emotion at the moment of change, at the particular moment when something is realized, then what K said was right. To my younger self, K's kindness was astonishing, and it always made me uncomfortable and distant whenever I was with her. But she never changed a bit. One afternoon, we were on the snow-covered hill in front of our school when K, who was a couple of steps ahead of me, suddenly turned around and threw a snowball in my face. I stared at her blankly, standing there as the snowball made contact, with bits of snow sticking in my hair and melting on my face. It didn't feel cold at all. I walked slowly toward K.

"You should've thrown one at me, too, you silly girl," said K. I smiled just like a silly girl would. Quietly approaching me, K suddenly reached for the front collar of my school uniform and stuck her hand, so cold it should have made me scream, inside my shirt. It wasn't me who screamed, but K. She burst out laughing and ran away up the hill. I stood there vacantly, watching her. The snow smeared from K's hand melted down between my breasts. Running away, K was beautiful. A sad, tender wind blew through my heart. As my body shivered, I felt cold; but then a wild sensation washed over me. It was a new kind of feeling, one that I had never experienced before. I was confused and afraid.

"What about you? Tell me about yourself. Even though you're not married, you must have a boyfriend, right?"

The question was to be expected.

"Aw, why are you making a face like you're a virgin? You were popular with the boys at school."

K was wrong. They hadn't chased after me; they just wanted to know more about K, who was always with me.

"I got married early, you know. In fact, once I was married I felt like none of my previous relationships had been 'real.'"

"Yours was a real relationship, was it?" I heard my voice grow unintentionally harsh. We had come together to study abroad, but I had to go back alone. Before she had met that man, K and I would often drive ten hours to see each other.

"No, I don't mean relationships that lead to marriage. I mean something more like a deeply affectionate but sad kind of love."

K's face suddenly looked lonely. Was her man married? Why would a man and a woman fall in love and drive themselves into a pit with no way out? If this was a story about people who loved each other deeply and should never have met, then enough: I had heard it all before.

For instance, when Mom would talk about Dad, she said, "There are people who live together just for the sake of being together in the world. One of them is already married, and it can't be taken back." Her face looked sad but dignified. She had looked the same way when she sent me off to that house, saying "You'll do fine." Mom repeated the same things over and over for days as she gathered my clothes, sorted my books, and packed for me. I didn't ask her why I couldn't live with her any longer. Although no one had taught me, I knew I shouldn't ask. I cut her short whenever she tried to talk about it because I couldn't stand to see her looking so sad.

When she said, "When you get there, you will have three sisters," I interjected, "I'll get along with them." When she pointed out Mother, saying, "There's the mother of your sisters . . ." I reassured her, "Don't worry, I'll call her Mother." Mom was a cheerful and optimistic person. A beautiful person who knew how to smile and how to be as sweet as her pretty face. As a little girl, I thought there had to be something left for her. If her cheerfulness disappeared with me, then she would be lost, too. I imagined meeting my cheerful, lovely mom, I imagined her waiting for me and quietly holding her breath after school—it was sad, and at the same time sweet.

"Love sounds nice. Well, I could tell from your face. You look prettier."

I tried to turn the conversation to her, but K didn't take the bait. Neither K nor I opened our mouths for a while. The names of men and women, S, Y, and others, who had met me as H, J, or O, crossed my mind and faded just as quickly. I told all of them that I loved them. I never had any ill intention. I thought that a little game to endure the boring, monotonous days was something that could also be called love.

"Didn't you ever . . . Was there really no man that you wanted to live with? Or maybe not live together, but even just be involved with? Even at your age?" K asked. Her face seemed genuinely curious.

A man I wanted to live with . . . A man I wanted to be involved with . . . I mumbled, following K.

"There . . . was. Just once."

My voice was hoarse. My throat hurt, as if a nail were stuck in it.

"Hey, you look like you're about to cry. Was it that serious?"

It was. I had wanted to hold him and touch him from the day I met him. I still did, even after I saw a picture of his graceful wife and children on the desk in his office. I thought I would endure anything, any pain if I could have him . . . I had been so foolish.

"Not serious. It never went beyond dinner and drinks."

I felt tormented by the need to tell her about him.

"Are you serious? Just dinner? As an adult?"

A sharp pain stabbed my heart. I thought again of the tension when I had finally seduced him in a motel outside the city. I couldn't begin to talk about it. I could barely speak.

"Yes, we just ate together. Often."

K smiled despondently.

That day, we had both been a little drunk. How else could I explain what happened afterwards? He had caressed me all over, kissing and undressing me, but for some reason my body grew more and more cold to his touches. At some point, he burst out laughing. His hard penis became small like a child's.

"You're rejecting me. I think that's why." His voice was low. The awkwardness, when he had said, "Oh, how embarrassing," had passed. Lying next to him, I kept looking at him with a serene face, as if I were just watching TV. Had I rejected him? I wanted to say I hadn't, but I didn't know. Would I have been sad if I said I hadn't? I didn't know that, either. All of those moments when I wanted him, when my desire kept me from sleeping, when even in my dreams I longed for him — if they had only been illusions, then . . . If my desire, which was so intense I felt I could touch it, was a lie, then what on earth was I? Was I even alive? Was I a phantom? I was confused, but I couldn't find any words to express it. My strength leaked slowly out of the tips of my fingers and toes. I felt as if my veins were open and all the blood in my body was draining out of me. I felt like a horribly ruined woman.

Had I cried? He turned around and held me in his arms. "I'm sorry," he said. Why was he sorry? I couldn't say any of this was his fault. It wasn't his fault that he casually said, "You're cute," or, "The way you hold the steering wheel is pretty," or that his hand, patting my back when he was drunk, was warm. Because it was me who had forced us together, no matter how much he avoided me . . . But then again, had I really been myself? His arms were warm, but my heart had stopped racing. I wanted to go back to the first day I met him. I wanted to start all over again slowly. I wanted to go through every hour, every moment again. Even if I didn't get his heart, I wanted to feel that desire, so stormy and intense. Now that it was irrelevant to my hollow, frustrated heart, his hand stroking my back failed to excite me. It was a calm, warm embrace like that between brother and sister. It was like a scene from a dream, illogical and incomprehensible.

"*Is there anything else you need?*" The waitress approached us. The crowded room had already emptied out. As we asked for the check, K's mobile phone vibrated.

"I was wondering why he had been so quiet today." It was her son. "Yeah, yeah. No, it's Mom's friend. *She just came from Korea. No, she's my best friend. Don't worry. I won't be late.*" Her English sounded nasal. I almost thought I was hallucinating, listening to a conversation between K and her husband. After she got off the phone, air leaked out of her lips, "Pfff," and she smiled.

"My son acts like he's the head of the house. He's eleven, you know. When I got a divorce, I thought he was too young to know, but maybe he wasn't. Whenever I couldn't sleep and left my room, the kid would just be sitting there on the couch, aimlessly. When I would ask, 'Why are you still awake?' he'd say, 'If Mommy doesn't sleep, I don't sleep, either.' And then . . . he and I would sleep in the same bed, holding each other tightly. We did that until he got quite big. He still comes into my room every once in a while with a pillow in his hand."

How old had he been when I saw him last? Her son had tottered over to me in his diaper. The baby smelled like K.

"He says he's the man of the house. And he always tells me, '*You don't need a boyfriend.*'"

I asked her if she had a picture of him. She opened her wallet and showed it to me. A boy with a pale face. The boy's face looked strange to me even though he looked exactly like his father.

"The boy has to know about everything. He's just like his dad. My ex was like that. He couldn't stand anything ambiguous, even about himself. But you know me. I think I could be this kind of person or that kind of person . . . And I don't have a problem passing the time doing something totally frivolous . . ."

K still didn't know that it was impossible for some people to live that way.

"He was, well, at first, I thought his being that way was great. He seemed perfect. No, he was, in fact, perfect. Oh well, it's a divorcée's rule not to talk about *ex-hus*, but I broke it today because of you."

There was one more thing, in fact, that she didn't know. The man who was supposed to be perfect: his perfection had ruined him.

We had been at the lakeside that day. It was in K's neighborhood. K, her husband, and I were each holding a fishing pole, but the surface of the lake was completely still. The sound of birds and of trees shifting in the breeze shook the forest and dissipated, and we gradually grew tired. K was the first to put down her fishing pole. Fumbling in the basket on the grass, she sighed, "Whew." We had been planning on catching fish and making spicy Korean fish soup, and all the basket contained was a few pieces of *kimchi*.

"I'm going to starve to death. I'll just run home quickly and grab something to eat." As K's figure disappeared over the road, I felt like our surroundings had been blanketed with tranquility. Putting down the fishing pole and turning around, K's husband opened the thermos and asked, "Would you like some coffee?" As soon as he asked, he made a strange face.

That morning, I had put salt instead of sugar in his coffee. Salt and sugar were in identical bottles with the same cork lids. Looking at K's round letters spelling out *sugar, salt*, I picked up the bottle labeled salt. K was busy making an omelette and playing with a stray cat that had just walked up, so she didn't see what I had done. I furtively tasted the coffee. It was salty and bitter, and tasted unspeakably strange; nevertheless, I silently put the cup in front of him. After taking a sip of the coffee, a peculiar expression appeared on his face.

"The oil probably wasn't hot enough. Isn't that omelette too greasy?" K asked.

"No, it's fine. The soup is good, too. I thought you might be a terrible cook, but you're actually quite good at it," I said with a calm face. The soup, which she had made with frozen vegetables and chicken, tasted metallic. Sipping my soup, I didn't take my eyes off his face. If he had said, "You must have put salt in the coffee. It tastes weird," then I only needed to say, "Oh, dear. I guess I was confused because the bottles look the same." Escaping my eyes, he picked up the newspaper on the table. He slowly sipped the coffee with an indifferent face. I stared at him intently, cutting up sausages and chewing bacon. Every time a sip of coffee traveled down past his Adam's apple, I felt as though some part of me was also being swallowed.

"He likes Korean food, but he hardly eats the soup or other things like that when I cook them. I guess it's because it's not like his older sister's cooking."

K made some more comments on the menu, but he only smiled faintly and kept quiet. Maybe he grew up in an environment with no regard for a sense of taste. I thought of his father, who had been an almond farm worker, the tan-faced old man had never taken a break, working from dawn till the middle of the night until he had set up his own dry-cleaning shop, and his wrinkled sister who didn't mind being called his father's wife. This taciturn man, who supposedly had never slipped below first in his class, who had received a scholarship to complete his studies, and who was immediately recruited by Boeing upon graduation. I was afraid of this man who didn't even blink an eye about coffee with salt. I feared that K was going to become thin and pale with him, that she was going to become just like him.

My back tensed at the sight of him holding the thermos. I knew he was looking at me and that he knew I had done it on purpose. Then something broke the surface of the boundless water. The floating cork was pulled deep down under the water and a heavy feeling reached the tips of my fingers.

Just as he said, "I think you got a bite," the reel started unraveling fast.

"Loosen it up a little first," he called out, coming over to me. A carp or a bass or some other type of fish had taken the bait and was swimming away, farther out into the water, with all its strength. Rippling waves moved across the surface of the water.

"Now, wind the reel back in slowly," he said. Once or twice while reeling it in, I saw a dark object suddenly jump up on one side. I screamed involuntarily. It was my first time fishing, and I hadn't known what to expect. The fish nosedived again and the reel took the brunt of it, loosening and making a whistling sound.

Although he shouted, "Slowly, slowly," the reel wouldn't budge an inch.

"Is it stuck somewhere?"

Approaching me from behind, he stretched out his arms to hold the fishing pole.

"They drag it into the rocks." He raised his arm up high to lift the pole. "It's heavy, isn't it? It's a big one." He seemed excited.

Even his breath became wild. As he came close to me I noticed that his eyebrow was drawn up sharply. The fishing pole suddenly cracked and he, who had been keeping me from falling over onto my back, fell down . . . All these things happened at once, as if they were predetermined. I tore open his shirt and unbuckled his belt. I plunged my hands in deep.

An unknown ruthlessness possessed me. A cold wind blew in the forest. The sky I looked up at was endlessly blue and gorgeous as I held his slender back. A deer, passing by under a tree, looked over at us. I looked down the path where K had disappeared and waited, hoping both that she would show up and that she wouldn't. His wild, seemingly angry movements suddenly stopped, and he looked down at me with helpless eyes. He stretched his hands out towards my head and removed a fallen leaf sticking to my hair. It was a blood-red maple leaf.

"Do you want to come down with me to the lakeside for a while? I want a smoke."

I walked along the street, following K. Without the neon bar lights, the street was dark. It was hard to get the lighter to catch because of the strong wind. I stood close to K and opened my coat. Inside my coat, K, lowering her head, lit the cigarette carefully.

"One for me, too," I said.

K was delighted. "Since when? You used to be repulsed by a woman who smoked."

When had that changed? I couldn't remember. I had left the country the day after that afternoon by the lake. K's husband, who stayed with K for several more years after that, ended up leaving her.

"Marlboro Lights, I like these cigarettes."

The taste was strong. It was the kind K's husband used to smoke as well.

"I secretly smoke in the backyard away from my kid. I wear a shower cap on my head and gloves on my hands. Isn't that pathetic?"

I suddenly wanted to see that boy who had appointed himself *man of the house*. Although the rain had stopped, the night air was still humid and damp.

"He . . . got remarried soon after. I heard that he might even have another child."

I stared at K's trembling hand, though her voice was steady and nonchalant.

"I still don't understand why he did that."

I listened silently to her words . . . That he suddenly seemed like a different person. How he stopped going fishing, his only indulgence. That they still talked to each other, sometimes, because of their child. K's tone was low, sad, and monotone. It seemed like she didn't really see him as an ex-husband. Maybe she didn't have a boyfriend after all. K would never really know what had happened and why it happened to her.

"I don't mean that I regret it. Where would I have gotten such a good son if not from him? And if I hadn't come to this country, would I ever have become interested in helping the homeless and people like that?" K asked, throwing the cigarette butt far away. The spark bounced and disappeared. K's husband, his back looking meager and pitiful, flashed across my mind and disappeared.

"Did you say your flight is tomorrow morning? When are we going to see each other again?"

"I'll probably come back soon," I said. It was impossible for me to know if I would contact K again, if I would meet with the man who used to call me H again, if I would shut up the memory of both of them in the attic of my mind. I threw away the cigarette butt, following K. The cold wind blew in from the ocean. K frowned, standing to face the wind. Her distorted face suddenly looked like an old woman's. A wind blew inside me as well. Agony, sadness, pleasure, and something unknown were sucked into the whirlwind.

"By the way, when did you change your name? The front desk didn't recognize it." K asked, turning around and walking.

"A long time ago," I said.

Who Are You?

It was by coincidence that the woman happened to go for a walk that night, as was coming across those books. As she opened the door of the used bookstore, the book seemed to have been placed there, waiting just for her. She thought that novels, especially the ones she wrote, were expendable. This one had sold seventy thousand copies and gone into twelve editions, so it was hardly unusual to meet it in a place like this. Though it had been tossed away like a dead battery, this was neither surprising nor unfair.

"It's been a while." Even when the owner, putting down some books, greeted her from inside the dark hallway, she just nodded silently.

Only when he said, "Let me know if you need anything—we're closing next week," did she look up at the man.

"The building is going to be demolished. Didn't you notice that the hardware store and the rice-cake shop had moved out?" The man was unusually talkative. He added, "You've been our customer for ten years and we are truly sorry." It was, indeed, regrettable, but it was also true that she had had a feeling that it was going to disappear soon. When she first moved here, back when low-slung houses with trees and flowers sat behind short red brick walls, the bookstore was a place that invited relaxation, like a hidden playground or the neatly organized attic of a large house. However, the trend for restoration and remodeling had passed, and now Italian restaurants and wine bars lined the streets—the building that housed the bookstore had long become an outcast in town. As they passed the old building on the secluded street, some people tossed their cigarette butts at it, as if it deserved them, and most people paid it no attention at all. When she visited the bookstore, the woman sometimes bought several books and sometimes none. The books were either ridiculously cheap or expensive, but she usually just paid without remark. She liked this place that was indifferent to the principles of competition and compensation, as if they were irrelevant to life, the space like a tomb of books, full of dusty books, and she liked the owner who usually wouldn't even greet you when you walked in. She tended to keep friendly or talkative people at a distance.

"The books that you are likely to be interested in are still over there . . . and let me just see if anything's come in for you." Picking up several books and putting them down, the man said, "Oh, by the way, I have some books of yours. Signed copies, too." Plodding toward her, he pointed at the corner. They were the books that had first caught her attention. Instead of looking at those books, she looked straight at him. The long, triangular eyes under the brimmed hat twinkled at her. She was a little bewildered to find that the man who was always searching for something in a corner, the man whom she only knew by his voice, saying, "That's one thousand won," "Just give me three thousand won," and "You can leave it there for me," looked much younger than she had guessed, and the words "books of yours" and "signed copies" took her completely by surprise.

"Oh, maybe you thought I didn't know, but I realized a long time ago." He smiled a little awkwardly. Since she had started writing these things, novels, there had been people who recognized her once in a while, but this was the first time she had met one in her own town.

"I knew the first time you came into my store. You had won some kind of award. You came in the day after I saw your picture in the newspaper," he said. "I've read almost all of your books even though I don't really read novels by women writers." It was hard to tell if this was a compliment or something else. She took a deep breath and straightened her back.

She always felt uncomfortable meeting someone who read her books in these unofficial settings. It was even worse in a case like this, when he was openly showing interest.

"Did I offend you? Because I didn't tell you?" Even though it had been ten years, she had hardly had any conversations with him and had never seen him this close before, so his kindness now was uncomfortable.

"I didn't mean anything by it. I just thought you might not come anymore if I told you I knew who you were." He had guessed right. The bookstore was in the middle of her town. She found the title *Seonsaeng-nim* tiresome whenever it was addressed to her — during her weekly lectures at the university, in a conversation with readers, at award ceremonies, or at book signings to launch a new novel. The first person in town who discovered she was a writer was the security guard of her apartment building, and sometimes her neighbors, who heard about the rumors, would ask.

"Oh, wow. I heard you're a writer. Writing dramas, that's such a headache, huh? What are you writing these days? Let me know and I'll watch it." Whenever she was asked, she winked and politely said that there was no show currently airing, but that she appreciated their interest. She felt comfortable living in a town where a writer was automatically assumed to write TV dramas, without stress, and without concern for earning one's daily bread, and where her neighbors lived their lives as if novels didn't exist. He was still looking at her with his gleaming eyes. She was lost, feeling like a child caught in a clumsy lie, or a spy whose identity had been exposed, but she remembered that the bookstore would disappear next week and soon recovered her calm.

She asked gently, "Well, why didn't you tell me? Have I ever acted weird? Been rude or cursed?" The man burst into laughter.

"That's curious. Everything just changed. *Seonsaeng-nim*'s tone and eyes, and . . . I wish I had a mirror so I could show you."

She thought, "What's so curious about that?" Although she knew that as a man who read old books, selling them and even sleeping with them under his head, he was capable of thoughts like that, she still found it irritating.

"In fact, I've been always curious about you. When you're wearing glasses like that and stretch pants . . . You seem just like any other *ajumma* . . . But when you appear in an interview, or in photographs, or on a TV program, you look like a model . . ." She had to cut him short right there. She felt almost suffocated by the sour smell of sweat emanating from this man who was standing so close to her.

"Are those the ones? The signed copies?" He held up the books she was pointing at. There were seven of them in all. She spied her first collection of stories and two of the novels, including the latest one. It seemed that somebody had been very determined to clear out his bookshelves. Whenever a book was published, she used to sign copies, piled high on the huge desk at the publishing company, until her arms felt numb. Critics, established writers, younger writers, poets, and former teachers . . . It usually added up to five hundred, sometimes six hundred. While she had never really thought about, didn't have time to think about whether the recipient would appreciate it or even read it, it seemed reasonable that some would end up selling the book. Whoever it was, it was only a matter of dropping their name from the next list. She picked up the book on top.

"It might be someone you know, so I thought about putting them away and . . ." She didn't hear any more of what he said. Opening the hardcover, she turned pale. Her signature, the date of a day last autumn, and above them, there was K's name. She held her breath as she opened the covers of the other six books. She confirmed that each book was made out to the same name and had the same signature; only the dates were different. A book fell from a high shelf elsewhere in the store, making a loud bang. Several smaller piles of books also toppled over, and this was followed by a moment of heavy silence. The dust stank. After a while, a deep sigh escaped her mouth.

"It was someone I knew casually, but it seems like the person has moved or something. Thank you for keeping them, but it would feel strange for me to buy them back. You can dispose of them as you wish," she said in a calm voice.

It was just this: when the sun started to set, when afternoon was ending, the woman became a little anxious, as usual, so she hung around the living room before finally going out. In those days she was troubled by many small things—her son who was dealing with being a senior in high school, her husband who had become noticeably talkative recently, and insomnia. Unlike her husband and son, insomnia was an opponent that she could not fight, ignore, or nurse. How was it that some people could just fall asleep when night fell? When the sun set, was it just habit that made them sleep, or was it exhaustion? Looking at the dark windows on the far side of her fourth-floor living room, from which she could see the garden of the apartment next door, it sometimes seemed like the world had disappeared.

Insomnia, in fact, was like an old friend to her. She had always been a sleepless child. Would it have made it better if her mother had been more attentive, dozing off while waiting for her daughter to fall asleep? She couldn't remember anything like that ever happening. It wasn't that her mother didn't care about her insomnia. Her mother, a Home Economics teacher at a junior high school, was a very responsible person. She washed her hands as soon as she came home from school and always prepared something to eat, even if it was nothing special. At night, if she seemed to have trouble falling asleep, her mother made her drink warm milk or told her the usual tricks, like counting with her eyes closed or wrapping her feet in a warm towel, and above all, and most often, asked over and over if something had happened that day.

"There must be something that's keeping you from sleeping." Although her mother's voice was gentle and soft, the girl felt vaguely guilty, as if she had done something wrong. "My grades dropped," "My period has been irregular," "A friend has been bothering me," she always gave that kind of answer. Because when she looked into her mother's eyes—those big, clear eyes—she had to come up with some reason. After listening attentively to her words, her mother would smile and say, "You should write a novel. How come you're so good at making up stories?"

'With her help, could I have turned those stories into novels?' It might have happened, but in her seven books that caught her eye in the bookstore now, there wasn't a single story about her mother. She never wrote stories about people who were close, people who ate together and slept together. She picked up the first book and flipped through the pages inattentively. She noticed that some pages were dog-eared and some passages underlined with a thick pen. She had a habit of reading her own published books calmly and carefully. The stories seemed unfamiliar and unnatural, and the sentences were loose like the wind was blowing through them. This novel, as the man at the bookstore knew, was the one that had won her a leading literary award. "I wanted to write a story both fearful and comical . . ." Her eyes stopped at the epilogue.

K had said, "Your novel is neither frightening nor funny." K had once made a face about the large picture of her printed above a newspaper interview. He had probably said something like, "Isn't your skirt too short? It looks nice, but how old do you think you are?"

'Why had he sold the books? Had something happened to him?' She felt foolish to be so worried that a couple of her books ended up in a used bookstore, as if she had been deserted by someone. But she couldn't resist taking out her mobile phone. 'I have to call him,' she thought, even if it was just to listen to his sarcastic comment, "You couldn't possibly think your books were worth keeping, could you?"

She pressed eleven buttons and waited as the phone rang. When was the last time K had called her? Had he called her or had she been trying to reach him? She couldn't remember. She hadn't thought about it until now and there had been no reason to remember. K's number wasn't stored in her phone. She hadn't written down any appointments with him in her calendar and she hadn't recorded their conversations, where they went, or the films they saw, not in a notebook, research notes, or even on scratch paper. She stored them away in her mind, hiding them deep inside her memory. K's way of speaking and the stories he told her were hiding in her novels, in the sentences, and at the end of scenes like puzzle pieces. She never told him, but she knew that he put those pictures together as he read the novels. She also knew that it sometimes pleased him and more often than not infuriated him, but she didn't concern herself with that. Her novels were the reason she had gotten to know him and kept seeing him, and she thought that he must be well aware of this. She tended not to see him when she wasn't writing a novel. Keeping everyday life separate from novels was a principle she had adhered to since she started writing.

The phone rang repeatedly, but the call never connected. After trying again several times, she looked in her address book and found one name. K's old school friend said, "K? I haven't seen him for a while, either. Was it last fall? No, was it summer? Well, I heard somewhere that he quit working at the magazine. You know he never stays anywhere long. But what's going on with him now? If you lent him some money, forget about it. He only knows how to borrow money, not return it." When he didn't hear any response, he asked again, "You seem like you really did lend him money. Was it a lot?" After calling three more people, it became clear. K was not in Seoul. No one knew his whereabouts . . .

When she realized this she was shocked. The fact that she was shocked made her angrier, and then she realized that she had already been angry for a few hours, which made her even angrier. She was working herself into an uncontrollable rage. 'How could he do this? How could he sell my books and disappear?' She knew that impossible and incomprehensible things happened in life, but she still thought, 'This is not right.' At that moment, the other phone number crossed her mind. She impulsively dialed the number. It was exceptional for her to act this way; rage usually made her quiet and calm. Her tranquility was long gone by this point.

"Daddy's not home," a little girl said.

"Do you know where he is? I'm your dad's colleague." Just as she was thinking, 'It isn't a lie to say that I'm his colleague,' another voice came on the line.

"Who am I speaking to?" She recognized the voice at once. It was K's wife, the woman whose presence next to K at K's wedding had seemed so inexplicably unnatural.

"Oh, hello, this is A. I need to speak with him, but he's not answering his phone," she explained calmly and politely. Why shouldn't she? She thought it was enough that she lied in her novels.

"Oh, you are A *Seonsaeng-nim*," K's wife said and grew silent. The silence was heavy and uncomfortable. She didn't know whether K and his wife were a happy couple or not, and she had always imagined that his wife was a nice woman. Regardless, she had always assumed that K was still with her, or at least that K's wife was still with him.

"He, well, um . . . In fact, I don't know where he is. He said he was going to go away for a few months, and . . ." Her ambivalent tone suddenly became decisive. "I don't know what this is about, but you might not see him for some time. I'll tell him if I hear from him." K's wife hung up first. Still holding the phone in her hand, A sat there vacantly for a moment. The hostility pouring out of the phone was jarring. It felt like cold water had been poured over her, like she had received an undeserved insult.

'K's testing me,' she thought. 'It's just a coincidence that he cleaned out his bookshelves, sold the books, and I saw them . . .' It was all too unreal. Reality, unlike novels, was not hospitable to coincidences. But she believed that whatever coincidence there may have been, it hadn't started out as one. K was the person who had read her first novel for her. He was the person who had handed her a picture torn from a magazine, saying, "Your ending was weak. Why don't you fix it? This might help." The person who suddenly called her up and handed her a ticket to *Jeju* Island, saying, "Sitting here doesn't make a novel. Right now the snowy season is at its peak." That was K. He was the person who was there at the beginning and who remained there, waiting where she could always find him. She never doubted his dependability, or even really noticed it, just as she had never doubted that she would write novels until the day she died.

Her husband, who came home just before midnight, was a little drunk.

"Oh, wow, you're really getting into exercise," her husband

smiled at her as she sat on an exercise bike. "I'm so grateful for you these days."

"What? Did something happen?" she asked, sweaty and out of breath.

"Well, it's just that," he said, plopping onto the couch by the bike, "These women . . . I mean, my friends' wives. It seems like they think they can do anything now that they've been married for twenty years. They have no shame. You know H. His wife called me today and told me not to hang around her husband. She carried on for about half an hour, making a long speech about how her husband's breaking her heart, and I couldn't just hang up, and oh, dear . . ."

Unable to cut him off, she ended up getting off the bike before she had finished her forty minutes and saying, to raise his spirits, "She did? Well, she went too far. So, how did you leave it?" After listening to her husband's explanation, she continued, sweetly cajoling him:

"She must have been very frustrated to call you like that. I think she just did that because she knows you're a kind person. I still say that being a good person is your biggest weakness." Speaking to him in this way always made her feel a bit squeamish, but these little daily problems required patience, humiliation, and above all, acting. As she expected, her husband stood up from the couch looking satisfied.

She lay awake as she did night after night. Her bed felt like a cross where she had been hung in eternal punishment.

"There must be something that's keeping you from sleeping . . ." She thought of her mother's comment from her childhood. If she had to blame it on something, it would have to be the change in season. When the season changed, insomnia tormented her like a persistent virus. Whenever the temperature rose or fell, she felt the new season's wind passing through her body, and a peculiar feeling as if something was slipping out of her. Lying motionless, she suffered from the terrifying sensation that all the cells of her body, from her head to her toes, were slowly dying, growing smaller and smaller, until nothing would be left but an empty shriveled space. If one considered the world in which she lived and the pictures that made up her daily life, it was hard to understand her insomnia. When a stranger, or even an acquaintance, looked at it, the daily problems and insufficiencies of her life were invisible.

The woman happened to write a novel and became a novelist, but writing novels, like other coincidences, didn't particularly change her life. Even though three of her books became bestsellers, for her—with a rich father, married to a rich man, and owning stock in financial technology, which was rare for a novelist—the economic benefits were trivial. This was true even when she won an award accompanied by a considerable cash prize. Although she had been unable to control her emotions as she spoke her few words at the award ceremony, her voice trembling and tears welling in her eyes, she knew that the effect of winning this award would have worn off by the time the newspaper print faded. She believed that she was just lucky, and that luck was like the wind that blew randomly here and there, with no one knowing where it came from. One could say that her way of living was very practical. When she got bored writing a novel, she went to look at plots of land, ascertained their investment value, bought them and then sold them at the appropriate moment, earning a good return. She hedged her bets by investing in several different funds and reinvesting in them when it was favorable to do so. Some people, including her husband, doubted that a novelist could be well-informed about such things. But if one didn't mind reading books on economics when one wasn't studying history and culture, attending two-hour meetings with the PB Center's team twice a month, and keeping up on news regarding stocks, the world economy, capital, and physical distributions, it wasn't that hard. She sometimes thought, why is it considered strange that I would attend a book signing today, sign the contract for the purchase of an empty lot in *Pyeongtaek* tomorrow, and decide to repurchase an emerging market fund the day after that? Sometimes she lost, but it didn't bother her when she did. Even if her bank balance went down a little, nothing much changed; but more than that, this was just how she was. She thought it was foolish to be upset about something that had already happened. If the interest rate on an investment went up, she increased the donations she sent to several different charities—in order to put her guilty conscience to rest. In terms of responsibility, she was just like her mother. She had never asked anybody for a favor and was not indebted to anyone. The situation with K still weighed on her mind. His disappearance smelled like a plot. She mulled over what to do and how high a price she would have to pay.

The next day, after leaving home, she sweated for forty minutes at the gym and then had an hour-long facial at the salon downstairs. After checking her face for any lingering traces of insomnia, she treated her hair with oil and a protein supplement, giving it proper attention for the first time in ages. She dressed herself elegantly, left the house, filled the car with gas, and drove out of the city at high speed. She accelerated, leaving other cars behind. As she drove, she enjoyed the sound of the engine and the momentary pressure on her back when she stepped on the gas pedal. The car, with its logo of four interlocking circles and its slick design, wasn't exactly appropriate for a writer in her forties, but she thought that standards of propriety should change according to one's situation. With her financial circumstances and personal disposition, she believed the car was perfectly appropriate and didn't care much about being hated for it. Fearing people's judgment: wasn't that just as vulgar as being proud of one's car? This was what she thought, at least.

When she reached *Cheonan–Nonsan* Expressway, the rain started to fall. Despite paying attention to the road signs, she almost missed the intersection. Now she had to make a sudden stop and a quick turn, but her car easily handled it. She drove on Interstate 1 for about thirty minutes, until it turned into a two-lane road. There weren't many cars on this road, which had been widened in the last ten years. Soon a field with peach blossoms in full bloom came into view and she saw the sign for the lake.

She slowed down outside the village and observed the surroundings. In the distance, the house, her destination, came into view. Although there was no sign of anyone in the village and the house was secluded, she knew that she shouldn't get too close. Passing by the front gate of the house and continuing a bit farther, she parked her car on the next corner under the shadow of a tree. She walked around the neighborhood slowly, looking like it was her first time there and she had fallen in love with the picturesque views. Her high-heels stuck in the wet soil, and her steps naturally slowed down. The short flowers at the base of the fence were wet with rain. Flowers grew in dense clumps or withered in isolation, as if they had grown from seeds that someone had scattered in boredom. The metal gate with its paint peeling like fish scales was unlocked. As it opened, it squealed unpleasantly like steel being scratched. A field of thick weeds welcomed her, reaching almost to her waist, and the rain sank silently into the ground beneath. At first glance it seemed like no one had lived there for a long time. Where there had once been a garden, a tall persimmon tree beaming with exuberant green leaves looked down on the untimely visitor. She moved cautiously towards the door, unimpeded.

Shards of glass and fragments of chopped wood . . . Passing through the front door, she turned pale, looking like she might be sick. Dark mold was growing in between the torn strips of wallpaper. It seemed like something might fall through the huge hole in the ceiling at any moment. To enter the living room, she had to remove the spider webs in front of her with a stick she found on the floor. Two spiders slowly disappeared from view, as though they saw no reason to rush. Piles of dust, like fine soil, fell on her feet in a puff and dirtied her shoes, but she silently continued forward into the house. There was a room and a space that looked like it had once been a kitchen . . . Following her memory, she looked at the space where a bedroom used to be. The linoleum floor was ripped and covered with mold. A small insect ran past her feet and into the walls. Her eyes passed over a desk, a small wardrobe, and a bed.

K had said that it was a friend's place, but she hadn't believed him. Everything in the house—a small dining table, a couch, a pair of chairs, and a potted plant by the front door—was new. As were the clumsily-papered walls. It was like a film set improvised for a few days of shooting. The place had no past. This realization had moved her. In this space, when she had run into an obstacle with her newly-begun novel, she felt like she could describe a story and characters so new that no one had ever seen or could even imagine them.

A dry lavender plant sat by the window. Dirt and dust was layered on the long, dried out branches, entangled like a skein of yarn. She left the bedroom, then dusted off one corner of a couch in the living room and cautiously set her body down. The couch looked like it had been intentionally shredded and gutted, two empty bottles of *soju* were lying on the floor, and a barely-hanging blind, cracked in the middle, drooped down in front of the window . . . She looked at each of them slowly. She had leaned against these walls struggling with a novel about a man and a woman who got angry, argued, reconciled, and fought again—a pretty typical story up to that point. The man wanted to turn back time; a certain supernatural being was moved by his desperation, and he was granted the ability to go back in time. He went back to the moment when hesitation had caused him to lose a woman, but the timid man still hesitated and hesitated and couldn't act. Even knowing how he felt, some kind of obstinacy and uncertainty made her close her heart to him . . . in the end, just as time was running out, when he was about to be absorbed in the wall of time forever, he finally confessed to her. The novel had a happy ending. It was like a cartoon or the kind of story they turn into a movie, but surprisingly, it sold well. K said it was probably because of the fantasy, fairytale-like space it was set in. This house had helped her describe the isolated house of the novel, a peaceful place in a mountain village with a view of a field of peach blossoms, where one could hear a goat bleating in the distance, where butterflies, bees, and birds came and went like neighbors . . . But now the house had become something suited only to a horror movie. She thought of that novel, which didn't sell anymore and had been forgotten by everyone, and her heart grew heavy. Seeing that the house had become deserted made her feel that the book, which was already out of print, was truly and finally forgotten and had disappeared. She didn't wonder whose house it was or why it was deserted. The house would gradually rot and eventually fall down. Through the closed blinds, she could see the streaking rain as it hit the window. The world outside was silent, and so was the house. She suddenly felt very weary. She wasn't naive enough to think that her works would endure in literary history, so it puzzled her that she suddenly felt so dejected.

On the way back, the rain shower turned into a downpour. 'What do I do now?' She thought about K as she flew past the hesitating cars in the rain. Although she hadn't expected to be able to see him if she went to the house, his absolute absence left her feeling groundless and empty. She had always treated K carelessly; it was common for her to be two hours late for a rendezvous or to even forget about meeting him, and she would sometimes call him inconsiderately in the middle of the night to ask if there was a problem with this sentence or that scene. She never thought of those things as rude because he always answered her call as if he had been waiting for it. He responded with comments like "Make that like this, and this like that," "It'd be better to kill the guy off," or "Why don't you just drop that scene?" She didn't always take his advice and, unlike K, she wasn't always glad to see him. Sometimes she dreamed of a final parting from K, a permanent farewell. The dream was sweet, pitiful, and tormenting. K was the only person who knew her novels, their origin, creation, and extinction, as a whole. Traffic started backing up around the *Pangyo* interchange. Two tow trucks were driving on the shoulder with loud sirens blaring. It was almost time to pick up her child. Jamming on the gas and brake by turns, she ferociously sped past the other cars. She hoped that the weather would be clear tomorrow. She knew she had to go somewhere, but she didn't know where.

The next day, as soon as her son had left the house, she went out. She wore a broad-brimmed hat and sneakers. As she drove through a tunnel and along various different thruways and highways, she felt vaguely anxious. She couldn't explain why she was going this way, so she tried not to think about the question. Although it was the way she had always gone with K, she wasn't driving in his direction in the hopes of seeing him. Sometimes things must be done for no reason, and she just felt that she had to go this way. *Bibong, Namyang, Sagang,* and *Seosin* ... The signs whizzed by until she reached the sea. She handed over a thousand *won*[52] bill at a cart on a street overlooking the sea and received a cup of coffee. The hot coffee soothed her empty stomach and, now tranquil, she stood looking at the serene spring sea and the silent sky. The guard post was located on a road so narrow that a car could barely make it through, but which suddenly turned into a four-lane highway. A set of stately tour buses parked along the road, spilling forth children and women with unkempt hair who looked like they had had an early start to the morning. Some small boys ran toward the sea cheering.

She drove along the coastal road, watching the people rolling up their pants and digging at the water's edge. The road would be submerged when the tide came in at six p.m. Until then people would hang around in the muddy water. They would dig up short-necked clams, oysters, razor clams, and maybe even find an octopus. Before that it would be impossible to look over the desolate sea with nothing but lights floating on it in the shape of a human shadow. As she approached the little island, she was greeted with a more dramatic view. The sky along the coastal road that embraced the sea was covered with billboards. A *Jokgu*[53] court, seminar rooms, and barbecue facilities were all ready and group reservations were welcomed ... *The beach experience ... All equipment provided ... Bring back the memories* ... She read the phrases one by one. When she had just made her publishing debut, she visited the island with nothing but a newspaper clipping in her hand. It had been a very long trip, driving on the long mountain road that twisted and turned along the shore. It had been a cold, gloomy day with severe winds. After three more visits to the island, she had finished a novel that gained her some attention for the first time. She returned twice after that, once for the shooting of a TV

---

52 A thousand won is a little less than a dollar.
53 A leisure sport commonly played in Korea, mostly by men. It resembles volleyball but is played with the feet instead of the hands.

show about the setting of a novel, and once for that other event . . .
Each time, the island was slightly changed, like a woman changing her clothes, and at some point, after it became a vacation destination, it was an entirely different place. There was no spot left
on that island where one could escape the smell and smoke of
grilling clams.

The recently constructed buildings up on the hill looked down
on her overbearingly. The little hotels had diverse names: Il Mare,
The White House, The Memory of Sunset. Spelled out in large
letters that could be seen from a mile away on a billboard as big as
a house: Seawater Bath, Germanium . . . A local bus stopped and
men and women crowded onto it. She drove by a gaudy amusement park at the end of the coastal road, passing its hanging Viking
ride, cheap-colored bumper cars, and songs that drummed in her
ears. She didn't want to criticize the people who had decorated
this island like this. It was only natural, since there were people
who needed a place to go and people who needed them to come.
It was just that the inevitable thing happened and the change occurred, and it didn't seem to be anybody's fault. Just as she was
passing the coastal park, which was as tasteless as the gardens of
the nouveaux riches, the sun reached the apex of its arc.

The open waterway to Hawk Rock was also packed with people.

A young man who had pulled up his shirt sleeves scaled the
side of the rock and a woman in a red dress followed after him.
She could see that the woman had picked up one of the candles
that sat in every crevice and had lit her own candle with it. The
man smiled brightly and took a picture of it.

"Why don't you light one, *ajumma*? Your wish will come true.
It's two thousand *won*." A peddler who sidled up to her held out
a white candle. Had there been a candle peddler back then? There
probably had been. Because she didn't believe that her wish would
come true even if she lit a candle, because she didn't have much to
wish for, and because, on top of everything, the tide would soon
come in and consume the candle, she didn't buy one.

"That's your problem," K had said. "No one wants nothing."

They just hide what they really want."

Her novel started like that. It was the story of a secret: something was revealed after having been hidden for a long time, returning as an irreversible wound; denial wouldn't keep it safe and confession would only lead to being reproached and ultimately deserted. The female protagonist, who had been repeatedly compelled to be patient and accept a predictable life, finally crossed the line, and couldn't or wouldn't come back to the other side . . . The novel was sad and quite beautiful. To preserve that sad feeling, she had not allowed herself to go out, watch sad movies, or listen to sad music. That was back when she didn't separate daily life from writing. When she used to stay up all night in a writing frenzy. When her passion rose in flames before her eyes.

She stayed until the tide began to change. The sound of the waves being pushed by the spring wind gradually became louder and the water started to flow in from far out. People returned from the shore, splashing and reveling. She calmly watched as Hawk Rock was taken over by the water, slowly disappearing from the bottom up. When the top of it rose like a candle still standing, the people who had been on the waterway had all gone and new people had emerged, hoping to see the sunset. She slowly stepped through the water that licked her ankles. The water in her heart was filling up as well. Her eyes were sore. Looking out at the sea, she blinked. She didn't wipe away the tears that gathered.

As she was getting into her car, her phone rang. It was the man she had spoken to, K's oldest friend, who told her he had run into K. He had been on his way to go fishing with some friends.

"It's around *Tongyeong*. There's a place called *Yokjido*. He was going fishing there. I didn't know he fished but he said he does it once in a while. I asked him where he was staying but he didn't tell me. He said, 'I don't have any particular destination,' and he looked like a vagabond."

Although the man seemed to want to find out why she was looking for him, she hung up. K, by his nature, was a man with the heart of a wanderer. It wasn't due to his unkempt hair, or because he didn't wash for days and always wore the same clothes. It was something in his expression and his wild eyes. Also, his unpredictable streak. He had a different address and a different business card with a new title every time she saw him, and with a mischievous face he would always say, "I'm not going to stay there for long. It's just a favor to them."

She knew *Yokjido*, too. She had scoped out the place for a sea-fishing scene when she was writing her third novel. K had gone with her, as usual, and even told her the story of *Yeonhwa-do*, in which a lotus flower turned into the island. The character she chose was a man who visited an island that had appeared before his eyes while he was fishing. The novel was boring: a story about a nonexistent place that seemed to exist, a person with an ungraspable existence, and a constant switching between fantasy and reality. The market rejected it because it was a hard read, but the novel earned her a different award. After reading a review that said that the novel expanded the philosophical perception of Korean literature with a new approach, he burst into laughter.

"Do these kids even know what they're talking about? In fact, you didn't even know what you were writing about, did you?" he said. She had been hurt by this but couldn't deny what K said. Indeed, she had been confused the entire time she was writing it. She had even wondered if it was ever going to be complete. But she felt that he had no reason to be so harsh, since she had just written about not knowing when she was in the state of not knowing, and perhaps it was that honest question mark in her writing that had attracted certain readers. This strange feeling had produced an unusual image. K's response was exceedingly sharp.

'So, should I go to *Tongyeong* to look for K now? What do I say when I see him? If I don't go look for him, will all my anger and excitement from the last few days just disappear?' She felt as though she were heading towards a dead end.

That night, she saw K. No, she saw K's back. He was holding a fishing rod, standing on the rocks of the shore. Even as she approached him, she didn't know what she would say to him if he actually turned around. If she could just say, "It's so great to see you in a place like this. Have you caught any fish?" and stand beside him looking out at the sea . . . Then, she thought, she would be able to forget about his arrogance and sudden disappearance. As she got closer, an unfamiliar fear rose in her heart. When she was within ten steps, three rocks away, K's back said, "Don't come near me."

She understood his words even though the waves were particularly high in that spot. Feeling insulted, she screamed, "That's impossible. You can't leave me." Deep in her heart she felt a penetrating pain. "You can't desert me like this. You just can't. Even if you wanted to terribly, you can't help it. You can never ever escape me." Her voice reverberated off the sea like a wild wind. K's back was silent. As if something had taken his bait, his fishing rod tightened. The spooled rod quickly unwound. The tides were rising and the loosened rod stretched far, far out, shaking as if it were dancing with the swells.

Looking at K's hand winding the reel back, she slowly approached him. When she was about ten steps away, she heard K's voice.

"It is you who can't get away. Not me."

It was a low, frightening voice. A foreign voice she had never heard. She gazed at his moving shoulder muscles, holding her breath. She didn't ask, "Why the hell are you doing this? Why are you torturing me? What have I done that was so terrible?" The sincere desire to give up and the fear of loss mingled in her heart, weighing it down. She realized, painfully, that it had been a mistake to believe that she wasn't tied to him, and that he couldn't hurt her with a look or a word.

Looking toward K's expressionless back, she asked, "Why are you playing with me like this? How could you hurt me so much? Who are you? Who were you really?" If she could reach his heart, if she could get down on her knees in front of him, if she could hold his hands or look into his eyes and say, "It's me" . . . If K's eyes recognized her and began to shine again . . . She felt all her hopes and wishes were in vain. The feeling was vivid and sharp, as if she could touch it with her hand. The pain choked her.

"K," her voice was mixed with tears. His back didn't answer. "K," she called again. K's back resembled an enormous wall.

Finally, K said, "Don't call me by that name. I'm not K anymore."

The next moment, violent hostility swallowed her up. She carefully stepped toward K. The rocks on the shore were slippery, covered with moss. The high waves knocked against the sides of the rocks she walked on. The waves were rising up from somewhere far out to sea. When she got close enough to hear his breath, her hands stretched out automatically toward K's back. His black shirt and thin back were right in front of her. The time spent with him, the despair he caused her, his vicious and cynical way of talking, and the tiresome love and hatred suffocated her. He was right. She realized that she could never escape him as long as he lived. 'I just have to dismiss him.' She clenched her teeth. Shaking the foggy feeling from her body, she pushed him into the sea with all her strength. K flew up into the air without so much as a shriek, like a piece of straw, like a broken kite. His fishing pole flew into the air, and then something hanging at the end of the rod tumbled in the air with a whoosh and fell in front of her. The objects flapping at the end of the string were the books he had deserted at the used bookstore. The damaged black letters scattered like dust before her eyes.

It was her cry that woke her. It was dawn. The time when early birds look for food. She heard cuckooing from somewhere nearby. Entering the bathroom, she turned on the cold water and took a shower, shivering. Goose bumps broke out all over her skin like scales. The vivid dreams that had flashed across her mind during her short sleep still remained, spinning around in her ears.

The day broke and she waited until the parking lot and streets were less busy before leaving home. Although she accepted that dreams were the products of her unconscious repressions, she didn't believe in granting them special meanings. She was now confused about who K was, what kind of being he was, and whether the K she knew was the real K. She didn't know if she should go to see him or if she would be intent on murdering him as she had in her dream. She pushed the image of K standing against the wind and the silhouette of his thin back out of her mind. She had things to take care of first. The books in her dreams, those wet books falling at her feet . . . she couldn't get them out of her mind. She thought that she would never forget the wet, flapping covers. She felt as if her heart was filled with clods of wet tissue.

Turning a corner, she stopped automatically. She looked out across the street at the broken bricks, the rusty steel bars that stuck out, the building where only a frame remained. A worker was sweeping the concrete ground. The place where the bookstore used to be looked especially dark. It was a small space, making one wonder how the poorly assembled steel bookshelves, the old ladder, and all the books had fit into it. She thought of the moment when she was putting down her books, her deserted books in a corner. A feeling passed over her . . . she couldn't tell if it was thirst or pain that swept through her heart. She went into a new convenience store and drank a bottle of water in a single gulp. The bookstore had disappeared and the books with it. She inhaled deeply. 'It's not worth being melodramatic,' she thought.

"Oh, you're out early. You probably have errands to run." The young man at the counter was delighted. The man, who was wearing a hat, was the owner of the used bookstore.

"I haven't decided what to do yet. I'm working part-time for a while. It's not that I wasn't worried about what would be left after closing the store, but the price for recycled paper was less than I expected." The man, who had been somewhat curt in the dark bookstore, like a soldier in a fortress, was now lively and kind under the bright lights.

"Even though I quit the business, I'll keep on reading your books without fail."

She smiled at him and left the store. She slowly walked down the street, with white pollen flying like snow. The town seemed to have changed entirely in the past few days. She looked at the streets as if it were a strange town and the people were strangers. If she kept writing books that would be sold as recycled paper for pennies, if she kept writing stories that would scatter in the empty air . . . She didn't know if she had to go on searching for K.

The Little Thing

1

They said that the document had been posted to the company's online bulletin board. It was accessible to anyone in the company, so the rumor spread instantly. People were shocked, not at the content of the message, but just by the names mentioned in it.

The person to whom it was first reported was Chief Inspector Min in the Department of Internal Affairs. Having arrived at work, about to have a cup of green tea, he put down his cup and clicked twice on the computer screen with the mouse. His face turned pale. He scanned the information in twenty seconds, printed it out, called Technical Support, and directed them to delete it.

He read through the material slowly several times. It was written in a calm and unemotional tone, like a report, using clear, unadorned sentences. The writer revealed her real name. Young-joo Yi? That name didn't readily come to mind. That meant that she wasn't a known troublemaker, but he knew from experience that a problem was always likely to come from an unexpected person at an unexpected time. At forty-three, he had worked in Internal Affairs for fifteen years and nothing surprised him anymore. Director Min-ho Shin ... He underlined the name in the document. 'To encounter his name in such a place ... that is a surprise,' he thought. Director Shin and he were upper- and lowerclassmen at the same college and residents of the same apartment building. A graduate of the not-so-famous K University, rather than the prestigious K University. If Min getting stuck in the Inspection Department for so long was due to not being a graduate of a well-known college, like the majority of the company staff, the appointment of Director Shin could be said to be a symbol. Director Shin was a beacon of hope to the outsiders in the company. The Shin he knew was a kind, sincere, and hardworking person. He thought of Director Shin's face when he met him once during a walk. Shin said he had started jogging to help with the insomnia he developed when he sent his wife and younger daughter to Canada. Thinking about the white breath coming from Shin's mouth, who waved his hand and continued on his way, Min's heart fell. To Min, Director Shin, who had taken care of him like an older brother since his early days in the company, was more thoughtful than his actual brother.

Min's hand, holding the phone, about to call Director Shin's extension, hovered in the air for several moments. He immediately replaced the receiver. He thought it would be inappropriate to call through the company's phone lines. Looking back and forth between his two mobile phones, one white and one black, he shook his head again. Any communication system provided and paid for by the company could not assure security, he thought. Even his personal mobile phone wasn't safe. He turned off the phones and put them in a drawer. In a few days he would be having conversations that wouldn't be a problem no matter who was listening in on the landline. His habitual sense of security momentarily satisfied him. Being cautious and still more cautious ... He was well aware that an organizational system was a monster that could attack him and knock him down at any moment.

2

At five after ten, the Chief Inspector called a meeting. Section Chief Yi, Supervisor Pak, and Administrative Investigator Jung came in, with Chief Inspector Min entering last. The heavy door closed silently behind him.

"Is the file deletion complete?" There was no indication of anything unusual in Chief Inspector Min's tone.

"The technical team deleted it, but . . ." Jung finished his words vaguely and smacked his lips.

"Are you saying that it was already leaked?" the Chief Inspector asked.

"It's possible. It was posted at five to nine and the deletion was complete at nine fifty-nine. It was up for about an hour."

The world was such that in an hour it could have reached even the South Pole, crossing the Pacific Ocean. If the rumor got out, if the reporters and netizens caught on to it, it would come crashing down on the company. It would be a huge crack in the image of the company, which had just broken into the top thirty companies with the motto of "ethical management."

"Let's just monitor things for a while. Contact the technical team, check how much was leaked, and tell the public relations department to watch the reporters. Isn't the Chairman's annual speech scheduled for tomorrow? They could do a staff dinner or something before that. Tell them to be careful not to give the impression that they are taking any special measures."

While the Chief Inspector looked carefully at the documents in his hand, Section Chief Yi's mobile phone rang. As Yi opened his phone and looked at the screen, a strange look came across his face.

"It's Director Shin . . . What do you want me to do?"

"Answer it. Tell him to stand by until he's summoned."

The Chief Inspector's tone was clear and decisive. He thought Director Shin would probably have already called his mobile phone several times. Shin was simpleminded. He was a righteous and foolhardy person who didn't try to avoid obstacles. Quickly rising through the ranks as a new recruit, a supervisor, a section chief, and a section director, to finally become a director, his philosophy, which had protected him until he became the symbol of the company, was a textbook of morality: hard work, patience, earnestness . . . He could probably be called a symbol of the epoch. But surely even people like him found that their time comes to an end eventually. The Chief Inspector felt his heart sink but he finished what he had to say.

"Let's talk about the reliability of the posting first. What do you think, Section Chief Pak?"

Pak looked startled as if to say, "Oh, me?"

"The way I see it is . . . There's a little bit of a leap in logic, but it sounds plausible. I know Young-joo Yi a little."

"Do you know her personally?"

Pak's face turned slightly red. "It's not that, but she's known in the sales department."

"How is she known? According to her picture, she's quite pretty. Is it because of that?"

"Supervisor Pak is still single, so . . ." The middle-aged Section Chief Yi casually broke in. The room was filled with smiles for a moment.

Pak hesitated and then said, "Ms. Young-joo Yi got married last month. I met her at a hobby club."

The Chief Inspector quickly asked what kind of club it was, whether it was a registered association, how often they met, and what kind of people were in it. Pak, speaking quickly, explained about the Internet game club, and the Chief Inspector took notes.

"So, Supervisor Pak thinks that Ms. Young-joo Yi's words are reliable, right? How about the rest of you?"

Section Chief Yi and Administrative Inspector Jung expressed similar opinions. It was Jung who made the point, which seemed more serious, that her writing wasn't exaggerated. The four of them examined the posting's sentences one by one for twenty minutes. At certain passages some of the men turned red and frowned.

"We'll confirm the facts today and report this to the upper division tomorrow. Let's call Ms. Young-joo Yi in first. Mr. Jung, examine the company's regulations and draw up an estimate for a settlement."

A heavy mood pervaded the room. Yi reached for the handset.

"Yes, this is Young-joo Yi." The voice that came from the speaker phone was clear and beautiful.

3

A twenty-nine-year-old graduate of K University's Business school, entering the company with the best record, and promoted to a representative in the shortest time. As her résumé verified, Young-joo Yi looked smart. A navy-blue suit, dignified eyes, and sleek forehead, with soft hair hanging past her shoulders and full lips that were closed as though she were nervous. It was a face suitable for the bulletin cover.

"You called for me." After saying this and sitting down, Young-joo Yi didn't open her mouth until after the Chief Inspector had asked and then offered the answers to several brief questions. She looked embarrassed every once in a while, but didn't look pitiful, sigh, or turn red like most of the people who reported this kind of thing.

"So, you are saying it should be handled according to the regulations?" the Chief Inspector asked her after a round of questions and answers.

"I learned that there is an Equal Employment Opportunity Law and an Anti-Sexual Discrimination Law."

"Would you explain what those are?"

She looked at the Chief Inspector with her mouth clamped shut. Her well-shaped forehead furrowed, but when she opened her mouth after taking a deep breath her voice was calm.

"As far as I'm concerned, sexual harassment is bullying by verbal or physical harassment of a sexual nature in relation to work, or intimidation by illegal employment discrimination on the conditions of verbal and physical abuse of a sexual nature. Harassment can include offensive jokes and remarks, sexual comments and estimation on appearance, unwanted physical contact, and coercion by sitting next to one and pouring a drink at the staff dinner, the staff picnic, and so on . . . All of that is written in the document."

Section Chief Yi and Supervisor Pak looked deeply impressed. Administrative Inspector Jung seemed rather crestfallen. The Chief Inspector thought, 'She has a great memory.' Anyone who got involved with a woman like this would never get away with anything.

"And to what does Director Shin's action correspond in the above?"

"If you insist on me pointing it out . . ."

For the first time since she had entered the room, she looked hesitant.

"Did he make an indecent joke?"

"It might not be correct to call it indecent . . ."

"'Ms. Young-joo, your husband seems to be a fine person. You should feel confident.' Is this part problematic?"

"No, that's . . ."

"'Even so, treat Representative Choi and Representative Kim nicely.' Is it this part?"

"I think it is unfair to look at them separately in that way."

"Then let's look at them all together. 'Ms. Young-joo, your husband seems to be a fine person. You should feel confident. Even so, treat Representative Choi and Representative Kim nicely. Be generous to them . . .' Where is the problem?"

"I think the problem is that I was made to feel sexually humiliated. You might understand if you had read my explanation that Representative Kim and Representative Choi had both proposed to me. And the Director was well aware of it."

According to Young-joo Yi, she received proposals from three men in the same department and she refused all three of them. She had dated all of them and as soon as she refused their proposals she ended the relationships. An attractive single woman drew attention from single men and it happened that they all wanted to marry her . . . It was a very natural thing. Moreover, it was in the past. And almost all the staff members in her department had attended her wedding ceremony last month. Director Shin left his name in the guest book, gave them a thick envelope, and ate *kalbitang* [54] and rice cakes.

"Let's move on to the other story. Instant barbecue beef . . . What is that about?"

"That is . . . as I explained, what Director Shin said at the staff

54 Beef rib soup.

dinner. I think all of you here should be familiar with it."

Chief Inspector Min looked around the room. Jung lowered his head, looking awkward. Yi and Pak looked away, making themselves busy with other things.

"On a business trip, he recommended that Ms. Young-joo Yi, who was staying at a different hotel, change hotels. How about this part? Don't you think it would be convenient to stay at the same place for the sake of work? It's difficult to understand that it was such a problem for you."

"Chief Inspector." Her eyebrow flinched. Her breath seemed heavier, too. "That situation is explained in the document . . . the circumstance in which the comment was made and at which time he told me to switch hotels. On that trip, I wasn't even working on the same project as the Director."

Min quietly glared at her and Yi stepped forward instead.

"It says here that he proposed the change at the staff dinner after the daily work. It's written that Director Shin was drunk. Weren't there other people there at the time? Since it wasn't a dinner between just two people . . ."

Young-joo Yi took a deep breath and collected herself. "Two of the men from the local office joined us."

Min, staring at her surreptitiously, immediately turned his head. "Well, Ms. Young-joo Yi, let's get the circumstances straight. You had a scheduled staff dinner on this business trip, you were with two local staff members, and there Director Min-ho Shin suggested a private proposal. Wouldn't that have been awkward? Even if he were drunk, this is too much. In other words, are you sure you weren't being too sensitive?"

Too sensitive . . . She was stunned into silence for a moment. She thought about how men are all the same. She felt that they didn't try to understand what they didn't feel themselves and wondered why there were no female staff members in the inspection department. She thought about her husband's reaction a few days ago.

"Aren't there any sexual harassment cases in your company?" she asked him as she hesitated over whether to post the document.

"Pff," he smiled and shook his head. "I work at a manufacturer.

I mean, there are only men there." Flipping the pages of a weekly news magazine, he glanced at her and asked, "What is it? Did
something happen at your office?"

"Not something, more like . . ." Her voice became cautious.

"Did someone do something? Is this about the staff dinner
yesterday?" He closed the magazine. His face looked threatening,
as though he would go after whoever it was.

"No. It's not just a recent thing. Men are really weird. Why do
they think they have to comment on how their female coworkers
look?" She sighed.

"A comment . . . Is that all?" His face relaxed.

"Is sexual harassment only a matter of touching someone, or
telling dirty jokes?"

When she asked him this, he said, "Everyone says things like,
'You look pretty today,' or, 'You look like you've lost some weight.'
Don't you like to hear comments like that? There are plenty of
women I can't say that about. What is so bad about telling you
you're pretty in a world where your beauty gives you a competitive
edge?"

She gave up trying to explain after that. She thought that it
was too much to ask him to understand. If she tried to tell him
how their comments made her feel, or some of the uncomfortable situations they created for her, he just wouldn't understand.

'Isn't it enough that I feel this way? Who has the right to say
that I shouldn't feel like this?' she thought as she quietly clenched
her teeth. Looking straight into the Chief Inspector's eyes, she
spoke precisely.

"It's wrong for you to just assume that I've intended to do this
from the beginning. The state of affairs became overwhelming because the same situation was repeated again and again, and as you
know, this is an extremely personal matter, so it's not easy to make
other people understand. For myself, I didn't want to be involved
in this ugly situation, but . . . If you are asking me whether it was
impossible just to avoid it, forget it, or take it as a joke . . ."

She stopped talking for a moment and fidgeted with her hands.
The four men looked at her long, pale fingers.

"Was it impossible?" the Chief Inspector asked her.

"I . . . didn't want to. I knew it would cause problems for me, but I also knew that if I didn't say something then it would never stop."

Chief Inspector Min thought, 'Isn't she acting like a fighter? Isn't this a typical K University graduate's attitude, like she can't imagine being wrong?' but he kept his mouth closed. Listening to Young-joo Yi's statement, he was convinced that the content of the document was mostly true. As she said, it was possible to interpret it in different ways depending on how one felt about it, but the solution to this problem seemed to have already been decided by the person bringing it up. Being smart, she didn't mention not getting the promotion last fall. The problems she raised were trivial, passing words and minor acts. Now, it was impossible to avoid this. The Chief Inspector felt his heart grow heavy.

4

In the afternoon at Director Shin's office, while he was waiting to be summoned by the inspection department, a man showed up in the vestibule where all the staff members sat holding their breaths in anticipation. The secretary was surprised and hurriedly stood up from her seat but the man just nodded at her, knocked on the door, and opened it without waiting for an answer. Director Shin's eyes opened wide as he paced around his office.

"Can I sit down?" the man asked, smirking at Shin and flopping down on the couch without waiting for an answer.

"What brings you here out of the blue?" Director Shin looked unhappy to see him.

Tut-tut. Clicking his tongue, the man asked, "What happened here? You and I have been through everything; how could you get yourself into this mess because of a woman? I thought you weren't interested in women, but I guess I was wrong."

"Does this make you happy?" Director Shin wanted to ask. The man, who sat looking at him disapprovingly, had entered the company at the same time as Shin and had always been one step ahead in promotions, all the way up through representative and section chief. For a while, Shin had hated him. The man, who was good-looking, had a rich wife and children enrolled in the smart kids' school, causing one to wonder if there was anything he lacked . . . had he been angry when he didn't get promoted to director last fall and Shin got the position instead? Was Shin thrilled about it himself?

"By the way . . . what're you going to do? Everyone's talking about you now. The whole house is bustling."

"I suppose so . . ." Shin nodded his head feebly.

"What did the inspection department say? Have they called you yet?"

"They will soon, I guess. I'll know once I get there."

The man, Managing Director Pak, looked straight at him. "Those inspection fellows are nasty. Don't expect even the chief inspector, Min whatever, to help you get out of this just because he's your man. I got the brush-off last year, as you know."

Last fall, a woman wrote to the inspection department. The letter reported on their insignificant love affair, which everyone in the company already knew about. Since she didn't reveal her identity openly, he insisted that he was being set up. Even though it ended there, he couldn't prevent it from blocking his promotion.

"When they call you, they'll ask questions about the content of the document first. My guess is that they already called the woman in and they'll call you in to confirm the facts with you."

"Facts or whatever . . . It just feels ridiculous. I mean, wouldn't it to you?"

"I completely understand how you feel. Everyone thinks it's unfair to you. But I . . . If I can give you some advice, it would be wise to admit it and quietly go through the process . . . You see, I think if you fight it, it will only get worse. The general opinion doesn't seem good, either . . ."

"The general opinion? Whose opinion do you mean?" Director Shin's raised his voice, "You said everybody thinks it's unfair to me, and you mean the general opinion isn't what everybody thinks?"

His colleague was silent for a while. He clicked his tongue as if he felt sorry for him.

"There's something you don't know. Women, you see, they are weird animals and it's utterly impossible to talk to them when they hold a grudge. That woman, I could tell right away, looked like she was never going to give up."

If it was about women, there was a chance he might be right.

"The problem is that it was announced on the bulletin board. Even though they're blocking it, it will be in the gossip section of the newspaper by tomorrow. Keep your head clear so you can make a decision. It doesn't matter what the truth is."

Shin looked at him blankly. If the truth didn't matter, then what did? He couldn't think straight.

"In my opinion ... You should stop the ethics committee from meeting. As you know, there are quite a few members of that committee who are jealous of you."

As he said, if the ethics committee met, he might not be able to avoid disciplinary action. Even a quiet retirement might not be possible.

"Look, Director Shin. Think about it. We're already fifty. That would mean retirement at almost any other company. Since you've risen to the level of director at this kind of giant corporation, you could find a position elsewhere. They would probably compete to bring you to their company. If you fight it, go through all the trouble, submitting to disciplinary measures, and having your retirement benefits cut ... That is not a joke. You should think about your kids. Besides, you have daughters."

He wanted to ask, "Did someone put you up to this?" He wanted to ask, "If I quit, are you going to take over this position?" He wanted to say that he didn't want to retire like this, which would mean disgrace for the rest of his life. But his mouth wouldn't open. He didn't think that what Pak said was wrong. But it was difficult for him to understand this situation, being driven into a corner in one day, in a matter of a few hours like this. "It feels unfair. It feels really unfair. It feels really, truly unfair . . ." He wanted to cry, but naturally, he couldn't.

5

The opinions of the male employees were varied but could generally be summed up by, "Isn't this a bit much?"

"He didn't even touch her ass or grab her tits. They say he just put his hand on her shoulder. What the hell is he guilty of?"

One of the men made a face like it was all ridiculous.

Someone replied right away, "That girl must have an erogenous zone on her shoulder as well."

They broke out into boisterous laughter.

"My boss . . . whenever I hear her nagging, my blood pressure goes through the roof. She never opens her mouth without saying 'as a man,' or 'a man ought to do this or that,' and isn't that sexual harassment? Someone ought to be talking about that."

As if they had been waiting for this moment, the men who had female bosses now started talking about their troubles.

"It's so bad that this society acts like all men are perverts. It assumes that men go crazy at the drop of a hat, that their loins are on fire, and they are always groaning like puppies about to take a dump."

All the men in the small lounge looked resentful.

"No kidding. There is supposed to be some executive who got fired for asking a female employee what an aphrodisiac was. I heard, at least, that they waited a month before firing him. It turned out his wife came in and begged them to wait because it was going to be twenty years in a month and there would be a huge difference in his pension and retirement benefits."

"What's an aphrodisiac?" someone asked.

"It's a love drug, idiot," came the answer.

Someone said something like, "It's similar to Aphrodite? Of course, it must come from her name. To have the power to make all the women look as beautiful as Aphrodite. It probably means something like that."

"In fact, what do women know about men? When you really think about it, you see that women just cause problems." The man from the sales department who added this insight was known to be an expert on women.

Having gained their attention, he continued talking. Women think that all men think about is arousal, erection, endurance, and withdrawal, and that those are the only things men dream about and hope for. Men are so simple and ignorant that even on a seemingly simple course, a visual or psychological stimulus is necessary; the cerebral cortex receiving it becomes excited, and the excitement has to go through the optic thalamus in the cerebrum and the hypothalamus . . . Women ignore these facts. The signal, which passes through the spinal cord, is delivered to the erection center in the sacral spine, which is the bottom part of the spinal cord, then that signal, which is delivered from the erection center, vasodilates the vessels towards the penis, and in a short while blood enters the cavernous tissue . . . Women aren't interested in this series of processes that happen in organic actions of the nervous system, the cardiovascular system, the endocrine system, and the musculoskeletal system, which is extremely delicate, subtle, and even artistic. In other words, they often forget that men are also beings with a brain, back, waist, and on top of everything, a heart . . .

Just as his long explanation was about to end, someone asked, "By the way, that aphrodisiac or whatever you mentioned a while ago, is it like Viagra? Do they sell it in Korea, too?"

The man in the role of lecturer smiled.

"Oysters, eels, pumpkin seeds, sesame seeds, shrimp, and beans . . . All of those will work. Don't go looking for the non-existent seal penises in vain. These things all have a lot of zinc in them. Eat things like oily fish, garlic, and onion. They contain a good dose of a mineral called selenium, that's the so-called 'sex-mineral.'"

The eyes of the men were shining with curiosity and admiration. Somebody let them know lunch was ending soon. They went back to their offices in groups.

6

"Do you have some kind of grudge against me?" Director Shin spoke quietly. He wondered why this woman, his nice, charming, and talented subordinate, had pulled a knife on him. How long had she been sharpening that knife?

"I . . . have no such thing, Director." Young-joo Yi's voice was quiet as well. To this woman, he was now nothing but a middle-aged man one would run into on the street. He was no longer a director she had to gaze up at from below.

"Well, why did you do this? Even if I said, as you wrote in that report, certain things to you. It was just because you were lovely and . . ."

He caught his breath for a moment and tried to think of the right words. It seemed like the whole thing was over now, but he couldn't be sure. Who could know if she was going to put today's conversation on the bulletin board? His thoughts ran to the ongoing settlement for his retirement benefits. From now on, he would have to hesitate, take a deep breath and think twice about whomever he met and whatever he said.

"I said those things out of admiration for you . . . Didn't you know that?"

"Director." Young-joo Yi chose her words carefully, too. She had been informed of the decision by the inspection office late that afternoon. The chief inspector told her respectfully, "We intend to wrap this up with Director Shin's voluntary resignation. There'll be no additional disciplinary action. Would you accept that?" and she responded simply, "I understand."

It wasn't the solution she wanted, but she had no more strength left in her to push it any further. At this point, when it was over, she didn't want to cause him any more damage. However . . . she realized that he still does not know what he had done wrong. Quite the contrary, he must be thinking that he was suffering from really bad luck. Since he was an executive at a company like this, there might be another company making a great effort to bring him in. No, of course there would be. An executive director, a managing director, or probably a vice president . . . She thought of what her mother used to say, 'A good connection lasts a lifetime.' She looked straight at him.

"You say you admire me, but . . . there were more occasions I experienced as insults. I do not appreciate being admired in that way. I'm aware that I might be considered a strange, eccentric woman, but . . ."

"No, no," Director Shin waved his hand. "What I'm saying is . . . No, that's not it. I admit I didn't know those were insults to you. I admitted all of it to the inspection team . . . the same interrogation you went through . . . I'm not saying I haven't done anything wrong. Even if I did, I just want to know why you didn't tell me about it. You were a person who seemed, I don't know, straightforward."

His face grew sad. The face of Young-joo Yi darkened as well.

"I wasn't hoping for your resignation. I wanted an apology. I wanted to let you know that I was suffering when you did that. I wanted to tell you that not only me, but also many other female staff members experience these incidents. Not just being unhappy, but coming to hate the company and to hate themselves for feeling so timid, like they're walking on eggshells . . . There are even staff members who suffer from insomnia and depression. I wanted to bring these stories to light. I just wanted to talk. I didn't intend to make you resign like this. But, if I'd told you about it, would you have said, 'I understand. I'm sorry about that'?"

Her voice trembled. Her eyelashes quivered. Finally, she shed tears. Tears she had been holding back for a long time. At that moment Young-joo Yi's phone rang and her husband's number showed on the screen.

"Are you busy? Can I have a minute with you?" His voice was trembling with tension. "What have you done? Everyone is calling me and it's total chaos. It's the first time I've ever experienced rumors like this. The rumor is all over my company that I married a witch."

While she remained silent, her husband's anger washed over her.

"He . . . is responsible for the well-being of his family. They say he has two daughters . . . How can he face his daughters? How can you be so cold-hearted? . . . How much must he have gone through to get there? Having someone fired . . . Are you happy? I feel like it's happening to me as well . . ."

She calmly folded her phone.

7

The house was quiet and dark. Once again, he was hit with a wave of loneliness at the fact that his wife and younger daughter had left, but right now his wife's absence felt fortunate. Luckily, the light was on in his older daughter's room. He opened the door.

"Dad, you're late." His daughter, sitting in front of her computer, called out to him. He looked at her with drunken eyes. His heart ached. He flattened his hand and made a gesture, sweeping down his chest with his palm. 'My heart, my heart is aching . . .' His daughter's eyes opened wide.

"You know sign language."

She had been taking care of handicapped children in the suburbs of Seoul since the year before last. She started after she failed to get into college for three years and announced that she wasn't going to take any more entrance exams. It was practically unpaid volunteer work.

"You know, your dad . . . I mean, a long time ago . . ."

He sat at her feet. A long time ago, when he was twenty years old, he was a good-for-nothing in the city where he was born and raised. He wandered the dirty alleys, hanging out with his poor, worthless friends, boys of his age, with nothing to be afraid of and nothing to lose. His father signed him up for a new college in the region and waited patiently.

"A man's gotta know how to enjoy himself in order to work," his father used to say. When he went to school, pushed by his father's tenacity, he found that he was enrolled in the Special Education department.

It was one of his few training days. While getting used to his schedule of washing a severely disabled child—a quadriplegic—dressing him and teaching him songs, he realized that every part of him was drawn toward the door. Although he was deeply disappointed in himself for wanting to leave, his back bending like a magnet was pulling him, what struck him more clearly was the feeling of the child's excrement. The sticky, muddy feeling wouldn't leave his mind all afternoon.

That night he told his father, "Father, I thought I was a reliable, sincere person."

His father didn't say a word.

"Now I realize I'm . . . a lazy and shallow jerk."

His father stared silently at him.

"Now I'm going to live the life I'm capable of. Please send me to Seoul."

"You know, when Dad was studying to retake the college entrance exam . . . When I attended an institute in *Yongsan*, there was a deaf child in my boarding house. Whenever he was in trouble, I helped him and took care of things for him . . ."

His father made up a school record for him and sent him to Seoul. He paid his tuition, was proud of him even though it wasn't the famous K University, was delighted when he got married and had a baby, and cried with happiness when he bought his first home. His father took care of everything for him. He wanted to do that for his two daughters, too. He wanted to be a father who took care of everything for his children.

"That guy . . . What was his name?"

Strangely enough, only his own name came to mind.

"Min-ho Shin . . . It's a good name, isn't it?" He mumbled with his eyes half closed. His body slipped down.

"Dad, you're drunk. You're cute when you're drunk, Dad."

His daughter covered his shoulders with a blanket. When he first entered the company, his father kept touching his ID card over and over again, as if it were a thing of wonder. Today, if his father saw him, he would have held him without saying a word. He would have patted his back, saying, "It's okay. It's okay." He missed his father, who was gone now, so much. 'If I could see my father, even in my dreams . . .' Tears rolled down from his closed eyes.

The going-away party was cancelled. There was a rumor that Director Shin's former secretary, Ae-ry Jung, had burst into tears while emptying out her desk; there were no other stories of staff members feeling sad about his resignation. That afternoon, a rumor circulated that Managing Director Pak's visit to Director Shin, in which he convinced Director Shin to leave quietly, had been arranged by Chief Inspector Min, though the two men had very different motives; however, the fact couldn't be confirmed. A company, like any other place, was sensitive to rumors and conspiracy.

The office, belonging to no one, underwent remodeling for a few days. The wooden door was changed to glass and the blinds covering the windows were removed. The office was left empty for a long time until a rumor appeared and just as naturally evaporated that a female executive in her forties would soon be placed in that office, which was now fully exposed to everyone's eyes. Some people had started to suspect that it might have been a conspiracy to reduce the number of executives at the company.

Young-joo Yi was transferred. She became an auditor at the *Yeongdeungpo* branch. It was technically a supervisory title, but could be seen as a demotion for a representative in the sales department at the head office. She silently took up her new work as a matter of course. The company still bustled along. If there was anything different, it was that the male staff members who used to eat at the underground staff cafeteria now usually ate outside the building. They went to a restaurant, right in front of the office building, that specialized in steamed oyster rice.

About the Author

SEO HAJIN was born in 1961 in Youngcheon, North Nyungsang Province. She studied Korean literature at Kyunghee University in Seoul, Korea, and is currently an assistant professor of Korean Literature at the same school. Her story "Tidal Path" was short-listed for the Yi Sang Literature Award.

About the Translators

AMY C. SMITH and ALLY H. HWANG have together translated two collections of Seo Hajin's short stories. Smith is an Associate Professor of English at Lamar University (TSUS), and Hwang is currently completing a book on Virginia Wolf.

LIBRARY OF KOREAN LITERATURE, VOL. 1

KIM JOO-YOUNG
STINGRAY
Translated by Inrae You Vinciguerra
and Louis Vinciguerra

"Stingray should be savored, read slowly ... the author has managed a perfect reproduction of the way people spoke in the late pre-modern era, relying on circumlocution rather than direct statement ... the beauty of silence and metaphor both are presented wonderfully due to the author's exquisite craftsmanship." —*Donga Ilbo*

Hailed by critics, *Stingray* has been described by its author as "a critical biography of my loving mother." With his father having abandoned his family for another woman, little Se-young and his mother are forced to subsist on their own in the harsh environment of a small Korean farming village in the 1950s. Determined to wait for her husband's return, Se-young's mother hangs a dried stingray on the kitchen doorjamb; to her, it's a reminder of the fact that she still has a husband, and that she must behave as a married woman would, despite all. Also, she claims, when the family is reunited, the fish will be their first, celebratory meal together. But when a beggar girl, Samrae, sneaks into their house during a blizzard, the first thing she does is eat the stingray, and what follows is a struggle, at once sentimental and ideological, for the soul of the household.

Available at **www.dalkeyarchive.com**

LIBRARY OF KOREAN LITERATURE, VOL. 2

HYUN KI-YOUNG
ONE SPOON ON THIS EARTH
Translated by Jennifer M. Lee

"This novel is one of the most outstanding bildungsromans in
the history of Korean literature, showing us the ways in which
a human being interacts with history ..." —*Hankook Ilbo*

An autobiographical novel that takes a life to pieces, putting
forward not a coherent, straightforward narrative, but a series
of dazzling images ranging from the ordinary to the unbeliev-
able, fished from the depths of the author's memory as well as
from the stream of his day-to-day life as an adult author. In-
terweaving flashes of the horrific Jeju Uprising and the Korean War with pleasant family anecdotes, stories of schoolroom
cruelty, and bizarre digressions into his personal mythology,
One Spoon on this Earth stands a sort of digest of contempo-
rary Korean history as it might be seen through the lens of one
man's life and opinions.

Available at **www.dalkeyarchive.com**

Library of Korean Literature, vol. 7

Lee Ki-ho
At Least We Can Apologize
Translated by Christopher Joseph Dykas

"Do you want to laugh? do you want to cry? Read Lee Ki-ho
… He is the weathervane of Korean fiction in the 2000s."
—Park Bum-shin

This story focuses on an agency whose only purpose is to offer apologies—for a fee—on behalf of its clients. This seemingly insignificant service leads us into an examination of sin, guilt, and the often irrational demands of society. A kaleidoscope of minor nuisances and major grievances, this novel heralds a new comic voice in Korean letters.

Available at **www.dalkeyarchive.com**

YI KWANG-SU
THE SOIL
Translated by Hwang Sun-ae and Horace Jeffery Hodges

"Matching the fame of its author, who is perhaps the most studied fiction writer in the history of modern Korean literature, *The Soil* is in the center of numerous academic and critical discussions, debates about nationalism, philosophical literature, agrarian literature, pro-Japanese literature ... literary theory and the history of literature itself." —Moonji Publishing

A major, never before translated novel by the author of *Mujông/ The Heartless*—often called the first modern Korean novel— *The Soil* tells the story of an idealist dedicating his life to helping the inhabitants of the rural community in which he was raised. Striving to influence the poor farmers of the time to improve their lots, become self-reliant, and thus indirectly change the reality of colonial life on the Korean peninsula, *The Soil* was vitally important to the social movements of the time, echoing the effects and reception of such English-language novels as Upton Sinclair's *The Jungle*.

Available at **www.dalkeyarchive.com**